"You have my word I will do what I can to get the boy released."

"Why?" Janey asked suddenly, "You are a stranger here and can have no interest in what becomes of Jem."

Jonathan shrugged his shoulders. "I can never resist a distressed damsel, so long as she is passably pretty, of course," he added self-mockingly.

"I am not distressed, sir! I am angry! And neither am I passably pretty!"

"No. Any man who considered you merely passable would be lacking in judgment and taste," he said lazily, his eyes warm and teasing as they met her gaze.

D1353720

MARIE-LOUISE HALL

Rake's Reform

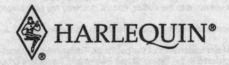

HARLEQUIN®

TORONTO • NEW YORK • LONDON
AMSTERDAM • PARIS • SYDNEY • HAMBURG
STOCKHOLM • ATHENS • TOKYO • MILAN • MADRID
PRAGUE • WARSAW • BUDAPEST • AUCKLAND

ISBN 0-373-30358-0

RAKE'S REFORM

First North American Publication 2000

Visit us at www.eHarlequin.com

Printed in U.S.A.

MARIE-LOUISE HALL

studied history at the University of London, where she met her husband. Now living in rural Aberdeenshire, she has had the ambition since marriage to find time to write. Domestically incompetent, she was thrilled when her husband took over the housework so that she could write. She also works for her husband's oil industry consultancy and looks after her young son, six cats and three delinquent donkeys.

Chapter One

The courtroom was small, crowded, but utterly silent as the judge, resplendent in his crimson, put on his black cap and began to intone the words of the death sentence. Above in the gallery, a young woman sat as still and as rigid as the ashen-faced boy who stood in the dock, his hands clenched upon the wooden rail.

Miss Jane Hilton stared disbelievingly at the judge, her hazel eyes ablaze with anger beneath the wide brim of her black straw hat. This was nothing short of barbarism. This could not be happening! Not in England! Not in the supposedly civilised, well-mannered England of King William IV in this year of 1830. And she was not going to let it happen.

She was on her feet before she had stopped to think.

"How can you?" Her question rang out in the hushed room. "What crime has this child committed? Any farmer or labourer in this room could tell you that a rick of poorly cured hay may heat to the point where it catches fire without any assistance."

There was a murmur of agreement from the more

poorly dressed onlookers as every head in the lower part of the courtroom turned and looked upwards, including that of her guardian, Mr Filmore, who regarded her first with astonishment and then with tight-lipped fury as he gestured to her furiously to sit down and be silent. The judge's hooded eyelids lifted as he, too, stared at her with bloodshot blue eyes.

"Silence in the court, madam, or I shall have you removed from the building," he roared.

"I shall not be silent!" Janey retorted. "I know Jem Avery is not guilty of arson. On the morning and at the same time as he is supposed to have set the rick alight, I passed him upon the road some five miles from the Pettridges Home Farm yard."

"Indeed?" The judge's bushy white brows lifted. "I trust you acquainted the defence counsel with this—" he paused "—alleged meeting."

"Of course I did, but—" Janey began.

"M'lud?" The defence counsel stepped forward and said something in an undertone to the judge. American, unstable and prone to female fancies were the only words which Janey caught, but it was enough, combined with the smug smile of her guardian, to tell her why she had not been called as a witness.

"It seems your evidence was deemed unreliable," the judge said, lifting his head again to look down his long nose at Janey. "So I must ask you a second time to be silent."

"I will not!" Janey repeated furiously. "I have seen better justice administered by a lynch mob in St Louis than I have here today."

"Then perhaps you had better go back there," the

judge sneered, earning sycophantic smiles from both defence and prosecution counsels, who were already surreptitiously shuffling their papers together. "Gentlemen," he said laconically to two of the ushers who stood at the back of the gallery, "remove that woman from the courtroom."

"I suppose I should not have lost my temper." Janey sighed heavily a few minutes later as she stood next to her maid upon the steps of the courthouse, attempting to push strands of her flyaway fair hair back into the rather workmanlike chignon in which it was usually confined. "But that judge is a pompous, port-sodden old fool!"

"Yes, miss," Kate agreed as she handed her the wide-brimmed hat which had become dislodged from Janey's head during her somewhat undignified exit from the courtroom between the two ushers.

"It makes me so angry, Kate," Janey went on as she rammed the hat down on her head. "Jem Avery has never hurt a soul in his life. The worse he has ever done is poach a rabbit or two to prevent his family from starving. I know he did not fire that rick, though Mr Filmore gave him reason enough in the way he treated him! It is monstrous to even suggest he should hang."

"I know, miss," Kate said sympathetically. "And there was not a Christian person in that room who did not agree with you."

"Then why didn't they all get up and say so!" Janey said, her American drawl more pronounced as it always was when she was angry. "Why don't they demand a retrial?"

"Because that's just not how it's done here, miss.

People don't dare make a fuss, for fear they'll lose their places or trade if they're in business. You have to know someone, one of them...if Jem were a Duke's son, then it would be different.''

"I know," Janey said gratingly as she retied the grey silk ribbons on her hat beneath her pointed chin. She was almost as angry with herself as she was with the judge. After four years in England, she should have known better than to expect an instant public protest. Kate was right. That wasn't how things were done here in this genteel and ancient English cathedral city, where the law was enforced to the letter and property valued above lives.

She glanced upwards at the serene, awesome spire of the nearby cathedral, which seemed almost to reach the grey November clouds, and sighed. Even the buildings in this corner of England seemed to have that air of superior certainty which she had encountered in so many of her English acquaintances.

God in his Heaven and everything and everyone in their proper place, including Miss Jane Hilton, colonial nobody, she thought, feeling a sudden overwhelming homesickness for the handful of ramshackle timber dwellings strung out along a muddy track, half a world away. That had been the nearest to a town she had known, until her parents' death had forced her to return to St Louis, where her grandfather had found her.

The log cabins in which she had spent her childhood had had no attractions with which to rival either the medieval splendour of the cathedral or the exuberant prosperity of the timbered Tudor merchant's houses that clustered about its close. And the people who had lived in them had often been rough and illiterate. But they would not have condemned a boy like Jem for the loss of a hayrick, which had in all probability set alight by itself.

No, she thought, Lilian, her parents, the Schmidts, the Lafayettes and the rest would all have been on their feet with her in that courtroom—and one way or another the judge would have been made to see reason.

She shut her eyes, seeing them all for a moment as if they were stood beside her. Her mother, fair, calm and beautiful, even with her apron besmirched with smuts and her sleeves rolled up. Her father, weathered and strong as the trees he had felled with his own hands to make the clearing that they had farmed. Proper Mrs Schmidt, looking askance at red-haired Lilian, who was as tough as the trappers she allowed to share both her cabin and her body. And Daniel, quiet, brown-eyed, brown-haired Daniel Lafayette, who had moved through the forest as silently as their Indian neighbours.

Daniel, who had been her childhood sweetheart and the first to die of the smallpox that had swept through the small frontier community. And with all the innocence and intensity of a fifteen-year-old, she had thought nothing worse could ever happen to her. And then her parents had become ill, and she knew that it could.

She shivered, remembering the sound of the earth being shovelled on to their rough wooden coffins by Lilian who, since she had had the smallpox as a child and survived it, had taken on the responsibility of nursing the sick and burying the dead.

"Miss?"

She started, wrenched back into the present by Kate's voice.

"They'll commute it, surely—give him transportation, won't they?" Kate said hopefully.

"I don't know," Janey said flatly, swallowing the lump which had arisen in her throat. Hankering for the past and feeling sorry for herself was not going to help Jem. This was not Minnesota, this was England. Green, pleasant, and pitiless to its poor. And if she was going to save Jem's neck, she had to think clearly and fast.

"They wouldn't hang him, they couldn't," Kate added with a distinct lack of conviction. "He's just a child, really."

"I know," Janey replied grimly. "But everyone is in such a panic of late because of the labourers' riots in Kent and Hampshire that they are seeing the threat of revolution everywhere. If you had heard Mr Filmore and his fellow magistrates at dinner last night, you would have thought them in danger of being carted off to the guillotine at dawn. They see harshness as their protection."

"But it's not right!" Kate's blue eyes brimmed with unshed tears. "If Mr Filmore had not dismissed him, this would never have happened. I don't know how we're going to break this to Mrs Avery, miss."

"Nor do I, but I promised I should call and tell her of the verdict as soon as it was known," Janey said grimly. "Where's the gig, Kate?"

"That way, around the corner—I paid Tom Mitchell's boy to hold the pony out of the master's sight, like you said," Kate replied.

"Thank you—I'd better go before Mr Filmore arrives and tries to stop me," Janey said as others began to trickle down the courthouse steps. "Can you stay here and see if the warders will let you see Jem for a moment, or at least get a message to him that I will do everything I can for him? I saw Jem's uncle, Will Avery, over there. I am sure he will give you a lift back to Pettridges if you ask him."

"Yes, miss," Kate agreed. "Miss—you'd better go. There's Mr Filmore."

With an unladylike oath acquired from Lilian, Janey picked up the skirts of her grey gown and pelisse coat and ran.

"Be careful, miss," Kate admonished from behind, "that leg of yours is only just healed. You don't want to break the other one."

"Jane! Jane! Come here at once!" Janey increased her speed a little as Mr Filmore's rather shrill tones overlaid Kate's warning. But flicking a glance over her shoulder, she slowed a little. Mr Filmore's over-inflated idea of his own dignity would not allow him to be seen chasing his ward down the street.

There would undoubtedly be a scene when she returned to Pettridges Hall, she thought resignedly as she scrambled into her gig and took up the reins. Not that she cared. While her grandfather had been alive, she had done her best to turn herself into the English lady he had so wanted her to be, out of affection for him. But she had no such feeling towards the Filmores, and what they thought of her had long since ceased to matter to her in the slightest.

Five months, she thought, as she cracked the whip over the skewbald pony's head and sent it forward at a spanking trot. Five months, and she would be twenty-one, and she would have control of her fortune, her estate—and would be able to tell the Filmores to leave Pettridges.

Heads out, extended necks flecked with foam, the blood bays pulled the high-wheeled phaeton along the narrow lane at full lick. Bouncing from side to side on the rutted surface, the wheel hubs scraped first the high stone wall on one side then the other.

"You win, Jonathan! I still consider this contraption outmoded and damned uncomfortable, but I will grant you it is faster than anything in my carriage house. So, slow down!" the fair-haired man, sitting beside the driver, gasped as he held on to his tall silk hat with one hand and the safety rail with the other. "We'll never make that bend at this speed and if there's anything coming the other way—"

"You're starting to sound like my maiden aunt, Perry." The Honourable Jonathan Lindsay laughed, but he pulled upon the reins and began to slow the team of matched bays, who were snorting and sweating profusely. "For someone who was cool as a cucumber when Boney's old Guard came on at Waterloo, you've made an almighty fuss for the last twenty minutes about a little speed."

"At nineteen, one has not developed the instinct for self-preservation one has at thirty-two," Perry said, sighing with relief as his dark-haired companion brought the bays down to a trot. "And I can assure you, I was far from cool..." A faraway look came on to his fresh ruddy face. "Is it really fifteen years ago? I still have nightmares about the sound of the damned

French drums as if it were yesterday. And at the time, I didn't think either of us would see our twentieth birthdays.''

''No.'' Jonathan Lindsay sighed. ''Neither did I, and sometimes I begin to wish that I hadn't—''

''Begad! You *have* been bitten by the black dog!'' Lord Derwent said, giving him a sharp look from his brown eyes. ''What the devil is up with Jono? First, you announce you are giving up the tables, next, that you are going to bury yourself in the country—'' He stopped and gave a theatrical groan. ''You have not been spurned by Charlotte?''

Jonathan shook his fashionably tousled dark head.

''Or Amelia, or Emily Witherston?'' Perry frowned as Jonathan's craggily handsome face remained impassive. ''Tell me it is not that ghastly Roberts girl—''

''Margaret? Allow me some taste!'' His friend sighed again. ''I have not fallen in love, Perry, and I have not the slightest intention of doing so!''

''Then what is chewing at you?'' Lord Derwent persisted in asking. ''Go on like this and you will be in danger of becoming positively dull.''

''Exactly!'' Lindsay sighed again, checking the bays as he looked ahead and saw a small ragged-looking child swinging precariously upon one of the gates that interrupted the run of stone walling here and there. ''Don't you feel it, Perry, creeping in from all directions since the old king died? And it'll get worse if Wellesley steps down for these reforming fellows—''

''Feel what?'' Lord Derwent looked at him blankly.

"Dullness, respectability, worthiness and rampant hypocrisy! You can't enjoy an evening in a hell without these new Peelers turning it over. And as for society—the most innocent flirtation sends young women into a simpering panic, and let slip the mildest oath and the mamas look at you as if you have crawled out of the midden! Conversation is all of profit and industry, new inventions and good works—everyone fancies themselves an archaeologist or scientist or writer—no one confesses to idleness or sheer self-indulgence any more. I begin to think old Bonaparte was right—we're becoming a nation of shopkeepers with a tradesman's morality—damnation, I am even beginning to feel that I should be doing 'something useful' with my life!"

"But you do…you do lots of things. You hunt and fish, and you're damned good company at the club—"

"Amusements, Perry, that's all," Jonathan said gloomily. "Amusements of which I am beginning to tire."

Lord Derwent's brow furrowed. "Well, you're a Member of Parliament. That's useful, ain't it?"

"Parliament! I rarely visit the place and I've made *one* speech in five years—and that was for a wager to see if I could make old Beaufort's face go as purple as that young Jewish fellow's waistcoat."

"Caused more of a stir than most, though." Derwent laughed. "When I read it in *The Times,* I thought you'd become a raving revolutionary. If every landowner gave land to his labourers for their use, we'd all be penniless and I doubt they'd bother to work for us at all!"

"One can hardly blame them," Lindsay answered drily. "The price of bread is up, wages are down, and the common land has been fenced in for sheep. Their work is being taken by machines in the name of profit and the poor relief has been cut to subsistence."

"Well, at least they're spared all that nasty dusty work—and the farmers do well out of it," Lord Derwent said lightly. "All the clever chaps tell me that the health of the nation is dependent upon the creation of wealth—"

"And also, it would seem, upon the creation of paupers," Jonathan said glancing towards the pinched face of the child as they passed him.

"The lower orders have always gone without when times are hard, they're used to it. A bit of hunger toughens 'em up and keeps 'em grateful for what they do get. They're not like us, Jono, they don't have the finer feelings—look out!"

But Lindsay had already reined back the bays almost to their haunches as they rounded another bend, made blind by the gable end of a cottage built into the wall, and almost collided with a pony trap slewed across its width.

There was no sign of its driver. The reins were looped loosely about the post of a small gate to one side of the cottage, and the skewbald pony was nibbling at a weed growing in a crack in the wall.

"Damned silly place to leave it!" Derwent announced loudly. "All Curzon Street to ninepence that it's driven by a woman."

"The Rector's wife or daughter, I'd wager," Jonathan agreed wryly, glancing at the weathered straw hat with a plain ribbon trim that lay discarded upon the seat of the trap. "Calling upon the downtrodden and irreligious with some tract, no doubt. Jump down and move it, would you, Perry? Or we'll be here all day. There's a field gate a bit further on—put it in there while I pass—"

"Must I?" Lord Derwent looked down doubtfully at the chalky mud of the lane. "It took my man hours to get this finish on my boots." His face brightened as he noticed that the tiny downstairs window of the cottage was open and leant across to pick up the whip. "No need, watch!"

He stretched out the whip and rapped upon the window sill. "I say, you there, would you like to earn a shilling—?"

"Go away! Go away!" A woman's voice, choked with sobs, replied. "You're murderers! All of you!"

"Murderers! I assure you, we are no such thing!" Perry shouted back cheerfully. "All we want is for someone to move this trap—surely you have a good strong lad—"

The woman's sobs became a low keening wail.

There was a bang as a door was thrown open. A moment later, Janey was at the gate. Tall and slender in her grey gown and white apron, she glowered up at them, as she settled a grubby-looking infant more firmly upon her hip.

"Can you not just go away?" The voice was low, educated and furiously angry with the faintest of accents, which puzzled Lindsay for a moment. He had heard that accent before, but where? His brows furrowed for a moment. And then he remembered. Jack de Lancey, the young American officer who had served on Wellington's staff at Waterloo before being mortally wounded.

"Whatever is the clergy coming to? She sounds like a colonial," Perry hissed in an all-too-audible whisper at the same moment.

"Perhaps that is because I was born in America and spent the first sixteen years of my life there," Janey snapped. She was in no mood for condescension from a pair of aristocratic dandies who were probably incapable of tying their own cravats. "Now, if your curiosity is satisfied, will you please go away!"

"With pleasure," Lord Derwent moaned, "but this—" he wrinkled his nose distastefully as he gestured to the trap "—this vehicle is in our way."

"You have my permission to move it!" she retorted, brushing back a strand of dishevelled fair hair from her face with her free hand. "Unless you would prefer to hold the child? I thought not!" she said scathingly as her hazel eyes blazed across Derwent's horrified face. "It might spoil your gloves!"

"But surely there is a lad—" Derwent said.

"Not any longer! You hear that woman weeping—she has just heard that 'her fine lad' is to be hanged for the firing of a rick, which he was not even near—"

"Hanged! Bigod!" Lord Derwent's fair brows lifted. "Damned inconvenient timing, but I suppose he deserves it."

"Deserves—" Her voice came out of her throat as a hiss of contempt. "Do you think anyone deserves to die for the price of a hayrick, when his employer is a mean-minded cheat who will let men, women and children starve to death? Is hanging a just punishment for such a crime?''

"Should have thought of that before he set fire to the rick. Common knowledge that arson's a capital offence," Lord Derwent drawled.

"He did not fire the rick!" Janey found herself almost choked with rage. If they did not go soon, arson would not be the only capital offence to be committed of late. She could easily murder the pair of them. "I do not know how you can be so complacent! So arrogant!" she said fiercely.

"Quite easily, really. Someone has to support the rule of law, you know."

"The trap, Perry?" Jonathan interposed quietly, speaking for the first time when he saw Janey's free hand clench upon the crossbar of the gate as if she were intending to rip it off and hurl it at Derwent like a spear. "Now, if you would not mind?"

"Must I?" His companion's answer was one sharp glance that sent Lord Derwent down from the box in a moment.

The hazel eyes followed Derwent, and the soft rose lips silently framed an epithet that the Honourable Jonathan Lindsay had never heard from a lady, and certainly not from a Rector's wife. His cool blue gaze flicked to the hand she had put up to push away another stray strand of hair from her eyes, leaving a smudge of soot upon her slanting cheekbone. No ring upon the slender fingers—the daughter, then?

A pity, he thought. With her great angry dark eyes, slanted dark brows and wide, soft mouth, she was all passion and fire, a veritable Amazon. Quite unlike the insipid blue-eyed misses who were English society's current ideal, but put her in Paris and she'd have 'em falling at her feet. If she had been married, country life might have proved more entertaining than he had expected, but he had a rule of never seducing unmarried girls. There were some depths to which one could not sink, even to relieve boredom.

And then, with a start, he realised that those extraordinary hazel eyes were fixed upon his face, regarding him with a coolness that he found distinctly disconcerting. He was not accustomed to women looking at him as if he had just crawled from beneath a stone. Possessed of a large fortune, and good looks since the age of sixteen or so, he had always been the recipient of frank admiration, dewy-eyed adoration or thinly veiled invitations from females of all ages.

"Lord Derwent is not as unkind as he sounds, I assure you," he said, wondering why that cool dark gaze should make him feel as if he should apologise to her. After all, why should he care what she thought of him?

"No?" The fine dark arch of her brows lifted as she glanced to where Lord Derwent was somewhat ineffectively coaxing the unwilling pony away from the weed in the wall. "Perhaps I misjudged him...perhaps he is merely stupid."

"Derwent is far from stupid. He is overly flippant at times," he said tersely, knowing that it was equally true of himself. "It has been a habit of his for so long he no longer notices himself doing it."

"Flippant!" Her voice was as contemptuous as her stare as she looked at him a second time, taking in the studied carelessness of his Caesar haircut, the immaculately tailored grey topcoat that emphasised the broad width of his shoulders, leanness of his waist and hips, the glossy perfection of riding boots that did not often have contact with the ground. "If you think that an excuse, then you are as despicable as he is."

Her gaze came back up to his, defiant and decidedly judgmental, he thought. She might as well call him a dandy and a plunger and have done with it as look at him in that fashion. Well, if that was how she wished it—

"Oh, no, I really cannot allow you to insult Derwent in such a fashion," he drawled and returned her scrutiny with a blatancy which sent the colour flaring in her cheeks. "I'm worse, much worse, I assure you."

"That I can well believe," she replied, involuntarily lifting her free hand to the little white ruff collar at the neck of her grey gown to be sure it was fastened. And then, aware that his mocking blue gaze had followed the gesture, she let her hand drop swiftly back to her side and lifted her chin to glare at him again.

"But I do have my saving graces," he said, drily feeling a flicker of satisfaction that he had succeeded in disconcerting her. "A sense of humour, for instance."

"Really?" Her faintly husky voice was pure ice as her gaze blazed into his eyes. "I cannot say I find hanging a source of amusement." Hitching the infant more firmly upon her hip, she made to turn away.

"Wait! My apologies. You are right, of course— hanging is no laughing matter." He found himself speaking before he had even thought what he was going to say. "This lad who is to be hanged—if you tell me his name and circumstances, I might be able to do something. I cannot promise, of course, but I have some influence as a Member of Parliament.''

''You are a Member of Parliament?'' There was astonishment in her voice and in the wide hazel eyes as she turned to face him again, and, he noted wryly, deep suspicion.

''Difficult to believe, I know, but it is the truth,'' he drawled.

''For a rotten borough, no doubt,'' she said, half to herself.

''Positively rank, I'm afraid. My father buys every vote in the place,'' he taunted her lightly. ''But the offer of help is a genuine one.''

She regarded him warily for a moment. There was no longer mockery in either the blue eyes or that velvety voice.

''You mean it?'' she said incredulously. ''You will try—?''

''My word on it,'' he said, wondering how he had thought her hair was mouse at first glance. It was gold, he realised, as a shaft of weak sunlight filtered through the clouds. A warm tawny gold, like ripe corn under an August sun. And it looked soft. Released from that tight knot, he would wager it would run through a man's hands like pure silk.

''His name is Jem, Jem Avery, he's fourteen years old and he was sentenced at Salisbury Assizes, by Judge Richardson.''

Jonathan jerked his attention back from imagining the circumstances in which he might test his own wager and gave her his full attention. ''Fourteen? That does seem harsh,'' he said slowly.

"Yes. Fourteen. They seem to think that to make such an example will quell the discontent amongst the labourers and prevent it spreading to Wiltshire," she said flatly, as his blue gaze met and held hers for a moment. "You really will see what you can do? You will not forget?"

"No. No." He shook his head, quite certain that even if the unfortunate Jem slipped his mind, his advocate was not likely to do so for a week or two at least. "You have my word I will do what I can."

"Why?" she asked suddenly. "You are a stranger here and can have no interest in what becomes of Jem."

He shrugged his shoulders. "Must be my altruistic nature. I can never resist a distressed damsel, so long as she is passably pretty, of course," he added self-mockingly.

"I am not distressed, sir! I am angry!" she snapped with a lift of her chin. "And neither am I passably pretty!"

"No," he said, after a pause in which his gaze travelled over her face, taking in the breadth of her brow, the fine straight nose that had absolutely no propensity towards turning up, the clean, strong upward slant of her jawbone from the point of her lifted chin, and that wide, generous mouth, "you are not passably pretty."

"I am glad you realise your error—" she began to say, wondering why she felt such a sense of pique.

"Any man who considered you merely passable would be lacking in judgement and taste," he interrupted her lazily, his eyes warm and teasing as they met her gaze. And that was true, he thought, with a touch of surprise as his gaze dropped fractionally to the decidedly kissable curve of her mouth and then lower still to the perfect sweeping lines of her body beneath the plain grey gown.

Janey stared back at him. He was flirting with her. This laconic, drawling, society dandy was flirting with her! He was looking at her as if he wanted to kiss her, touch her... The image that arose in her mind was so shocking, so devastating, that she could do nothing for a second or so but stare back at him helplessly. And then, as the corners of his wide, clever mouth lifted imperceptibly, and the clear blue eyes dared her to respond, the breath left her throat in a small exasperated sigh.

"Have you no sense of propriety?" she found herself blurting out and then frowned as it occurred to her she had sounded all too much like Mrs Filmore.

"Afraid not," he answered with a complete lack of apology. "I blame it upon a youth spent in hells and houses of ill-repute, not to mention the houses of the aristocracy and Parliament, of course."

"Oh, you are quite impossible!" In spite of herself, in spite of everything, she found her mouth tugging up at the corners.

"You can smile, then?" he said lightly. "I was beginning to wonder if you considered it a sin."

"No." She sobered, feeling guilty that for a second or two she had almost forgotten Jem. "But I cannot say that I much in the mood for merriment at present."

"No." The hint of mockery, of invitation, left his face and voice as he glanced at the cottage. "That is understandable enough in the circumstances. You have not told me where I might send word. The Rectory?''

"No, Pettridges Hall," she said with inexplicable satisfaction, having overheard his comments about the likely owner of the trap through the open cottage window. "I have no connection with the Rectory and no fondness for reforming tracts."

"I am delighted to hear it," he said without the slightest trace of embarrassment. "Especially since it seems we are to be neighbours. I have just become the new owner of Southbrook, which I understand borders the Pettridges estate."

"You have bought Southbrook?" Janey's face lit as she looked at him with unhidden delight. "That is wonderful!"

The dark brows lifted, mocking her faintly. "I am flattered by your enthusiasm to have me for a neighbour."

"It is not for you in particular, sir, I meant merely that it is wonderful that Southbrook has been bought at last," Janey said, and knew as she caught the flicker of amusement in the pale blue eyes that she had spoken just a little too quickly to be completely convincing either to him or herself. "The land has lain idle so long and there are so many men in the village who desperately need work."

"I stand corrected," he said drily. "Though I feel honour bound to confess that I did not buy the estate from any sense of philanthropic duty. I accepted it in lieu of a card debt after the owner assured me it was no longer his family home. We are on our way to inspect the property now."

"Oh, I see," she said, her voice flat again suddenly. "You are not familiar with the estate, then?"

she asked, thinking that he and his companion would undoubtedly take one look and return to town forthwith, as had all the other potential purchasers.

"Not yet. Why?" he asked sharply. For a moment she considered warning him about the leaking roof, the broken windows, the last five years of complete neglect that had followed upon twenty of inadequate maintenance, but then she decided against it. There was always a chance that he might see beyond Southbrook's failings to its original beauty and decide to restore the estate.

"Oh—no reason," she replied, carefully giving her attention to the child in her arms who was beginning to grizzle and wriggle. "I'm sorry, what did you say?"

"I asked whom I should ask for?"

"Janey." Stupidly, for no reason she could think of, she answered with the name with which she had been known to family and friends for the first sixteen years of her life. "Miss Hilton, Miss Jane Hilton, I mean," she stammered slightly as the straight black brows lifted again.

"Jane," he repeated it with a half-laugh. "Plain Jane."

"Yes," she said defensively. It was a jest she had endured more times than she could count from her guardian's son and daughter. "What of it?"

"Nothing." Again his narrow lips curved. "Somehow I did not think you would be an Araminta or Arabella, Miss Hilton."

"Jono! Are you coming through or not?" Lord Derwent called impatiently.

"I must go. I think your trap would be better there by the gate, but if you wish—"

"No, your friend was right, it was a stupid place

to leave it," she admitted ruefully. "I was thinking only of how to break the news to Jem's mother. I am sorry for the inconvenience."

"It is of no consequence." He smiled at her as he gathered up the reins. "Good day, Miss Hilton, I shall send word as soon as I can."

"Thank you, Mr—" she began to say and then realised she did not even know his name.

"Lindsay," he called over his shoulder as he sent the bays forward, "Jonathan Lindsay."

She stood staring after him in disbelief. That was the Honourable Jonathan Lindsay? That laconic mocking dandy had made the passionate speech, demanding better conditions for the labouring poor that she had read in the paper? Surely not! And yet he had offered to help Jem, a boy he had never met.

For a moment, as she watched the phaeton disappear down the long winding lane, she felt like chasing after it and begging him to take on Southbrook. If she were honest, it was not only because a humane landlord would make such a difference to so many in the village, but because he had made her feel truly alive for the first time since she had arrived in England.

"Miss, miss..." The child who had been swinging on the gate came and tugged at her skirt. "Have you brought us something, miss? I'm hungry—"

"Yes, Sam. Some broth, some bread and some preserves," she answered, still staring after the phaeton, "and some gingerbread, if you promise to be a good boy for your mother."

She broke off, frowning as she watched the little boy who was already running for the door, his too thin arms and legs flying in all directions. Even with what she could persuade cook to let her have from the kitchen, they were not getting enough to eat, nor were at least half a dozen other families in the village.

As farm after farm took to the new threshing machines, there would be more men out of work this autumn—and she could do nothing, since she had no control of her estate, nor access to the fortune left her by her grandfather until she was twenty-one. And five months was far too long for Sam and the other families, who would starve and freeze this winter. There was nothing she could do, nothing—heiress she might be, but she was almost as powerless as poor Jem in his prison cell.

Biting her lip, she adjusted the child on her hip again as she limped slowly up the little herringbone brick path to the cottage door. As ever when she was tired, the leg she had broken a year ago had begun to ache. But there was no time to think of that now, not when Mrs Avery stood in the doorway, her face grey and desperate.

"He'll be so scared, miss, so frightened," the older woman blurted out. "I'd rather it was me than him."

"I know," she said helplessly.

"I've got to go to him, miss." Mrs Avery caught her arm. "I've got to!"

"I will take you tomorrow, I am sure they will let you visit," Janey said huskily as she guided the other woman back into the little dark room, where the other four Avery children were huddled upon the box bed, pale and silent. As she looked from one thin, pinched miserable face to another, the rage in her bubbled up afresh. If Jonathan Lindsay failed them, she would not let them hang Jem! She would not! Not even if she had to break him out of gaol herself.

Chapter Two

"Great God, Jono!" Lord Derwent broke the lengthy silence which had ensued after the phaeton drew up before the edifice of Southbrook House. "You took this in lieu of ten thousand? I should not give five hundred for the whole place! The park is nothing but weeds, the woods looked as if they had not been managed in half a century and as for this—" he gestured to the ivy-masked façade of the house "—look at it! There is not a whole pane of glass in the place, and what the roof is like I hate to think…"

"Perfect proportions, though," Jonathan Lindsay said thoughtfully as he, too, surveyed the house. "See how the width of the steps exactly balances the height of the columns on the portico. Come on, Perry, let's look inside now we're here."

Knotting the ribbons loosely, he leapt lithely down from the box.

"Do we have to?" Derwent groaned.

There was no answer. Jonathan Lindsay was already striding across the weed-choked gravel of the drive.

* * *

"You are not *serious* about intending to live here?" Lord Derwent pleaded an hour later, after they had inspected the house from attic to cellar. "It's damp, dusty and—" he paused, shivering in his blue frock coat "—colder than an ice house in December."

"Nothing that someone else's industry will not put right," his friend said absently, as he stared up at the painted ceiling of the salon adjacent to the ballroom. "This ceiling is very fine, don't you think?"

"It might be," Lord Derwent said unenthusiastically, "if you could see it for dust and cobwebs. I'm sorry, Jono, but I simply can't understand why you would wish to reside here when Ravensfield is at your disposal."

"I never shared my late uncle's taste for Gothic fakery, you know that, Perry."

"Yes, but it has every convenience, it's in damned good hunting country and the agent runs the estate tighter than a ship of the line: you wouldn't need to lift a finger from one year end to the next. Local society's not up to much, I'll grant you that, but it won't be any different here."

"Oh, I don't know." Jonathan smiled. "I thought the neighbourhood showed some promise of providing entertainment."

"You mean that extraordinary young woman?"

"Ah, so you thought she was extraordinary, too," he said, as he began to walk slowly back towards the entrance hall.

"Extraordinarily rude," Lord Derwent replied huffily. "It is scarcely my fault some idiot boy is going to get himself turned off, but she looked at me as if she'd have preferred to see me in a tumbril on the way to Madame Guillotine.''

"I'm sure you misjudge the fair maiden—I think she'd have settled for a horse whipping,'' Jonathan said drily.

"I don't!'' Derwent said with feeling. "I can't think why you offered to help.''

"No, not like me, is it?'' Jonathan agreed, deadpan. "I must have succumbed to this fever for worthiness.''

"Succumbed to a weakness for perfect proportions, more like,'' Derwent said darkly, "and I'm not referring to the portico.''

"Ah, Perry, you do know how to wound one's feelings,'' Jonathan said, grinning. "But you must confess, she was very easy on the eye.''

"And to think that, only two hours ago, you were telling me that you were going to give up women along with the tables.'' Derwent sighed. "But I'll wager you'll get not that one past the bedroom door, Jono. These radical females are all the same—they only give their affections to ugly curates or long-haired poets who write execrable drivel.''

"No gentleman could possibly accept such a challenge.'' Jonathan laughed. "So, what are your terms?''

"Triton against your chestnut stallion,'' Lord Derwent said after a moment's thought.

"Triton!'' Jonathan's dark brows rose. "I'd almost contemplate marrying the girl to get my hands on that horse before the Derby. Are you so certain of my failure?''

"Positive. I chased after a gal like that once. There

I was, in the midst of telling her about my critical role in defeating old Boney and waiting for her to fall at my feet in admiration, and all she says is 'Yes, but do you read the scriptures, Lord Derwent? Spiritual courage is so much more important than the physical kind, don't you think?' "

"Poor Perry." Jonathan sighed. "It must be a sad affliction to lack both good looks and natural charm—" He broke off, laughing as he ducked to evade a friendly blow from Derwent.

"And," Derwent went on, "she'll never forgive you for not saving her arsonist. You said yourself the local men were determined to make an example, so they're not likely to listen to a newcomer to the district, not even you, Jono."

"Who said anything about local men?" Jonathan smiled, a wide slow smile. "We are going to get some fresh horses, and then we're going straight back to town and I am going to see the Home Secretary."

"The Home Secretary! He wouldn't intervene on behalf of an arsonist and thief if his mother begged him on bended knee. And you are not exactly in favour with the government after that speech—the front bench did not appear to share your sense of humour."

"Oh, I think he'll lend a sympathetic ear," Jonathan drawled. "Remember I told you I was involved in a bit of a mill with the Peelers when the hell in Ransome Street was raided? Well, if I hadn't landed a well-aimed blow upon one of the guardians of the law, our esteemed Home Secretary would have found himself in an extremely embarrassing situation."

"Great God!" Derwent cried. "You mean you are going to blackmail the Home Secretary to win the admiration of some parson's daughter! It'll be you on the gallows next.''

"Blackmail—what an ugly word.'' Jonathan grinned. "I'm just going to seek a favour from a friend. And she's not the parson's daughter, her name is Jane Hilton and she resides at Pettridges Hall,'' he added, his grin widening.

"If she's not a clerical's brat, she must be a poor relation or a companion and they're as bad,'' Perry said huffily.

"You know the people at Pettridges?'' Jonathan's blue eyes regarded him with sharpened interest.

"Hardly describe 'em as acquaintances, but their name's not Hilton, so she's not one of 'em,'' Derwent said lazily. "I met the offspring last season: sulky-looking lad who talked of nothing but hunting and a distinctly useful little redhead that Mama was doing her best to marry off before she got herself into a tangle of one sort or another. Now, what the devil was the name—ah—Filmore, that's it. They must be comfortably off, though—Pettridges wouldn't have come cheap. My father told me old Fenton never spared a penny when it came to improving the place.''

"Fenton? I don't know the name.''

"Well, he was something of a recluse. He was a cloth manufacturer, worked his way up from millhand to owner and dragged himself out of gutter by clothing half the army and navy and, if the rumours were true, half Boney's lot as well.

"By the Peace of Amien he'd made enough for a country estate and respectability, even had an impoverished earl lined up for his daughter. But she reverted to type and ran off with her childhood sweetheart, a millhand. Fenton was furious. He never saw her again and cut her off without a penny. Affair made him a laughing stock, of course, and he never made any attempt to take part in society after that.'' Derwent sighed. ''Damned waste of a fortune and a pretty face by all accounts. Wonder who did get his money? They say he had one of the biggest fortunes in Southwest England.'' Then he brightened. ''I think I might look into it, Jono. You never know, there might be a great-niece or something, and I might land myself an heiress.''

Jonathan laughed. ''He probably left it all to the Mill Owners Benevolent Fund for Virtuous Widows, Perry.''

''Probably,'' Derwent agreed gloomily. ''I suppose it will just have to be Diana, then. My father has told me he wants to see his grandson and a generous dowry in the family coffers before next year is out or he will discontinue my allowances, and tell the bankers to withdraw my credit. You don't know how lucky you are being the youngest son and possessing a fortune to match those of your brothers—it spares you no end of trouble.''

''Yes,'' Jonathan said beneath his breath, ''and leaves you no end of time to fill.''

Janey sat in the window-seat of the morning-room, the copy of Cobbett's *Register* in her lap, still at the same page she had opened it at half an hour earlier. She stared out at the gravelled sweep of drive that remained empty but for the gardeners, raking up the fallen leaves from the beeches that lined the drive. Surely Mr Lindsay would send word today, even if he had been unsuccessful. It was eight days now, and time was running out. In five days' time Jem would be led out from Dorchester Gaol and hanged.

She dropped her eyes unseeingly to Mr Cobbett's prose. At least she had not told Mrs Avery, at least she had not raised false hopes there—

"Jane! Have you heard a word I have said?"

She started as she realised that Annabel Filmore had entered the morning-room. "I'm sorry," she said absently, "I was thinking."

"You mean you had your head in a book as usual," the red-haired girl said disparagingly as she studied her reflection in the gilt-framed mirror above the mantelpiece. "Mama says so much reading and brainwork ruins one's looks," she added as she patted one of her fat sausage-shaped curls into place over her forehead.

"You need not worry, then," Janey said, not quite as quietly as she had meant.

"I have never had to worry about my looks," Annabel said blithely, utterly oblivious to the insult as she turned upon her toes in a pirouette to admire the swirling skirts of her frilled pink muslin. "Just as well, with Jonathan Lindsay coming to live at Southbrook."

"He is coming!" Janey's face lit up. "When?"

"Oh, in a week or two, I think Papa said," Annabel replied carelessly still admiring herself in the glass.

"A week or two!" The brief flare of hope she had felt died instantly. A week and all would be over for Jem. No doubt the promise had been forgotten as soon as made. So now what was she to do?

"Yes, but whatever has Jonathan Lindsay to do

with you?'' Annabel asked, suddenly curious as she turned to look at Jane. ''You have gone quite pale.''

''Nothing, I met him in Burton's Lane a few days ago,'' she said tersely, Mr Cobbett's *Register* fluttering unnoticed from the lap of her lavender muslin gown as she got to her feet. ''That's all.''

''That's all!'' Annabel's blue eyes widened in exaggerated despair. ''You meet the most handsome man in England in Burton's Lane and you did not say a word to anyone!''

''I did not think him so very handsome,'' Janey said, not entirely truthfully. ''He was a little too much of the dandy for my taste.''

''Not handsome!'' Annabel groaned and flounced down upon a sofa. ''When he is so dark, so rugged— and that profile! Why, he could be Miss Austen's Darcy in the flesh.''

''That is not how I see him,'' Janey said, half to herself, as an unexpected image of his face, chiselled, and hard, lightened only by the slant of his mouth and brows, and the lazy amusement in the cool blue eyes, came instantly into her mind. Oh, no, she thought, Mr Lindsay was definitely no Mr Darcy. He was far too incorrect—far too dangerous in every sense.

She doubted he was afraid of breaking conventions, or anything else for that matter. In fact, strip him of his dandified clothes and put him in a suit of buckskins and he would not have been so out of place among the backwoodsmen among whom she had grown up. Whether or not someone would survive on the frontier was the yardstick by which she always found herself assessing people; in Mr Lindsay's case, she found her answer was a surprising ''yes''.

"It's so unfair that you had to meet him in Burton's Lane instead of me," Annabel complained as she toyed with one of the flounces on her gown. "You should have invited him back here. Do you have any idea of how hard I tried for an introduction when I was in Town last Season?" Then her sullen round face brightened. "Mama will not possibly be able to refuse to allow us to be introduced now he is to be a neighbour."

"Your mother would not allow you to be introduced to him? Why ever not?" Janey asked, curious in spite of herself. The son of an Earl, even if he were the younger could usually do no wrong in the eyes of Mrs Filmore.

"Because of his reputation, ninny," Annabel explained patiently, as if she were speaking to a child. "He is the greatest rake and gambler in England; at least, that is what Miss Roberts told Mama. She said that there were a dozen husbands with cause to call him out, if duelling had not been banned, and another twenty wives who would willingly give their spouses cause to do the same.

"And she told me that he quite broke Araminta Howard's heart—and very nearly her reputation. Miss Roberts says he cares for nothing but his pleasure—" Annabel's lips parted upon the word and she gave a little shiver.

"I can scarcely believe that of the man who made the speech that was printed in the paper," Janey said, feeling a peculiar distaste about hearing of Jonathan Lindsay's apparently numerous amours.

"The speech about the poor!" Annabel gave a shriek of laughter as her brother entered the room, and came to lounge sullenly against the mantle. "Piers! Piers! Jane admires the speech Jonathan Lindsay made on behalf of the poor."

"Then, once he has settled in, we must be sure to call so she can congratulate him in person," Piers drawled, an unpleasant smile on his rather too-plump mouth. "I am sure he will be delighted with her admiration."

"Oh we must—we must—" Annabel spluttered into helpless incoherent laughter.

With a resigned sigh, Janey bent to pick up the *Register* and made to leave.

"Where are you going, dear coz?" Piers stepped in front of her.

"Somewhere a little quieter," Janey said, staring back into Piers's rather bulbous pale blue eyes. "Will you stand aside, please?"

"Papa wants you in the library," Piers answered without moving. "He is none too happy about the food you've been doling out in the village. Quite choleric, in fact, says he won't have the estate's money wasted upon the undeserving poor who do no work."

"And yet he does not mind keeping you in funds," Janey said mildly.

"I am not poor," Piers said frostily, his heavy features taking on an expression of hauteur.

"Undeserving was the adjective I had in mind." Janey smiled. "Now let me pass, if you please. Perhaps you can convey my apologies to your father? I have other more pressing matters to attend to this morning."

"Like reading this insurrectionist rubbish!" Piers

snatched the *Register* from her, crumpled it into a ball and threw it into the fire.

"How dare you!" Janey hissed. "That was mine, you had no right—"

"I had every right, dear coz," Piers sneered, catching her arm as she went to turn away. "You know Papa will not have that paper in the house. And now you are coming to the library, as Papa wishes."

"Let go of me!" Janey said warningly.

"No."

"Very well." Janey brought her knee sharply upwards in a manoeuvre which no well-brought-up young English lady would have known.

There were definitely some advantages in a frontier upbringing, she thought, as she saw Piers's eyes bulge, and he crumpled into a groaning heap upon the floor.

"Jane! What have you done? You have killed him!" Annabel flew to her cursing brother's side.

"I fear not," Janey said unrepentantly. She picked up her shawl from the window-seat and turned for the door, a smile upon her lips. A smile that froze as she found herself looking over her guardian's shoulder, straight into Jonathan Lindsay's blue eyes.

How long he had been there, what he thought of her after the scene he had just witnessed, were of no consequence for the moment in which their gazes locked. She only knew that she felt a ridiculous surge of happiness that he had not forgotten his promise to her. He had come.

"Jane!" Mr Filmore, who had seemed transfixed, apart from the trembling of his moustache, finally found his voice in a tone of thunderous disapproval.

"I cannot think what you have to smile about! Brawling like some tavern slut! Has the money your grandfather spent upon your education, the effort Mrs Filmore has expended, counted for nothing?"

Janey made no answer, but stood, head held high, her gaze fixed upon a point somewhere over the rather short Mr Filmore's head. She had a very good idea of how the conversation would progress. Mr Filmore never lost an opportunity to remind her of her failings, her lack of gratitude for the belated, but expensive, education lavished upon her by her grandfather.

Or the fact that she had been discovered, at the age of fifteen, living in a boarding house in the care of a woman who thought little of hiring herself out along with the beds, a woman who taught her the very useful manoeuvre she had just tried out on Piers. And upon receipt of that information, Jonathan Lindsay would no doubt decide to discontinue their acquaintance at the earliest opportunity, she thought, her happiness evaporating into a sudden bleak emptiness.

"Have you ever had the misfortune to witness such behaviour before, Mr Lindsay? I should wager you have not!" Somewhat to Janey's surprise, Mr Filmore turned to address his visitor before berating her further.

"No." Mild contempt edged Jonathan Lindsay's voice like a razor. "But then, neither have I seen such provocation before, being accustomed to the company of gentlemen." He looked pointedly at Piers who, after being assisted to his feet by his sister, strode out of the opposite door without so much as a word to any of them.

Janey's hazel gaze flashed back to his in grateful

astonishment. She had not expected to find an ally in the aristocratic Jonathan Lindsay.

Holding her gaze, he gave her the briefest of smiles. A smile that made her heart stop and skip a beat. Suddenly, the imminent lecture to be endured did not seem such an ordeal.

"If you knew my ward, sir, you would know my son is blameless in this matter," Mr Filmore said huffily. "We make allowances, of course—she has never been quite herself since her betrothed died so tragically last year."

"Allowances!" Janey's hazel eyes took on a greener hue as her temper rose.

"Jane," Mr Filmore said firmly, "do not let us have another scene. You do not want Mr Lindsay to think you unbalanced, do you?"

"That is not an error I am likely to make," Jonathan said coolly. "In my opinion, Miss Hilton is perfectly balanced." He put the slightest emphasis upon the last word, and Janey felt her insides contract as his blue gaze skimmed downwards from her face to the sharp curve of her waist emphasised by the tightly fitting bodice of her lavender gown. "And it is a delight to see her again."

"Again?" Mr Filmore said, looking down his sharp thin nose. "I was not aware you had been introduced, Jane."

"We met by accident, last week," Janey said dragging her gaze from Jonathan Lindsay's face. A delight. Was that true?

"In Burton's Lane," supplied Annabel with deliberate malice. "That's where the family of that boy who fired the rick live."

"Not for much longer, if I have anything to do with it." Mr Filmore was curt, disapproving. "I might have known you were gallivanting about the countryside again, dispensing largesse to all and sundry." He drew himself up. "If it were not for me, Mr Lindsay, Miss Hilton would not have a penny of her money left by the time she is of age."

"Oh, Papa, I am sure Mr Lindsay does not wish to be bored with our little domestic disagreements." Annabel came forward, all smiles, swaying flounces and bouncing curls, as Janey stood, momentarily stricken, wondering whether Mr Filmore could evict Mrs Avery without notice. "And you have not introduced me yet."

"There is hardly any need," Jonathan said, with a smile that did not reach his eyes. "I know you by sight, Miss Filmore, and by reputation." His mouth curved a little upon the last word. "You were in Town last Season, were you not?"

"Yes, how clever of you to remember," Annabel simpered, fluttering her eyelashes. "I did not think you would have noticed me amongst so many."

"Oh, you are impossible to ignore, Miss Filmore," Jonathan said drily as his eyes flicked over the pink frills. "Quite impossible."

"Oh, Mr Lindsay, you are such a flatterer," Annabel said, twirling one of her red curls coyly about her finger. "Is he not shameless, Jane?"

"Utterly, I fear," Janey agreed mildly, the corners of her mouth curving in spite of everything. Only Annabel, whose vanity was overwhelming, could possibly have taken what he had said as a compliment.

"Jane," Mr Filmore said frowningly, as he glanced

from Lindsay to Janey, "have you entirely forgotten your manners? Go and order some refreshment for our guest."

"Of course," Janey said demurely. "If you will excuse me?" She waited for Jonathan Lindsay to step aside.

"A moment, Miss Hilton." He touched her arm as she made to pass him, stopping her in mid-stride. She stared down at his long elegant fingers, so brown and firm upon her thin muslin sleeve just above her wrist. It was the lightest, politest of gestures. There was no need for her pulse to beat wildly at the base of her throat, no reason at all for her breath to stop in her throat. And it was ridiculous to have this feeling that her whole life had been leading to this moment, this man's touch upon her sleeve.

Dragging in a hasty breath, she jerked her gaze upwards to his and found him staring at her speculatively.

"Yes?" Her voice was almost, but not quite, as steady as she would have wished it as his gaze held hers and she caught the gleam of amusement in the indigo depths of his eyes. No doubt he was used to women reacting to him in such a fashion and that piqued her. She did not want to be like the rest…not to this man.

"That matter we spoke of—"

"About the gardens of Southbrook, you mean?" she interrupted him warningly, willing him with her eyes to understand that she did not want Jem's case mentioned before Mr Filmore.

"Yes," he said after a fractional hesitation, "the gardens."

"You will find the camomile seat at the foot of the waterfall," she went on hastily. "Sunset is the best time to sit there, the light turns the water to rainbows—" She stopped, as close to blushing as she had ever been, as his brows lifted quizzically and he smiled at her in a way he had never done before, a wide slanting smile that reflected the warmth in his gaze.

"Rainbows at sunset?" he said with gentle mockery. "How very romantic for a Radical."

"It was merely an observation—you really do get rainbows—" she said tersely as Annabel giggled.

"Then I shall go there this very evening."

She exhaled with relief as he lifted his fingers from her arm. He had understood. But then he understood everything far too well, she thought wryly as she took a step back from him.

"Rainbows!" She heard Annabel snort as she left the room. "I swear Jane is becoming more fanciful by the day."

Chapter Three

The orange disc of the sun was just slipping below the distant horizon of the downs when Janey stepped out of the woods. A few feet ahead of her was an apparently sheer cliff, out of which sprang a small torrent of water, which foamed and sparkled as it tumbled into the shadowy pool some forty feet below. Above the noise of the water, she could hear the frantic excited barking of a dog; glancing down to the edge of the pool, she saw Jonathan Lindsay, throwing sticks for his liver and white spaniel into the calm end of the pool.

Cautiously she began to descend the narrow zigzag of a fern-lined path that threaded down the cliff, thinking ruefully that it would have been easier if she had been as close a follower of the fashions as Annabel and, hence, would have been wearing a skirt that skimmed her ankles rather than the ground.

The roar of the falling water drowned out the noise of her approach. It was the spaniel who sensed her presence first, dropping its stick at Jonathan's feet and raising its head to bark furiously.

"Hello! I was beginning to think you were not coming, or I had misunderstood you," he called up to her as he turned.

"No, you understood perfectly," she shouted back, wondering why it was that seeing him should give her this peculiar feeling of instant well-being. "I am sorry to have kept you waiting," she said as she drew nearer, "it was more difficult than I had expected to get away."

"You are still in disgrace, I take it?"

"For all eternity, I suspect," she said with feeling, her guardians having waxed long and lyrical about her outrageous behaviour.

"Wait, I'll help you—the path has collapsed there." He came forward, hands outstretched to help her down the last drop of two feet or so.

"Thank you," she said after a fractional hesitation, and put out her hands to rest them on his shoulders as his hands closed about her waist. It would have been ridiculous to refuse. As ridiculous as it was to feel so afraid of touching him. Daniel had lifted her down from a thousand such places when they had roamed the great forests on the long trail west, looking for firewood and berries.

"Ready?"

"Yes..." The word dwindled to nothing in her throat as she glanced down into his blue, blue eyes and everything seemed to stop: time, her heart, her lungs—even the roaring, cascading water.

For a second, no more, he stared back at her. Then, with a flicker of a smile, he lifted her down. Staring at his snowy linen cravat, she waited for him to release her waist, and then she realised that he could hardly do so until she removed her hands from his shoulders, where they seemed to have become fixed.

Snatching her hands back, she pulled out of his grasp, took two steps back and dragged in a breath. She had danced with several men, even been kissed upon the mouth once by Daniel, but she had never, ever felt anything like that sudden irrational sense of belonging, of wanting to touch, hold on and never let go—

Get yourself in hand, girl, she told herself impatiently, as he regarded her a little quizzically with a half-smile hovering upon his wide mouth. Sure, he was handsome, but he had not found their proximity in the least bit earthshaking—but then, no doubt, he was used to simpering society misses falling at his feet. She took another breath and lifted her chin, preparing to be as cool, as ladylike and as English as she knew how.

"Do you always look at man like that when he touches you?"

His dry question almost made her gasp. No one she had met since she had come to England had ever been so direct, so outrageously intimate. How *dare* he ask such a thing! And then she almost laughed—if he wasn't going to play by society rules, then neither was she…she would be what she was, a colonial who did not know how to behave properly.

"Only when they have dishonourable intentions." She gave him a blithe smile as she spoke and had the satisfaction of seeing surprise flicker across his face.

"Alas, you know me so well already." He inclined his head to her, his blue eyes sparkling with laughter.

"But at least you did not slap my face; I suppose I should be grateful for that."

"I have never cared for overly trodden paths," she said as they walked side by side towards the camomile seat.

"Oh, sharp, sharp, Miss Hilton, I am wounded to the quick." He put a theatrical hand to his breast.

"Not so much as Piers was," she said sweetly, thinking it would do him no harm to be reminded that she was very capable of defending herself.

"True," he agreed wryly, and then frowned. "You are limping. Have you hurt yourself?"

"It's nothing. I broke my leg in a fall almost a year ago and it still aches sometimes," she answered, as she sat down gratefully upon the springy cushion of herbs.

"Horses can be dangerous beasts, can they not?" he said as he seated himself beside her. "I broke a collarbone once, and that took long enough to mend."

"Yes." She let his assumption go. She did not want to have to explain about the accident, or Edward, just now. She was having trouble enough coping with his disconcerting nearness and the knowledge that she was as susceptible as any society miss to Jonathan Lindsay's very considerable charm.

"So is that why you like to come here often, because you do not care for the overly trodden paths?" he asked a moment later, giving her a sideways glance.

"How did you know I come here often?" She paused in the act of crushing a sprig of the camomile between her fingers, wondering if the herb's calming properties would have any effect upon her heart, which had begun to race from the moment he had sat down beside her.

"This—" he patted the springy camomile, his fingers a scant half-inch from her thigh "—has no need of weeding, someone has been doing it, and—" he reached into his pocket with his other hand and produced a glove worked with the initials J.H. "—I found this. You, Miss Hilton, have been trespassing for some time. Have you not?"

"Guilty, m'lud." She released the breath that had caught in her throat as she accepted the proffered glove and his fingers momentarily brushed hers. "It was the one place I could be sure of escaping my guardians and—" she glanced across the pool and upwards to where the tall pines clung to the edge of the cliff above the waterfall "—there is something about it which reminds me of home."

"Home?" His straight brows lifted as he looked about him, from the sparkling spill of water to the wild untidy tumble of ferns, brambles and once-cultivated shrubs, long since gone wild. "I cannot say this puts me in mind of the grounds of Pettridges Hall."

"I meant America," she said, still staring across the pool. "This reminds me of the Kentucky Trail and where we settled in Minnesota. Sometimes, sitting here watching the water and listening to the wind in the trees, I can almost believe I am back there—that if I turn around quickly enough I will see my father hitching up the team or my mother coming out of the cabin to call us in for dinner—" She broke off, wondering why on earth she was confiding such thoughts to him.

"You miss your life there?" There was the faintest note of surprise in his voice. A note she recognised all too well in carefully educated English voices, when she made the mistake of speaking about her past.

"Yes, I do," she said with a sharp lift of her chin, telling herself that she was a fool to think that he might be different from the rest, that he might just understand. "America has a great deal to recommend it. England does not have a monopoly upon natural beauty, Mr Lindsay."

"While you are resident in England, that is a subject upon which I shall have to disagree with you," he said, bending down to pick up the stick that the ever-hopeful spaniel had dropped at his feet.

"Then I suppose it would be churlish to argue—" she said after the slightest intake of breath. "Do you always flirt so outrageously, Mr Lindsay?"

He straightened, threw the stick and then turned to look at her, his eyes sparkling. "Only with women whom I find interesting or desirable."

"And into which category do I fall, Mr Lindsay?" she asked, surprising herself with the apparent uninterestedness of her tone.

"Both," he said softly after a moment, his eyes suddenly very dark as his gaze dropped to her mouth, and then lower still to the fullness of her breasts. "Very definitely both."

His voice had lowered to a velvety depth that made her skin prickle and grow tight, as if his hands had followed his stare, and she found herself staring back at his face, the wide slanting line of his mouth, his long clever fingers as he toyed with a piece of camomile.

Her mouth and throat grew dry as his gaze came back to her eyes and she knew that he meant it and that they had just stepped off the safe ground of light-hearted flirtation into some decidedly dangerous waters—for her, at least.

She swallowed and stared down at the glove in her hands. "Good," she said, as matter-of-factly as she could manage. "I should hate to be merely desirable."

He laughed, dissolving the tension that had been almost tangible. "I do not think you could ever be 'merely' anything, Miss Hilton."

"You are doing it again," she murmured, lifting her gaze to watch the spaniel heave itself out of the pool and shake the water from its coat.

"What?" he said innocently as he studied her detachedly, thinking that he had been right. She was not pretty: her fine nose was too straight, the upswept line of her jaw too clean and sharp, her forehead a fraction too high, her mouth too wide and feline. Oh, no—no insipid, dainty, English rosebud, this—more a lioness, lithe, fierce and very beautiful.

"Flirting," Janey replied, putting a hand to her face, ostensibly to push back an errant strand of fair hair, but in reality to shield herself from the piercingly blue gaze that was making her feel decidedly uncomfortable.

"And you are not?" he mocked softly.

"No. I have no talent for it," she said tersely, wishing that she were not quite so aware that, if she moved a matter of an inch, his shoulder would touch hers. "All I asked you—"

"—was whether or not I found you desirable?" He laughed. "If that does not constitute flirting, Miss Hilton, I don't know what does."

She shrugged, determined not to fall into another of his verbal traps as she glanced at him with what she hoped passed for indifference. "I was simply curious."

"I should be happy to satisfy your curiosity whenever you wish." He grinned at her and quirked a dark eyebrow. "You only have to say the word."

He was wicked. Quite impossibly wicked, she thought, the corners of her mouth lifting despite all her efforts to look stern.

"The word is no," she said a little too emphatically.

"Pity." He was almost sober suddenly. "You would not reconsider if I told you your hair was the colour of gold, your eyes as dark and mysterious as that pool, that I shall die if I do not kiss you—"

"No!" She laughed, but got up abruptly and almost ran to where the dripping spaniel had dropped its stick, before adding, with all the lightness she could muster, "but before you expire, do tell me of any last requests and I shall be happy to see they are carried out."

"Heartless—heartless," he reproached her softly as he watched her bend lithely and throw the stick with an easy competency not often seen outside of Mr Lord's new cricket ground. "How can you be so heartless at sunset, beside a waterfall of rainbows?"

"I daresay I have not read enough of the latest

novels,'' she said as she watched the spaniel plunge into the shallows of the pool again. ''But it is beautiful, isn't it? I shall miss coming here.''

''Why should you miss it? So far as I am concerned, you may come here whenever you wish.''

She started as his voice came from immediately behind her shoulder. He had moved as silently as an Apache warrior across the muddy grass until he was a scant pace behind her. She turned, and then wished she had not as he met her gaze. She felt her heart leap and race beneath her ribs as if she had suddenly found herself between a she-bear and its cub. It was ridiculous, she told herself, ridiculous to think he had meant that nonsense about kissing her, ridiculous as this soaring feeling of happiness because he seemed to like her.

''That is very good of you, but I should not like to intrude.'' Her words came in a rush.

''I should count your presence an advantage rather than an intrusion.''

His voice was soft, warm, like his blue eyes as he sought and held her gaze. ''So promise me you will come here again, whenever you wish?''

Annabel had been right, she thought wryly. He was seductive, far more dangerous than any of the trappers she had encountered while staying at Lilian's boarding house in St Louis. And this was no polite invitation from one neighbour to another to visit his garden. Any well-bred young lady would refuse such an invitation without hesitation.

But then, she wasn't a well-bred young lady, she was Janey Hilton, colonial and daughter of a mill-hand. And Janey Hilton was tired of a life that held no more danger and excitement than taking a fence on her horse...tired of trying to behave like an English lady and being constantly reminded that she had failed.

"Thank you, I will," she said, holding his gaze steadily.

"You will? Alone?" He could not quite hide his surprise.

"Yes," she replied with a calm that she was very far from feeling. "It is a very special place for me."

"And for me—now."

It was her turn to be caught off-guard by his sudden unexpected seriousness; she let her gaze drop to the ground.

"Why is it so special for you? Because it reminds you of home?" he asked as he, too, dropped his gaze, and flicked a stone into the water with the toe of his top boot. "Or did you meet with your betrothed here? No—don't answer that," he said as he heard her sudden intake of breath. "I had no right to ask such a question."

"No, you did not," she agreed, staring at the ripples that spread out from where the stone had sunk, wondering how they had come so far so fast. It was, she thought, as if they had known each other for years, not a few minutes.

"The answer is no," she said quietly. "Edward would never have considered meeting me in such a place alone, even if I had suggested it—he would have considered it far too improper. He was always very concerned for my reputation. He was a curate and very principled."

"They usually are, until it comes to getting a lucrative living or catching an heiress," he said cynically.

"That is unfair. He was a good man. He did a great deal for the poor and he cared for me, not for my money, I am sure of it." But was she? The words sounded hollow, even to her own ears. Of late, she had begun to wonder about Edward, wonder if he was all she had once thought him...wonder if he would have been so prepared to overlook her shortcomings, or quite so supportive of her efforts to improve conditions for the poorer families in the village if she had not been her grandfather's heir.

"I am sorry," he said as he watched her face. "Cynicism becomes something of a habit."

"Like flippancy?" She gave him the ghost of a smile, remembering their first encounter in the lane.

"I am afraid so." He smiled back at her ruefully. "But—"

"Jem!" she interrupted him sharply, horrified that for these few minutes she had forgotten the very reason she had come to meet him "Oh, have you had any success?"

"No, I am afraid not." He looked away as he answered. "I had hoped to call in a favour from the Home Secretary and obtain a pardon for him, but—"

"He refused," she said flatly. She had not realised, until this moment, just how much trust she had placed in him or how much she had hoped she would not have to put her other plan into action.

"Not exactly." He shook his head. "The government fell shortly after I reached town. Wellington has resigned and, unfortunately, we have a new Home Secretary."

"But couldn't you ask the new Home Secretary?"

"Melbourne?" He shook his dark head a second time. "Lord Melbourne does not hold any affection for me. I was a friend of his wife, Caroline Lamb, and of Lord Byron, you see." Then he gave a wry smile as he saw her blank expression. "You don't see...you were probably playing with your dolls then."

"I was more likely helping my mother deliver a neighbour's child or my father harness the oxen," she said shortly, feeling as if a chasm had suddenly opened up between them as she saw shock ripple across his face. She had been a fool to think him different, a fool to think that he might like the real Janey Hilton.

"I suppose it must be a very different life for young women who live on the frontier," he said after a moment of silence.

"Different is something of an understatement." She was brisk. The use of the word "women" rather than "ladies" had not escaped her after four years in England. "You have to grow up fast on the frontier, Mr Lindsay," she added sharply, as he opened his mouth to say something. "Just as the sons and daughters of labourers must in this country. Now, if you will excuse me—" she turned abruptly from the pool "—I really must go back, before I am missed."

"Wait!" He strode after her. "I did not mean to upset you and I am truly sorry I have not been able to do more for Jem."

She stopped and turned to look at him, and to her surprise found that she believed him.

"It is not your fault." She sighed. "And I am very

grateful that you at least tried to help him. You haven't upset me…it is not your fault that you are a—'' She faltered, struggling for the right words.

"A patronising, arrogant society dandy who has never had to step outside of his gilded and well-padded cage?'' His dark brows lifted quizzically.

"I should not have put it quite so rudely,'' she said a little ashamedly.

"No, but you thought it.'' He grinned at her.

"True,'' she confessed ruefully, "and I apologise for it.''

"Then will you allow me the honour of escorting you home? It will be absolutely dark in the woods.''

"Oh, there is no need,'' she protested politely. "I shall be perfectly safe. I am not afraid of the dark— it is not as if you have bears or Indians in England.''

"I insist,'' he said and turned away momentarily to whistle to the spaniel.

"You insist?'' Her brows lifted and so, for no reason, did her heart as he returned his attention to her. "Then I suppose I have no choice in the matter.''

"None,'' he said, offering her his arm.

It was politeness, she told herself, as she put out her gloved hand and tentatively let her fingers rest upon the sleeve of his coat and they began to walk towards the cliff path, falling easily into step, nothing but ordinary politeness. There was no reason for her pulse to race, her heart to pound. No reason at all.

"No, Tess! Down!'' His exclamation as they halted at the base of the cliff path came too late for her to avoid the spaniel's enthusiastic greeting as it caught up with them and transferred a considerable amount of mud, water and pond weed from its coat and paws to the skirts of her black wool pelisse.

"I am so sorry—she's still very young and gets rather out of hand," he apologised. "Lie down, Tess!"

Tess shot off up the cliff path.

He muttered an imprecation under his breath and then turned to her. "I hope she has not done too much damage—I have a handkerchief somewhere."

"It really doesn't matter," she said, laughing as she watched the spaniel turn and come back down the path again, so fast it turned a somersault at the bottom as it tried to stop at its master's feet.

"Idiot dog!" He laughed, too, as Tess put her muzzle upon the toe of his boot and gazed up at him soulfully, the very picture of man's loyal and obedient friend. "She was the runt of the litter and is terrified of guns. I should have knocked her upon the head at birth—still should, I suppose—"

"But you won't," she said with a certainty she did not stop to question.

"No." He gave a half laugh. "As you have obviously perceived, a tender heart beats beneath this grim exterior."

"I should not have called you grim," she replied, giving him a brief sideways glance. "A little weathered, perhaps."

"Thank you." He inclined his head to her in a mocking bow. "Dare I allow myself to be flattered?"

"I do not think you have any need of my flattery. I suspect even the youngest son of an Earl receives more than enough."

He laughed again. "That was definitely not complimentary, Miss Hilton, though I am afraid it was all too true. Have you always been so brutally honest with your friends?"

"Yes," she said sweetly. "I find real friends always prefer honesty to pretence."

He smiled and conceded her the victory with the slightest nod of his head. "I had better go first," he said, gesturing to the rocky beginning of the cliff path, "then I can help you over the difficult places."

"Thank you," she acquiesced politely with a fleeting smile. She had climbed this path a hundred times without mishap and, in her childhood, rock faces as sheer as the one the water tumbled from, not to mention trees. Daniel had always got her to do the climbing when they had been looking for bird eggs—of the two of them, she'd had a better head for heights.

But that had been a different world, a different life, she thought, as he turned and held out his hands to her after scrambling over the first few boulders. English ladies were expected to be fragile, helpless creatures, and for once, as she put her hands into his and he smiled at her, she found she did not particularly mind furthering the illusion.

The path was steep enough to preclude much conversation and they climbed mostly in a companionable silence, with Tess padding quietly behind them.

He had been right. It was almost pitch black once they entered the woods. Out of old ingrained habit, she paused, listening and cataloguing the sounds in her mind and relaxing as she heard nothing but the natural chorus of the wood at night: the cooing of wood pigeons, the flutter and swoop of an owl, the squeal of a shrew and the rustle of leaves beneath

Tess's paws as she nosed around their feet, seeking a scent. It was only as she went to move forward again that she realised he had also halted and was listening.

"Sorry——" he turned his head to smile at her in the gloom "——I've never walked into a wood at night without stopping to listen since my troop was ambushed in Spain."

"You were a soldier?" She was surprised. He was so unlike the army officers who dined with the Filmores from time to time.

"Briefly, in my misspent youth." He shrugged as they walked on. "I did not particularly enjoy the experience. The Peninsular War was savage enough, but Waterloo—that was simply a slaughterhouse, and killed any remaining hankering to cover myself in military glory. I decided twenty was far too young to die and resigned my commission the moment we were sure Napoleon was beaten."

"You were six years older than Jem is now," she said flatly.

"I know." The self-mocking tone left his voice. "And I wish to heaven there was something else I could do...I feel as if I have failed you."

"No. No," she protested, knowing she had been unfair. "At least you tried to do something for Jem, which is far more than I expected of a—"

"A worthless rake and a dandy?" he supplied wryly. "That is what you thought me at first glance, is it not?"

"At first glance, perhaps. But I could not count anyone who made the speech that you did to Parliament entirely worthless, Mr Lindsay."

"Speech?" He looked at her blankly for a moment.

"The one defending the rights of the labouring poor."

"Ah—" he stumbled suddenly upon a tree root "—that speech. There is something, perhaps, you should know—I am no radical, Miss Hilton. I sit on the Tory side."

"Why?"

"Why?" He echoed her question in astonishment, as if he had never considered any other possibility. "Well, because my father did, and his before him, I suppose," he said after a moment of silence.

"That's the worst reason I have heard yet," she said drily.

"Thank you," he said with equal dryness.

She sighed. "Oh, well, I suppose it is not the label which matters, it is what you say. And you said all the things I should like to, except that you did it a great deal better than I ever could—"

"I doubt that. I suspect you would make a formidable advocate of any cause, Miss Hilton."

She sensed rather than saw his smile in the gloom.

"And is that what you thought of me at first glance? That I was formidable?"

"No. My first thought was that I should like to take you to my bed."

"Really, how strange…" she said after a moment, biting her lip to stop herself from laughing. He was impossible. Quite impossible. But did he really think he could shock her so easily when she had lived most of her sixteenth year in a St Louis boarding house?

"Strange?" He sounded faintly piqued by her reaction. "No man would think so, I assure you."

"That was not what I meant," she replied, after the

most fractional of hesitations. "I thought it was strange because I was wondering whether or not I should like you to be one of my lovers."

"One of your lovers!" He halted so abruptly that she found herself dragged backwards. "Great God, how many have you had?"

"Not nearly so many as you, I fear," she lamented. "There are so *few* men that I find both interesting and desirable." She could hardly keep the bubble of laughter out of her voice.

For a moment he stared down at her, trying to discern her face in the darkness, and then started to laugh. "I have just been hoist with my own petard, have I not?"

"You should not have tried to shock me," she said as they started to walk on again.

"I am beginning to think that is impossible," he said, shaking his head. "But, do you know, what shocks *me* most, Miss Hilton, is that you came to be betrothed to some milksop of a curate. What did the poor devil die of? Heart failure?"

"No." Her expression became closed and the laughter left her face abruptly. "And he was not a milksop!"

"I am sorry." He held her arm more tightly as she tried to walk ahead. "I did not mean to intrude upon your grief and I had no right to say that of a man I have never met."

"No," she said as they fell into step again, "you did not."

"I suppose he would have helped you in your efforts to save Jem and succeeded, most like," he said sourly, and then wondered what the devil was wrong with him to behave so mawkishly.

"I am sure he would have pleaded for Jem to be treated mercifully," she said a little too quickly, then realised that she was not sure at all any more. There was something that nagged at her, something that had been at the edge of her mind since the day of the accident, but she could never quite remember what it was, what they had been discussing in the minutes before the staircase in the Tower had collapsed.

They walked on in an awkward silence, each sunk in their own uncomfortable thoughts. And then, quite suddenly, they stepped out of the darkness into the comparatively lightness of dusk that turned Pettridge Park to every hue of silver and grey.

By mutual, unspoken consent they both halted in the shadow of a large beech at the edge of the Hall's garden. Pools of light shone out from windows of rooms in which curtains had not yet been drawn. Glancing up, she could see Mr Filmore, reading beside the drawing-room fire, Annabel playing the piano, and Piers leaning lazily across its lid.

"It does not seem you have been missed," he said as a maid suddenly appeared at the window, and the scene was abruptly blotted out by a sweep of lined brocade.

"No," she agreed succinctly as she remained staring at the curtained window.

He stared at her, studying her face in the dusk. For all her sharpness, her apparent self-confidence, her fierce honesty, she suddenly looked so very young, vulnerable, wistful and alone that he wanted to take her in his arms—though for very different reasons to those he had had until a moment or so ago. But now—now he was getting distinct twinges of conscience about his pursuit of Miss Janey Hilton, and about what the consequences might be for her.

"I had better go back," he said. "Your guardians might think it a trifle odd for me to be walking alone with you in the dark."

"They'd think you odd for choosing to walk with me at all." She gave a slightly ragged laugh.

"Then they have no taste," he said softly.

"All these compliments, you could turn my head, Mr Lindsay." She strove to sound light.

"Like this?" He lifted a hand and placed his palm against her cheek, turning her face and tilting it upwards so she found herself staring into his shadowed face.

"I was speaking metaphorically," she said a second—or was it minutes?—later. She did not know. She only knew that her face was burning beneath his hand, and that the world had seemed to stop again the moment he had touched her.

"Really? How stupid of me not to realise," he mocked her softly and himself for being such a fool as to think she did not know the rules of the game. But there was no hurry, he told himself as his hand dropped away. Janey Hilton was like a rare vintage wine—she should be enjoyed slowly.

"You had better go in, Miss Hilton," he said as she remained motionless.

"Yes," she agreed, "but I cannot until you let go of my arm."

"Of course," he said, but still did not release her.

She swallowed. "Is there something else, Mr Lindsay?"

"Jem?" he said, not knowing where or how the sudden anxiety had arisen in his mind, but only that she had been too quiet upon the subject. "You have not any wild or reckless schemes for his rescue in mind have you?"

"No," she said. It was not a lie. Wild and reckless simply would not do. It was going to take careful planning to save Jem. And a miracle to save herself from falling in love with Jonathan Lindsay.

"Good." He exhaled and let go of her arm. "Because this is England, and in England, the rule of law is upheld mercilessly."

"You need not tell me that," she said, half-relieved, half-disappointed that he had believed her so easily.

"And neither need I tell you, I hope, that such strategies as exchanging clothes with the prisoner, or copying keys with wax and the like, only work in the pages of fiction."

"I know."

"Then I'll say goodnight."

"Goodnight." She turned and began to walk towards the house.

"Wait!" he called softly after her. "How are you to get in?"

She stopped, turned and looked back at him. "Why, through the door, Mr Lindsay. You did not think I was going to climb the ivy in my petticoats, did you? If I had meant to do that, I'd have worn my buckskins."

"Breeches?" He sounded shocked again, she thought with a smile.

"Buckskins are what the Indians wear, men and women—" she began to expound, and then laughed. "Never mind, Mr Lindsay, I'll explain another time. Goodnight."

"Goodnight, Miss Hilton." His voice floated after her as she walked across the drive. And she was aware of him standing in the growing darkness, watching her, until the moment the great front door swung shut behind her.

She stood for a moment in the dimly lit hall, a half-smile on her lips. Worried as she was about Jem, and the estate, somehow, she had the absurd conviction that everything would be all right now Jonathan Lindsay had come to Southbrook.

Outside, at the same moment, Jonathan Lindsay frowned. He was feeling unaccountably guilty and it was not an emotion he was accustomed to. The trouble was, he liked Miss Janey Hilton, liked the way she looked at him, liked her cool directness and the way she smiled. He swore silently. What the devil was wrong with him? He was thinking like some greenhorn. She was just another woman, another conquest to be made...wasn't she?

He turned away without answering his own question, whistled to Tess and strode back into the woods.

"Jane! There you are!" Mrs Filmore, her ample figure tightly upholstered in cherry silk, greeted Janey majestically from halfway up the broad flight of stairs. "I have been looking all over for you. Mr Filmore has relented. You may come down and join us—when you are suitably dressed, of course.'' She frowned as she glanced derisively at Janey's besmirched pelisse.

''I'd rather go to my room, thank you.'' Janey gave Mrs Filmore her most benign smile. ''I've been walking in the gardens and I am rather tired.''

''Walking alone in the dark!'' Mrs Filmore gave a long-suffering sigh. ''Really, Jane dear, you cannot go on like this. A little eccentricity in the first throes of grief is allowable, but poor Mr Grey has been dead almost a year now—though the ordeal you suffered would be enough to turn anyone's mind.''

''There is nothing wrong with my mind.'' Janey sighed as she began to climb the stairs. ''And I should prefer it if you and Mr Filmore would stop implying that there is to anyone who cares to listen.''

''Well,'' Mrs Filmore snorted, drawing herself up to her full, rather limited, height, ''would you rather that I had explained to Mr Lindsay that your extraordinary behaviour this morning was learned from the female brothel-keeper with whom you lived for the year following your parents' death?''

''Lilian was not a brothel-keeper,'' Janey retorted. ''She owned a boarding house.''

''A boarding house! A wooden hut where men drank liquor, and women sold their services.'' Mrs Filmore gave a theatrical shudder. ''If I had been your poor dear late grandpapa, I should never have brought you back here.''

''Sometimes, Mrs Filmore,'' Janey muttered as she began to climb the stairs, ''I wish that he had not.'' But she knew that was not true, not any longer. It had not been true from the moment Jonathan Lindsay had first smiled at her.

* * *

"About time, Jono, where the devil have you been?" Lord Derwent said complainingly as Jonathan entered the library of Southbrook House. "This place is freezing, and I've been ringing for ages for your man to bring some more wood for the fire. Had to put some books on—only Mrs Radcliffe," he added as Jonathan frowned. "Didn't think you'd miss those."

"Probably not," Jonathan conceded, as he stepped up to the fire and held his hands out to the blaze, "but I'd rather you did not burn any more. The reason the servants have not answered is because the bell wires are all in need of replacement. You will have to go to the door and shout."

"Shout? Didn't think of that," Lord Derwent grumbled, leaning back in a creaking chair upholstered with well-worn green leather and putting his feet up upon the brass fender. "And where have you been?" he asked as his brown gaze took in Jonathan's muddy boots.

"Playing in the garden and walking in the woods," Jonathan said with a grin, sitting down in the opposite chair.

"Playing in the garden! Walking in the woods on a November evening!" Lord Derwent scowled, his fastidious nose wrinkling as the wet and muddy Tess pushed against his boots in an effort to get closer to the fire. "And to think we could have been at White's, or eating Wilkin's steak and oyster pie."

"Woods have their compensations," Jonathan said, "in the very delicious shape of Miss Hilton."

"What!" Lord Derwent's feet dropped from the fender to the floor. "You've not had an assignation with Miss Hilton already! How the deuce did you manage that?''

"Very easily." Jonathan laughed. "I do hope you've told your horseman to get Triton fit for me, Perry. Winning this wager is going to be easier than beating you at cards.''

"After you've failed to save her arsonist?" Lord Derwent shook his head. "I'll believe it when I see it. A walk in the woods is one thing but—" he made an eloquent gesture "—is quite another.''

"I haven't failed yet. We are going back to Town.''

"Hurrah!" Lord Derwent's countenance brightened immeasurably.

"As soon as we have dined.''

"Tonight?" Lord Derwent groaned. "But it's just started to rain.''

"There's not much time and I want to see Caroline Norton.''

"Caro Norton." Lord Derwent looked at him in surprise. "I thought it was all over between you years ago.''

"It was. But we have retained a fondness for one another." Jonathan smiled. "Melbourne is besotted with her and, where he might not do me a favour—"

"He will do anything for the beautiful Mrs Norton," Lord Derwent said slowly, "and Mrs Norton will do anything for you.''

"Exactly, Perry, exactly." Jonathan laughed. "I don't know why I did not think of it before.''

"Probably because you haven't been thinking clearly since you first saw that female," Lord Derwent muttered darkly. "If it wasn't for her, you'd not have contemplated taking on this place for a moment.''

''What did you say?'' Jonathan said, lifting his gaze from the flames of the fire into which he had been staring.

''Nothing.'' Lord Derwent sighed dejectedly. ''I'll go and shout for Brown.''

Chapter Four

The chalky Roman road stretched like a pale ribbon ahead, in the pallid dawn light, as Jonathan Lindsay urged his tired horse on. The long ride from London had left him cold, hungry and impatient to see Jane Hilton's face when he told her that he had succeeded in saving her arsonist.

He checked his horse as the road dropped steeply down into a hollow lined with hawthorns and scrub. He let the animal come down to a walk, glad of the respite from the biting wind that had cut through even his many-caped topcoat and caused him the loss of a new beaver hat. For a county so soft and pleasant in summer, Wiltshire could be damned bleak in winter, he thought, especially the edge of Salisbury Plain.

But then, as he rounded a sharp turn, all thought of the weather left his head. A fair distance ahead of him was a female rider, a rider he recognised more by instinct than any logic.

"Miss Hilton!" His shout was lost in the wind. For a moment, as she brought her horse to a halt, he thought she had heard him. But then, as he saw her dismount without so much as a glance behind her, he realised she was still oblivious to his presence.

"What the devil is she doing?" he muttered to his mount, which responded by coming to an uncertain halt itself.

He watched the distant figure with growing curiosity as she seemed first to address the hawthorns, and then cast her horse loose, shooing it away. Next she took off her hat, threw it down and stamped upon it, and then cast herself down upon the chalky road to lie prone across its centre.

And then from behind him, he caught the sound of hooves and the clatter of a carriage wheel borne forward by the wind. Looking back along the straight road, he saw a dark chaise, one which seemed to have more than its share of guards and bars upon its windows. He stared at it disbelievingly as understanding came with devastating clarity.

Prisoners were being transferred from Salisbury to Dorchester for the hangings, the chaise would already have slowed for the steep descent into the hollow, and would certainly stop at the sight of a lady, apparently having fallen from her horse. And the hollow was a perfect spot for an ambush with its high banks and ample cover. An ambush. No he shook his head at his own thought. He had to be wrong. Jane Hilton might have a strong sense of justice, but surely she would not be so reckless, so foolhardy, not for the sake of some poacher's boy, would she?

He spurred his horse forward into a gallop as he answered his own question. The steep chalk track was slippery and he prayed his horse would keep its footing as it plunged and slithered towards Janey's prone form.

Hearing the rapid approach of hooves, Janey shut her eyes, praying that the chaise would be able to stop in time. If it didn't, it would run her over. But there was something wrong—the hoofbeats were far too light, too fast. There must be an outrider—why hadn't she thought of that? Supposing his pistol had not come from the Salisbury Gaol's armoury? She had been so sure she had arranged it so no one would get hurt.

She held her breath as she heard the horse and rider come to a slithering stamping halt upon the chalky mud, so near she felt the ground shake beneath her head as the rider dismounted. Then a moment later a hand was upon her arm, shaking her roughly, ignoring what she had hoped was a pathetic groan.

"Get up!"

She opened her eyes and stared in disbelief at the man bending over her. It was Jonathan Lindsay, his dark hair windswept, his eyes as dark a blue as his mud-bedecked top coat as he glared down at her.

"You!" She gasped with horror as he lifted her bodily to her feet, momentarily too astonished to resist. But then, as she heard the approaching rattle of the chaise, she began to struggle frantically.

"Go away," she hissed at him. "Please just go away, you will ruin everything!"

"And you will get yourself shot!" he retorted fiercely, dragging her forcibly to the side of the road, an arm clamped about her waist.

"Let me go! You don't understand—" She wrestled to free herself in vain.

"'Ere, you! Let her be!'' A burly looking man, his face masked with a red and white kerchief, arose suddenly from the hawthorns and there were other rustlings from the other side.

"Get down, Will!" Janey half-sobbed as she heard the squealing of the chaise's brakes being applied at the top of the hollow.

"You heard her! Get down, damn you! Unless you want to end up on the gallows as well!" Jonathan reinforced the instruction. "And leave the talking to me! All of you!" he added as he glimpsed the shadowy shapes of three or four others in the bushes on the other side of the road.

"Please, please help us, it's his only chance!" Janey turned her face up to his, her eyes pleading. "Everything is arranged—there is a boat waiting at Poole to take him to France—"

"No. Absolutely not. There's no need."

"There's every need," she protested, struggling furiously to escape his grasp.

"Shut up! And keep your face hidden or we'll be the talk of the county!" As the chaise was almost upon them, he turned her against him, and held her face against the wall of his chest, so tightly she could hardly breathe, let alone protest.

"Trouble, sir?" the driver of the chaise asked, giving them a wary look and nodding to the guards to have their pistols ready.

"No, no—" Jonathan gave them a cheerful smile "—a small domestic disagreement—that's all—" he said grittily as Janey kicked him in the shin. "On your way, there is no need to stop."

"Have the same trouble with me own woman, sir."

The driver grinned. "A good spanking usually stops her nonsense."

"Excellent advice, I am sure," Jonathan grated out as Janey kicked him a second time. "But, please, don't let us delay you."

The driver grinned and whipped up his horses again, and the chaise clattered on.

"I hate you!" Janey spat out, jerking back from Jonathan as he released her. "I hate you!" And then, as she stared after the chaise and saw the small pale face peering back at them from behind the barred window, she made a helpless gesture. "Look at him!" Her eyes filled with tears and her voice broke as she gestured to the disappearing chaise. "He is a child! Just a child."

"And you are behaving like one!" he snapped. "You and your—friends, you could all have been shot. The guards are armed!"

"I am not a fool! All their pistols have powder so damp they would not go off if you dropped them into a furnace!" she snapped, rubbing her hand across her eyes.

"How the devil can you be sure of that?"

"Because Will's cousin works in the armoury at Salisbury Gaol."

"My God! How many of you are there in this conspiracy?" He groaned. And then shook his head. "No, don't tell me that. I'm a magistrate and a Member of Parliament, for God's sake. I don't want to know."

He turned suddenly to where Will was standing looking at them uncertainly. "You, take the others and get out of here. This has not happened, I have not seen you, understand?''

"Yes, sir," Will agreed sullenly, and four other masked men all carrying staves stood up looking sheepish. "But Miss Hilton—''

"I shall see Miss Hilton safely home. Now, go before anyone sees you here!''

Janey stared despairingly after them as they strode off across the grey-green turf of the down, moving with the long, ground covering stride of countrymen. Then she rounded upon Jonathan, her eyes blazing close with fury, her hands balled into fists.

"How could you! We could have saved him and you have ruined everything! Oh! I hate you! I wish that you were dead! I wish—'' She broke off, incoherent with rage as she saw the amusement in his eyes.

Jem would die and he was laughing at her. She jabbed at him with her right fist, aiming straight for his arrogant, aristocratic nose.

"Temper, temper," he said, as he ducked aside and caught her wrist. "Didn't anyone tell you that ladies are supposed to slap—not deliver right hooks like a professional gentleman? Who taught you to fight? Surely not your namby-pamby curate?''

"No!" she seared, twisting to free herself. "Let go of me! If Edward were here, you would not dare to treat me so.''

"If your milksop of a curate were here, I should hand you over to him with pleasure, but—''

"He was not a milksop!" she shouted, swinging at him with her other fist. A blow which he did not duck quite quickly enough, so her hand grazed his cheekbone. "He was a good man! He helped people who were less fortunate than himself! He might not have had your wealth, looks and wit, but at least he made a difference to people's lives, which is something more than you will ever do!"

"A curate who practised what he preached." His mouth curled derisively. "He sounds too good to be true. Are you sure he did not merely have his sights set upon your inheritance?"

"That is a monstrous thing to say! But then, someone like you would never understand someone who puts others before himself!"

"And you do, I suppose? Were you really thinking of the good of those men who have just left by involving them in this hare-brained scheme?" He was scathing. "If things had gone wrong, which seems more than likely, what do think would have happened to them? This is England, Miss Hilton, not the backwoods of America! There is no wilderness for fugitives to disappear into and make a new life. They would have been hunted down, tried and most likely hung."

"I shared that risk," she began defensively.

He gave a derisive laugh. "A beautiful, young heiress is rarely judged the same as a labourer, Miss Hilton. You'd probably have got off with a plea of insanity—which I begin to think is not so far off the mark."

"Yes. You're right, I know you are right—" she said miserably as she met his relentless blue gaze. "But I had to do something—I had to try. Jem is innocent. I know he is innocent. And they are going to hang him..." Her voice cracked and she bit her lip to stop the tears she could feel welling up behind her eyes.

"No," he said more gently, "they are not going to hang him. I have a full pardon, signed by the Home Secretary, here—" he patted the pocket of his coat "—which, when you have done with assaulting me, I shall deliver to the Governor of Dorchester Gaol."

"What?" She stared at him, her eyes very wide and glittering with unshed tears. "You have a pardon?"

"Yes." He smiled at her. "Happy now, Miss Hilton? Jem should be home with his mother by tomorrow morning at the latest."

"Yes, yes," she said. "It's wonderful. I don't know how you managed it."

"Better perhaps that you don't," he said with a smile as he thought of the beautiful Caro Norton and the flattery he had employed.

"I don't know how to apologise. Or how to thank you—" She broke off helplessly.

"I believe a kiss is customary upon such occasions," he said matter-of-factly as he bent to pick up her hat from the ground.

"A kiss!" She stared at him, her hazel eyes wide, her heart racing faster than it had when she heard the chaise approaching.

"Yes." He smiled as he straightened and pummelled her hat back into some sort of shape. "Merely out of gratitude, of course."

"Of course." She did not quite succeed in matching his tone as he stepped up to her and placed the hat upon her head, standing so close she had to tilt

her head up to see his face. "So long as you understood it was for no other reason…"

"Perfectly," he said cheerfully, his gaze never
leaving hers as he crossed the satin ribbons and pulled
them up beneath her chin and tied them into a bow.
"Why else would you kiss someone you hate?"

"Oh, t-this is r-ridiculous!" she found herself
stammering as he stroked a strand of her dishevelled
hair away from her mouth with a gloved fingertip. "I
can't just kiss you."

"Why not?" He smiled in a way that made her
want to murder him. "I presume you know how, considering the legion of lovers you laid claim to the
other day?" The amusement in his eyes was barely
hidden.

Janey bit her lip. He knew, or was almost certain,
she had lied. But she was not going to admit it, not
so that he could laugh at her. She had made enough
of a fool of herself for one day.

"And you must have kissed your curate upon occasion?" he added innocently.

"Yes, but only once!" she snapped. "And that was
like this…" Some lunatic irresistible impulse made
her go on tiptoe and touch her lips fleetingly to the
corner of his mouth.

Now who was shocking who? she thought triumphantly, as she heard the catch of his breath.

"I see," he said after a moment of frozen stillness
in which his hands remained immobile upon the ribbons beneath her chin. "He did not do this, then?"

He let go of the ribbons and put his hands upon
her shoulders, and drew her to him. She shut her eyes,

knowing she had either just made the worse mistake of her life or—

"No." The word was no more than a shaken breath as he brushed his lips over hers, once, twice before lingering in the gentlest of kisses.

"Or this…" he murmured, as he folded her into his arms and kissed her again in an entirely different way—a way she had heard Annabel boast to her friends of having experienced. A way that made her momentarily freeze with shock at the invasion of her mouth. And then she was lost, melted by the warmth of his lips, his tongue. Her lips softened, yielding to him completely. She pressed closer to him, instinctively seeking relief for this new aching heaviness in her breasts, her whole body.

He was hard, both mouth and body, hard against this feeling of softness that was drowning her, until she felt boneless, helpless, utterly female. Her gloved hands moved involuntarily against his caped coat; she wanted to be closer, closer than these layers of cloth would allow. She belonged to this man, wanted to be one with him…it was as if everything, the long hazardous journey to England and the last four years of loneliness and boredom had all been bringing her to this moment, this man…

This man who would undoubtedly laugh at her if she ever expressed such ridiculous sentiments, said a cynical voice at the back of her mind. To Jonathan Lindsay, society rake, this was probably nothing more than an opportunity for amusement and she, if she had an ounce of sense left, should never let him know it was anything more for her.

She withdrew abruptly from his embrace. He made

no attempt to restrain her, but his eyebrows lifted as he met her wide dark eyes with a quizzical stare.

"Well," she said, a little more shakily than she would have liked, as he continued to stare at her in silence, "I hope you consider yourself properly thanked, Mr Lindsay?"

"No," he said and smiled, a wide slow smile as he lifted a hand to stroke back a wing of hair that had blown over her face. "Improperly, perhaps."

He was so sure of himself, so practised, she thought, so damnably composed and confident while she—she was dissolving beneath his touch like snow in sunshine, as probably had scores of simpering misses like Annabel, she told herself fiercely. Well, she would show him Janey Hilton was made out of different cloth!

"Well, if you are not satisfied, I suppose I could try again," she said, as flippantly as she could manage while his fingers slid through the silky mass of her dishevelled hair and came to rest upon her shoulder.

His hand stilled and she heard the short, sharp intake of his breath as he stared at her, and she had to fight down the impulse to laugh. For all his sophistication, she could still surprise him.

"Thank you for the offer," he said, very drily. "But perhaps I should warn you, Miss Hilton, that I am not likely to be satisfied with a kiss and our surroundings are hardly appropriate for a more thorough expression of your gratitude."

It was her turn to catch her breath. The darkness in his voice, in his eyes, and her body's instant response to the image his words aroused brought home to her quite suddenly that she was playing a dangerous game with a man who had long since thrown away the rule book. But then, she could hardly criticize him for that, when she had never even read it, she thought, the corners of her mouth lifting.

She lifted her chin and gave him a blithe smile. "I suppose it would be rather uncomfortable. Lilian always said the outdoors was not to be recommended in winter."

"Uncomfortable!" He gave a splutter of disbelieving laughter. "Is that all you have to say?"

"What would you have me say?" she asked with deliberate innocence.

"A little outrage, some hot defence of your virtue would at least assist me in my attempt to behave like a gentlemen should towards a lady—" he said gratingly. "And who the devil is Lilian? Was she your governess?"

"Not exactly..." Her mouth curved at the unlikely vision of Lilian as a governess. "She was a friend. She looked after me when my parents died until my grandfather came for me. She kept a—lodging house in St Louis."

"A lodging house. I see." His brows lifted. "And do I take it that Lilian also taught you the useful manoeuvre with which you laid Master Filmore low?"

"Yes, and a great deal more besides. I could have knocked you down, Mr Lindsay, the moment you set a hand on me, if I had wished to—but I guess I didn't want to..." she confessed with a shy, slightly uncertain smile.

"You didn't want to..." he repeated slowly, almost accusingly, as he wondered what was wrong with him. She had just about handed him an engraved in-

vitation to seduce her. The wager with Perry was as
good as won if her response to his kiss and her smile
was anything to go by. So why did he feel so damnably guilty as she smiled at him, her eyes still soft,
her lips still faintly swollen and dark from his kiss?
It was not as if she were some innocent fresh from
the schoolroom. By the sound of it, she had seen more
of life than many women twice her age.

"No." She shrugged, wondering why she felt as if
she were gambling with her life. "I suppose I must
like you, Mr Lindsay, perhaps more than I suspect is
wise."

"Really?" He gave a brittle laugh, as her blatant
honesty caught him completely off guard. "I cannot
think why you should. You would do better to trust
your first impression of me, Miss Hilton. You had me
down as a dandy who cares for little but his own
pleasure and amusement, did you not?"

"Yes," she admitted a little ashamedly. "But I
know now I am wrong. You have gone to such trouble to save Jem."

"An aberration in an otherwise conscienceless
life," he said scathingly. "So save your halo for your
beloved curate's blessed memory, it will not fit me."

"I am not likely to mistake you for a candidate for
sainthood," she said with a half-smile as she caught
the edge in his tone. "And in case you are wondering,
I am not some sheltered debutante who is likely to
mistake a kiss for a declaration, nor am I seeking to
entrap you."

She turned away as she spoke and putting two fingers into her mouth she whistled to her huge black

horse, which left off cropping the springy downland turf and came trotting up to her.

"Where the devil did you get that?" He could not quite disguise his opinion of the black gelding as it approached. It was practically a carthorse.

It was a carthorse, he amended as the gelding came up and nudged at Janey with its enormous head. It had to be a good eighteen hands and it had chest, quarters and legs that would carry a twenty-stone man all day without noticing. It was hardly a typical lady's mount, but then, he thought wryly, Janey Hilton was not a typical lady.

"Looks are not everything, Mr Lindsay," Janey said a little defensively as she stepped forward to catch the horse's reins. "He jumps like a chaser, but he's as mild as milk—and he could pull a wagon if he had to, which is more than that thoroughbred of yours could do."

"I don't doubt it." He smiled. "I only wish I had had the sense to choose something like him when I went on my first campaign."

"I still cannot imagine you as a soldier." She stopped in the midst of bundling up the twenty yards or so of her trailing habit skirt over her arm and stared at him.

"Wellington told me once I had the makings of a good one," he said as he put his hands about her waist in readiness to lift her up into her saddle. "You don't have to look quite so astonished, Miss Hilton. I understand that, as far as junior officers go, I acquitted myself very well."

"I don't doubt that." She gave him a mischievous glance from beneath the rather battered and lopsided brim of her hat. "For a dandy, you do have your compensations, Mr Lindsay."

"I am pleased to hear it." With a soft laugh, he caught her by the waist with both hands and drew her close. "I suspect you also have compensations for a radical, Miss Hilton," he murmured against her ear before dropping the lightest, most frustrating of kisses upon her mouth. "A theory I look forward to exploring…"

It was a statement of intent, she thought, her heart beating wildly as he lifted her into her saddle. And she should be outraged—not delighted that he still wanted to see her, even though Jem was saved and any obligation he had towards her more than discharged. She glanced down as he guided her foot into the iron and found herself wanting to reach out and touch his dark, tousled head. He looked up, as if sensing her thought, and smiled before turning away to catch his own horse.

She gathered up her reins and shook out her habit skirt, then smiled as she watched him swing lithely on to the large grey's back. He rode like one of the trail scouts, she thought, totally at ease and at one with his horse. With his muddied coat, windblown hair and weathered craggy face he did not look in the least like the dandified society rake she had first encountered—in fact, an outsider might consider that she had had quite an effect upon Mr Lindsay's elegant and well-ordered life.

She gave a half-laugh at her own foolishness. It was madness to feel so ridiculously happy on a muddy, windy road at dawn in the company of an out-and-out rake who had treated her with complete impropriety. But then, perhaps, that was because she knew instinctively that he liked her as she liked him. They were two of a kind—she not quite a lady, and Jonathan Lindsay, though he was an aristocrat to his fingertips, not quite a perfect gentleman. If he had been, he would never have kissed an unmarried young woman.

Jonathan, turning in his saddle to ask if she was ready to set off, found his breath catching in his throat as she smiled at him, her face alight and quite startlingly beautiful beneath the fluttering brim of her hat.

"Shall we go?" he said after staring at her for a moment.

"I'll race you—" she laughed back at him over her shoulder, already nudging her horse into a trot down the steep hill "—from the bottom of the hill to the market cross in the village."

She still felt elated as she strode into the entrance hall of Pettridges, tossing aside her hat and gloves, not caring how much noise she made. It was *her* house, after all.

"Rather unconventional time to ride, ain't it, dear Jane?"

A few days before, Piers's supercilious drawl would have destroyed her mood in a moment, but now she did not care in the slightest. She felt invulnerable to his taunts. Jonathan Lindsay liked her, liked her enough to ride to London and back to please her. So what did she care for the opinion of a louse like Piers?

She turned slowly to face him. He was lounging in

the open doorway of the dining room, tapping a crop against his muddy boots.

"I felt like some fresh air," she said coolly, "as you did, apparently."

"Oh, I've been riding all night, one way or the other." He smiled unpleasantly. "And what about you? Was it a satisfying ride?"

His gaze lingered on her face for a moment before dropping down with blatant insulting slowness.

Her chin came up, and she smiled. A deliberate, slow smile. "Very, dear Piers, very." She aped his tone and had the satisfaction of seeing his eyes widen in surprise. "Now if you will excuse me, I wish to change before breakfast."

Turning her back upon him, she swept up the skirt of her habit, and began to ascend the stairs.

"I do hope Mama and Papa don't find out about your extraordinary behaviour, Jane," Piers called after her. "They are already anxious about you after your little exhibition in the morning-room. People might begin to think you not quite right in the head."

She halted to glance down at him over the polished mahogany balustrade. "I am not a child anymore, Piers. Tell them whatever you wish, I am sure it will not do anything to change their opinion of me."

"True, it could scarcely be lower," he sneered.

"Then they will be delighted to be quit of me and this house when I attain my twenty-first birthday, will they not?" She smiled and, not waiting for his answer, continued on up the stairs.

"Jane, dear, here you are at last, we've all been waiting for you." Mrs Filmore's plump face was all benign smiles beneath her rather unnaturally black curls as Jane came into the dining-room for breakfast.

"I was not aware I was late. The clock has not struck the hour yet," Janey said, startled as Piers leapt to his feet to pull out a chair for her. Ignoring it, she went around the table to sit beside Annabel, who gave her a speculative look.

"No, no, of course not, it is we that are early," Mrs Filmore said hastily, shooting a glance at her husband, who was frowning at his kedgeree. "It is just rather a special day—sad, of course, but life goes on. Poor dear Mr Grey, how you must miss him."

"Edward?" Janey looked at them blankly. They had hated Edward Grey, hated her engagement.

"It is a year to the day, my dear—" Mrs Filmore's tone was reproving "—a year to the very day since that awful tragedy."

"Oh." Feeling more than a little guilty that, of all anniversaries, she had forgotten this one, Janey dropped her eyes to her Wedgwood plate.

"You can come out of your mourning, dear." Mrs Filmore reached across the table to pat her hand. "No one will think the worse of you for it now, nor of anyone who has already waited overlong to declare his affection for you." She sent an adoring glance to the sullen Piers, who forced his thick lips into the semblance of a smile. "He has suffered, too, my dear, seeing you every day, and not being able to speak, being so sensible of your loss. No wonder he has been a little out of sorts with you. But that's all forgiven and forgotten, isn't it, Frederick?"

"Forgiven and forgotten," Mr Filmore intoned gravely. Janey looked from husband to wife in total disbelief. In the past, the Filmores' attempts to persuade her to become betrothed to Piers had been mostly made upon the basis that someone of her background should consider themselves fortunate in the extreme to marry a distant cousin of the Duke of Westminster. But to suggest that Piers was suffering from unrequited love for her and expecting her to believe it—she put a hand to her mouth.

"Surely you are not surprised, dear?" Mrs Filmore smiled at her. "It would make us all so happy if you were to accept him."

Janey did not doubt that. Not for a minute. "Marry Piers?" she gasped breathlessly. "I will not marry Piers. Not now! Not ever!"

"Why ever not, dear? It would be such a match for you."

"Because—" Janey caught her breath and struggled to suppress the bubble of laughter rising in her throat. Because he is nasty, cruel, lazy and utterly despicable, she felt like saying. "Because—" she hesitated, as Mary, the housemaid who was standing behind Piers, bit her lip to stop herself from laughing "—he's too fat and I simply cannot abide fat men."

"Fat!" Mrs Filmore gasped. "He is simply well built like myself. Besides, he could always reduce a little."

"And he's too short," Janey added, carefully deadpan. "Perhaps you could stretch him a little, too? I expect one of your numerous aristocratic relations still has the odd rack or two tucked away in the family dungeon?"

Janey saw Mary turn hastily to the sideboard, her black-clad shoulders shaking with suppressed laughter. It was her undoing. She was utterly helpless to stop the laughter that spilled out of her mouth.

"Marry Piers!" she spluttered. "Oh, I should not marry him to save my life!"

"That's as well—" Piers got up so suddenly his spoonback chair toppled backwards "—because you might not be so lucky next—"

"Piers!" Mr Filmore's roar coincided with Mary giving a gasp and dropping a tray of crockery and silver with spectacular results.

Then all was bedlam, Mr Filmore storming after Piers, Annabel bursting into sudden tears and Mrs Filmore leading her weeping from the room, pausing only to call Mary a stupid girl and instruct her to clear up the mess.

"Sorry, miss," the maid said timidly to her as Janey got up and helped herself to bacon and eggs from the covered dishes upon the sideboard, "about the china."

"It doesn't matter. Accidents happen." Janey shrugged. "Another five months and breakfast times will be more peaceful, I promise you. What happened—did you trip?"

"Not exactly...it was just what Master Piers said—" Mary hesitated and shook her head. "Don't matter, miss, I was probably just being stupid. I'll just go and get the brush and shovel, if you don't mind?"

Janey shook her head and sat down to her breakfast. Standing up to the Filmores had given her an appetite and her head was too full of Jonathan Lindsay for her to give any more thought to Piers's display of temper. She smiled, her breakfast momentarily forgotten as she recalled the way he had looked at her, the way he had kissed her—

Oh, hellfire, she repeated one of Lilian's favourite oaths softly beneath her breath. She would not be foolish enough to fall in love with Jonathan Lindsay, would she? How could she fall in love with a rake, a dandy, an indulged aristocrat, when she had never fallen in love with Edward?

Good, kind, worthy Edward, who had shared so many of her ambitions for the village. Edward, who had loved her—or had he? Edward had been so eager to improve her, so full of helpful suggestions as to how she might mend the deficits in her education and manners so that English society would approve of her...unlike Jonathan Lindsay, who seemed to approve of her exactly as she was.

The thought brought another smile to her lips, and her breakfast grew cold as she let herself indulge in a daydream of Jonathan Lindsay riding up the drive to demand her hand in marriage before the astonished gaze of all the Filmores. Then she sighed. Dreams were one thing, reality quite another. When and if the Honourable Jonathan Lindsay married, it would be to some aristocrat's daughter of impeccable blue-blooded pedigree. It would not be to Miss Jane Hilton.

Chapter Five

"Ah, awake at last! I was beginning to think you were going to sleep the clock round a second time," Perry greeted the unshaven Jonathan cheerfully as he came into the morning-room and threw himself down upon a sofa. "Not that I'm surprised. London to Dorchester in thirty hours in winter is damned good going, even for you. You should have made a wager on it."

"I did." Jonathan yawned. "With Russell. And, speaking of wagers, I trust you have made up your mind to part with Triton."

"I doubt she'll be that grateful for saving her felon's neck," Perry said confidently.

"Gratitude, my dear Derwent, does not come into it. Shall we say, the attraction is decidedly mutual?"

"You've seen her again?" Perry looked at him in disbelief. "When the devil did you find time for that?"

"A chance encounter upon the Salisbury road at dawn."

"On the road at dawn!" Perry's brows lifted.

"What the deuce was she doing on the road at dawn?"

"Oh, being her usual extraordinary self," Jonathan said slowly. "Tell me, Perry, do you think you have ever made a difference to anyone's life?"

"A difference?" Perry's brown eyebrows knitted. "Wouldn't have thought so—" Then his face lightened. "Parents, I suppose, were pleased to have me, son and heir and all that. But why the deuce do you ask?"

"No reason," Jonathan said as he shrugged.

"You're not back on this being useful thing, are you?" Perry sighed. "If you are, Jono, I am going back to Town. You're starting to sound like—well—one of those Reform fellows."

"God forbid!" Jonathan laughed. "But you have to move with the times, Perry, and reform is going to come, you know. You can't deny the cities like Manchester and Birmingham representation in favour of the counties for ever."

"The day town tells country what to do is the day I retire to the family castle and pull up the drawbridge." Perry sighed, fending off Tess as she tried to jump upon the sofa to lick his face.

"Has it occurred to you that that is just what I have decided to do here?" Jonathan said as the thwarted spaniel returned to sit upon his feet.

"You're not serious?" Perry stared at him. "You're one of the clever ones, Jono, you always were. You're bound to get a cabinet post sooner or later and then you'd make your difference."

"Nice of you to say so, Perry—" he smiled "—but I doubt it after that speech I made. Besides, I have difficulty in knowing which side I wish to be on these days—yes, Brown, what is it?''

He lifted his head as his butler came in after tapping at the door.

''A person to see you, sir. A William Avery, the local blacksmith, says he met you yesterday morning, sir.''

''Then show him in to the estate office. I'll see him there.''

''Yes, sir.'' Brown retreated.

''Avery? What can I do for you?'' Jonathan said as he entered the estate office, and saw the burly man whom he had seen with Miss Hilton upon the road standing at the window.

''It's a bit delicate, like,'' Will said, turning his cap over in his large, weathered hands. ''But you seem to be a friend of Miss Hilton, and there's no one else I know round 'ere I can turn to. Doctor and Vicar, well, they're all mighty thick with the Filmores.''

''This concerns Miss Hilton?'' Jonathan's expression of indifference left his face abruptly.

''Yes. It's about the accident she had last year.''

''The fall from a horse?''

''No, no, sir, when the staircase in old Fenton's Folly collapsed.''

''Fenton's Folly?''

''The tower, sir, the one on top of White Sheep Hill. Miss Hilton and Mr Edward used to walk there every Sunday after church. You can see the whole of the Pettridges Estate from the top of the tower.''

''Ah, I know where you mean now,'' Jonathan said. ''That is how she broke her leg?''

"Yes, sir, and her fiancé his neck. The top landing gave way when they were on it. He fell from top to bottom of the central stairwell, she was saved by her skirts catching on a piece of broken timber. Trapped there for hours she was, poor girl, hanging over a void, until the search party found them."

"My God! I had no idea," Jonathan said. "I thought it was a fall from a horse."

"It always bothered me, you see, sir," Will went on in his slow drawl. "My uncle built that staircase and there was no better joiner in all Wiltshire. That timber should have lasted another fifty years easy, and it was only a week before it fell that Mr Piers asked me to check it over. Said he'd heard it creaking. I went over it with a finetooth comb and it was sound as the day Uncle put the last nail in. Not as much as a single wormhole from top to bottom."

"Really, Avery?" Jonathan's brows rose. "Are you implying the collapse was not accidental?"

"I don't know." William Avery shrugged his massive shoulders. "I never got a close look at it afterwards, what with having to stop Master Piers from rushing in like a bull in a china shop to save Miss Hilton. He nearly dislodged the timber before the rest of us could get a rope on her. If it hadn't been for Tom—he's a stonemason, so he's used to scaffolding and the like—well, she'd have fallen, too. To be honest, sir, I've tried hard to put it out of my mind—but when Mary told me what Master Piers had said—"

"Mary?" Jonathan said, bemused.

"My betrothed, though I'd be grateful if you'd keep that under your hat, sir, or she'll lose her post. She's housemaid at Pettridges, you see."

"You have my word on it. What did Master Piers say?"

Will replied with a lengthy description of the previous day's breakfast at Pettridges.

"Hardly evidence upon which to hang an accusation of attempted murder," Jonathan said drily when Will had finished. "I think it would be better for you if you did not mention this to anyone else, Avery."

"I know that, sir," Will said. "But I'd be a sight easier in my mind if I thought someone was looking out for Miss Hilton."

"I am sure Miss Hilton is more than capable of looking out for herself," Jonathan said with a smile, as he recalled the effective way in which she had dealt with Piers Filmore's churlishness.

"Maybe, maybe," Will said slowly, "but she's a bit inclined not to see what she don't want to, if you get my drift, sir. That curate…"

"What of him?" Jonathan asked with sudden interest.

"Well, all his fine talk and good works, it was only when he had an audience, if you know what I mean."

"Indeed," said Jonathan, after a moment in which his spirits inexplicably lightened. "Thank you for the information, Avery. Now, if you will be so good, I have a great deal to do."

"You will look out for her, sir." Will turned back at the door. "There's summat wrong, I can feel it."

"I shall do my utmost to see that no harm befalls Miss Hilton," Jonathan assured him.

"Thought you would, sir, and thank you again for what you did for Jem. T'was a good thing, even if it were only to impress her," Will said with a grin, as

Jonathan stared at him in astonishment. "I might not have your learning, sir, but I ain't stupid, I saw the way you looked at her up on the road. And we all wish you the best of luck, sir—you'd have to go a long way to find yourself a better wife. Good day to you, sir."

"And good day to you," Jonathan said weakly as Will left. Damned impertinence, he thought and then laughed. No wonder Miss Hilton was popular with her tenants. Wiltshiremen appeared to be as outspoken in their soft, slow way as she was...

"Trouble, Jono?" Perry asked as he knocked upon the open office door some fifteen minutes later and found Jonathan sat upon the circular rent table for lack of a chair, staring out of the window.

"No." Jonathan shook his head and laughed. "Just some rustic with a peculiar fascination for staircases. He seems to think the Filmores harbour dark designs against Miss Hilton on the basis of some altercation at breakfast yesterday and the accident she suffered last year."

"Oh, is that all?" Perry laughed. "I feared 'Captain Swing' might be about to raise his ugly head. I gather from the paper the disturbances have spread all over Hampshire. Apparently, the old Duke says organising the militia to quell the rioters is the best fun he's had since beating Boney."

"I don't doubt it," Jonathan said. "Wellington has always looked happier wielding a sword than the pen, though it surprises me he is willing to do it against has own people with such alacrity."

"Now you are really starting to sound like one of

these Radical fellows." Lord Derwent snorted. "People who riot deserve what punishment they get."

"And people also deserve to eat," Jonathan said absently beneath his breath. Then, straightening, he sighed. "You don't think there could be anything in what that rustic said, do you, Perry? He didn't strike me as a fanciful sort of fellow."

"Oh, you know what country folk are," Perry said blithely. "Where there is no mystery, they are sure to invent one. And, speaking of mysteries, have you taken a look at the lake lately?"

"No. What of it?"

"Seems to be disappearing," Perry said laconically. "Awful lot of mud, flapping fish, very little water and a frightful smell."

"Damn!" Jonathan groaned. "I suppose we had better go and take a look at the inlet."

"We?" Perry's fair brows lifted and his nose wrinkled. "Don't you have men to do that sort of thing?"

"I have not got myself an agent yet, let alone taken on any labourers. And Brown and the servants are already muttering darkly about the amount of extra work in making the house habitable, and supervising the joiners and builders. I can hardly ask them to go poking about in the undergrowth or they'll all hand in their notice."

"Better go and change my coat, then," Perry said unenthusiastically.

"Mmm," Jonathan replied, still preoccupied with his thoughts. "I'll meet you at the south end of the lake, that's where the feeder pipe is, according to the estate plan."

* * *

"Oh, I didn't realise you are coming with us." Annabel pouted at the very same moment as Janey rode up to join her and Piers in front of Pettridges Hall.

"It was Piers's suggestion," Janey told her. "And I think he is right. Mr Lindsay might be my neighbour for some years to come."

Her emphasis upon the possessive pronoun was not lost upon the brother and sister, who exchanged sour glances.

"Let's go, then," Piers said sullenly. "We'll cut across the park, shall we? I fancy a gallop. And Jane always enjoys a good ride, don't you? My American coz?"

"So long as it is in the right company," Janey returned mildly, smiling inwardly as she saw Piers scowl. "And I am not your coz."

"But we'll have to jump the Wren's Dyke and two walls," Annabel protested sulkily, "and my new habit is bound to get splashed when we go through the river."

"Oh, for pity's sake, Annabel, don't you think of anything but clothes?" Piers snapped. "We are going across the park and that is an end to it. Understand?"

"Oh, very well." Annabel gave in and set her heels to her horse's glossy side. "Shall we say five pounds to whoever gets there first?"

"Ten," Janey said quickly. Her allowance for the month had already been spent on paying the lawyers she had employed to defend Jem, and ten pounds would buy a substantial amount of bread for the families whose men had no work.

"So sure you will win, coz?" Piers drawled.

"Absolutely," Janey said blithely and meant it.

Brutus responded to the touch of her heel with his usual good-natured obedience and launched into a steady ground-swallowing gallop, leaving Piers and Annabel's highly bred horses plunging and rearing in excitement as they struggled to turn them in the right direction.

A few minutes later, as Brutus slithered and slid his way carefully down a steep bank on the approach to a ditch, Janey glanced back over her shoulder. Annabel and Piers were taking the longer and more gentle slope. Janey laughed and took a handful of Brutus's mane for safety as his great quarters bunched for the leap over the ditch.

Having come late to side-saddle, she might never gain the perfection of Annabel's elegant seat, but when it came to the scramble and scrape of a fast cross-country ride, neither Piers nor Annabel could match her—but then, she thought wryly, they'd never had to literally ride for their lives with a war party of Indians on their tails.

The inlet pipe cleared, after a considerable effort and no assistance from Perry, who had taken one look and hastily suggested that he should go and look for some rods or something, Jonathan strolled back across the park, his coat slung over his shoulder, and his usually perfectly tied cravat hanging loose about his neck. He did not bother even to chastise Tess as she leapt up at him with a stick in her mouth. A few muddy pawprints, added to the mud with which his breeches and boots were already bedaubed, were going to make very little difference.

Taking the proffered stick from the spaniel, he

brought his arm back and threw it in a lazy arc and then halted and shaded his eyes against the morning sunshine. It seemed he was about to receive his first callers.

His mouth curved up at the corners as he recognised the foremost of the three riders galloping across the park. A race by the look of it, and Miss Hilton was winning by a good quarter of a mile, riding as low on her horse's neck as a staff galloper delivering a despatch under fire. He grinned as the giant black scarcely broke stride to leap a fallen beech; the style might not be orthodox, but it was certainly effective.

"Miss Hilton! Over here!" he shouted through cupped hands, and then, snatching off his cravat, he waved it in the air to attract her attention.

A moment later she turned her horse in his direction and waved back.

Pink-cheeked beneath her veil, exhilarated, and for some reason, stupidly, ridiculously nervous at seeing Jonathan, Janey did not rein in until the last possible moment.

Then, without any warning, she was flying through the air, past the black's shoulder, almost beneath its plunging forelegs to somersault into an untidy swirl of black habit, white petticoat and windblown golden hair at Jonathan Lindsay's feet.

"Miss Hilton! Have you hurt yourself?" Letting go his coat and the cravat, he dropped to his knees beside her, his voice ragged with what she took to be laughter.

"I don't think so," she said breathlessly after a moment's careful thought. "Fortunately it rained a great deal last night, and the ground is very soft," she said ruefully, as she pushed herself up to a sitting position and swept a loose tress of soft gold hair out of her eyes, unaware that in doing so she had transferred a considerable amount of mud from her gloves to her face.

"Good morning would have sufficed, Miss Hilton." He grinned at her. "You don't have to throw yourself at my feet."

"It was not out of choice, Mr Lindsay—" She gave a slightly breathless laugh as his eyes met hers and she knew instantly that he had no more forgotten their encounter upon the downs than she had. Her heart drumming in a way that had nothing to do with her fall, she looked away as the black gave her a hefty nudge between the shoulder blades. "It's no use saying sorry now, Brutus, you beast." She twisted and pushed at the horse's nose. "And now you've trodden on my hat!" she said exasperatedly as she began to disentangle herself from the hampering skirts of her habit.

"Come here, before he treads upon you as well." He slipped an arm about her waist and straightened, lifting her on to her feet.

Her breath caught as she found herself standing almost as close as they had been the previous morning, and she felt his fingers feather out across her ribs, preventing her from drawing back and trapping strands of her waist-length hair, which spilled down over her back and shoulders.

"You are quite certain you have not hurt your leg again?" he said softly as he looked down into her face. "You've gone very pale."

"Have I?" Her voice shook a little as she let her gaze lift to his.

"And you have begun to tremble."

"Have I?" She could find no other words as his eyes held her gaze.

"Yes." He smiled, smiled in a way that melted something in the pit of her stomach. "It must be the shock of your fall, no doubt."

"No doubt," she echoed, still unable to think of anything except his nearness, the weight of his arm about her waist, the way his mouth curved at the corners.

"You've got mud on your nose."

"Oh!" Her hand began to lift and then fell as he dabbed gently at her face with the soft folds of his cravat.

"And here…"

He touched the fine linen to the corner of her mouth. A touch that left her body aching and heavy, yearning to be closer, to be kissed—

"And if mud becomes me as well as it does you, perhaps we shall start a new fashion," he said with a lightness that did not match the darkness of his eyes as he drew back a little, leaving his hand only lightly upon her waist.

It did become him, she thought as she returned his scrutiny, noticing for the first time the degree of his dishevelment. There was no trace of the slightly effete dandy she had first taken him for. With his buckskin breeches liberally bedecked with mud, his thick dark hair windswept and his fine billowing linen shirt clinging to his broad shoulders where they were damp from perspiration, he was all lean, muscular strength.

"A slight problem with the lake," he said drily, his brows lifting as he intercepted her gaze.

"Oh." She felt her face colour and dragged her gaze from the open neck of his shirt. "You have not taken on any labour yet?"

"I have not decided yet whether I shall remain here or sell the place on," he replied without looking at her, his gaze going to the Filmores, who were approaching rapidly.

"Oh. I see," she said flatly. She stepped back from him and gave her attention to the business of bundling up the trailing skirt of her habit over her left arm.

Aware that he was watching her intently again, she found herself fumbling as she searched for the loop to slip over her wrist.

"Here." He bent and offered her the fold which had the little black silk cord stitched to its underside.

"Thank you," she said without looking at him. "Whoever thought this was a sensible garment for riding can never have fallen off. What did happen, by the way? Did he put in a buck? It's not like him." She was talking too much and too quickly, she thought, but she could not stop herself.

"Your girth broke—" He gestured to her side-saddle, which lay on the ground behind Brutus, who was cropping the grass placidly. "You did not have a chance of staying on."

"My girth broke—? But it was new only last month." She frowned and then shrugged her narrow shoulders. "Poor leather, I suppose. These accidents do happen."

"Yes," he said slowly.

"Well, at least it did not happen when we were

jumping Wren's Dyke.'' She sighed. ''But I shall have to speak to my horseman. I cannot understand it—he is usually so careful about such things.''

''Wren's Dyke?'' he queried.

''It is a large bank with a hedge upon the top and a ditch on the far side. It runs along the boundary between the Pettridges and Southbrook estates.''

''Don't tell me any more, I don't think I want to know.'' He exhaled audibly and then smiled at her, his eyes so warm that she felt her heart skip with a half-formed hope that she could not define. ''Why is it I have the feeling you are going to prove a very troublesome female?''

''Probably because I am one, or at least that is what I have been told since I arrived in England.'' She smiled up at him and then sighed as the Filmores reined in beside them. ''And no doubt I am about to be told so again.''

But Piers and Annabel were all consternation and concern for her welfare, fussing over her, until Jonathan suggested firmly that they make their way to the house and find Lord Derwent and ask him to order refreshments, while he walked back at an easy pace with Miss Hilton.

''I'll take the saddle, if you care to pass it up,'' Piers offered.

''Thank you,'' Jonathan said. He strode over to the saddle and picked it up and walked back to Piers.

''Saddler ought to be shot,'' Piers said disdainfully, as Jonathan handed up the saddle. ''New leather should not give way like that.''

''No—it should not.'' The hesitation was infinitesimal, fleeting as the shadow that crossed Jonathan's face as he stared at the broken girth and thought suddenly of the broken staircase in the tower.

"I'll lead Brutus." Annabel nudged her mare forward, coming between Jonathan and Piers. "Jane is welcome to ride my horse in, if she wishes. I'd be quite happy to walk back with you, Mr Lindsay."

I don't doubt it, thought Janey. But she managed to smile sweetly, and said that she would rather walk.

"Whatever you wish," Annabel returned with an equally insincere smile from the back of her dainty flaxen-maned chestnut. "I wonder if you could pass me Brutus's reins, Mr Lindsay?"

Reaching up to take the reins over the black's large head, Jonathan passed them to Annabel, who gave a slightly nervous laugh as the horse lifted his head and tried to nip at the foliage upon her hat.

"Behave, Brutus!" Janey hissed at the horse, who turned his head to look at her reproachfully.

"Brutus." Jonathan gave a half-laugh as he looked at the horse. "How appropriate."

"Not in the least. He's a lamb, and certainly not treacherous—hats are his only real vice," she said a moment or so later as she and Jonathan Lindsay watched the Filmores trot away towards the house, Brutus dwarfing the chestnut mare.

"Eating them or standing on them?" he asked her with a grin.

"Eating, mostly." She smiled back at him, wondering why it was she felt this irrational surge of happiness every time he looked at her.

"I suppose all that fruit is rather tempting," he said as he watched Annabel Filmore's bobbing millinery confection disappear into the distance.

"If you like looking like a costermonger's barrow, I suppose it is." Janey could not quite keep a thread of jealousy out of her tone. She knew that if Jonathan Lindsay came to prefer Annabel to her, she could not bear it.

"Tempting for horses, was what I meant." His wide mouth curved as he glanced sideways at her. Then suddenly he frowned. "Your girth—did you say it was new?"

"One month old," she said. "Why do you ask?"

"Oh, no reason." He shrugged, deciding he was letting Will Avery's wild imaginings occupy far too much of his thoughts. Filmore had more than enough money of his own. And evil guardians plotting against their wards belonged in Gothic romances, not on sunny autumn mornings in Wiltshire.

But with her soft gold hair tumbling in disarray down her back, and her slender figure swamped by the voluminous skirt and petticoats of the muddy habit, he found himself thinking that the self-sufficient, self-composed, unshockable Miss Hilton looked uncharacteristically vulnerable. She could so easily have broken her neck if the girth had broken earlier.

The thought sent ice along his spine at the realisation that he was already fonder of Miss Janey Hilton than was at all sensible.

"What are you thinking?" she asked as she watched his face.

"I was thinking that you might have been killed."

"But I wasn't—" she smiled at him, her dark limpid eyes full of unconscious invitation "—I suffered nothing more than a dent to my pride."

"I know a cure for that…" His voice was soft as velvet as he reached out and drew her into his arms.

"Do you?" There was the slightest of shakes in her voice as she looked up at him, and her heart began to race. He was going to kiss her again. And she wanted him to. Very much. Too much—it did not matter that she knew his intentions were not in the least honourable. All that mattered was this…

She shut her eyes as he bent his head and kissed her. Kissed her mouth, her eyelids, her throat, kissed her as if he could not stop. Kissed her until she felt boneless, floating, anchored only by his hands, his mouth. She gasped, her knees buckling suddenly, as his fingers found the aching tips of her breasts beneath the layers of wool and linen.

He caught her to him, one hand spread against her back, the other cradling her head against his chest. For a moment neither of them moved. She could hear his heart thumping as furiously as her own beneath his ribs, feel the rapid rise and fall of his chest.

"We had better go in," he said slowly. "The Filmores—"

"Yes," she agreed. But still neither of them moved, except for his hand that had begun to stoke her silky fair hair, smoothing it back from her brow.

"Jono!" It was Lord Derwent's distant shout that broke the spell.

They jerked apart and turned as one to see Perry striding across the park towards them. "Filmore said Miss Hilton had fallen. I thought you might need some assistance—" His voice tailed off as he looked from one to the other of them.

"My God!" he laughed good-naturedly. "You

both look in dire need of a large brandy and bed—''
He choked off the last word as Jonathan fixed him
with an icy blue glare. ''For Miss Hilton, I mean, best
thing for nasty shock and all that...''

Janey's face went from ashen to scarlet as she realised suddenly that a considerable amount of the pond-
weed which had bedecked Jonathan Lindsay now decorated her habit.

''I've no doubt you're right, Perry,'' Jonathan said
coolly. ''Miss Hilton has been feeling a little dizzy.''

''So I saw.'' Lord Derwent gave Janey a conspir-
atorial smile which increased her embarrassment.

''I'd be very grateful if you would go back quickly
and reassure the Filmores,'' Jonathan said, a distinct
warning note in his voice.

''What? Oh, yes, see what you mean. Glad you
weren't hurt, Miss Hilton.'' With the most unsubtle
of winks at Jonathan, Lord Derwent strode ahead of
them.

By silent and mutual consent they began to follow,
walking side by side and falling easily into step.

But as they came close to the house, Jonathan
halted suddenly. Janey stopped and turned her head
to look at him.

''If we continue like this, we will undoubtedly cre-
ate a scandal,'' he said slowly.

''Would you mind if we did?'' she asked, lifting
her chin to look him in the eyes.

''No,'' he said after a fractional hesitation. ''I am
no stranger to scandal, Miss Hilton. But perhaps you
should mind. Society will forgive behaviour in the
son of an earl that it will not countenance in a—''

"In a colonial of no breeding or consequence," she interrupted him wryly as he hesitated again.

"An unmarried lady, is what I was about to say," he reproved her softly.

"A lady?" Her brows lifted as she held his blue gaze. "Is that really how you consider me, Mr Lindsay?"

"You are generous, brave and honest, therefore I consider you a lady in every sense that really matters," he said with a conviction that made her heart flip over beneath her ribs. "Which is why I should not care to see you the subject of malicious gossips. It would perhaps be wiser if we took care only to meet in company in future."

"So that we may discuss the weather or the last run of the hounds?" she said with a sudden passionate anger that surprised even herself. "If that is being wise, I should rather be foolish. At least when I am alone with you I can be myself, rather than have to behave like some oversized wax doll without an opinion of my own or thought in my head except for the colour of my next new gown or the fitness of my horse! Every time I open my mouth upon any subject, the others all stare at me as if I am weak in the head."

"The others?" he queried.

"The people whom the Filmores have deemed me fit to be introduced to, all of whom seem to care for nothing but fox-hunting and their family connections. And their rules, of course. Their endless rules!"

"Rules?"

"The unspoken, unwritten ones, which you only know you have broken when they get that look upon their faces!"

"That look?"

"You must know the one I mean," she said bitterly. "Down the nose, with the faintest suggestion of a superior smile. The look that says *I am an English gentleman* or *woman,* and *you are a colonial nobody* with pretensions above your station."

"Ah, *that* look," he said with a wry smile. "They're not all like that, you know, and those that are...half the time I doubt they are even aware they are doing it."

"Just as half the time they do not appear to be aware that their labourers are starving! And even if they are, then they do not show any concern! Why is it in England that, if you show any compassion, any feelings about anything at all, you are made to feel as if you have committed a crime?"

"All this fire and passion. Lord Byron would have adored you, do you know that?" he said softly as she paused for breath.

"I had the impression the only person Lord Byron adored was himself," she said tartly. "Besides, I would rather you did," she added, her anger evaporating suddenly into something approaching a plea. "Adore me, that is."

"Miss Hilton!" He gave a gasp of laughter. "How the devil am I supposed to do the decent thing when you say things like that?"

"Not at all, I hope," she said with total honesty as she met his gaze. "And from what I have heard, except for the fact that I am not married, that will not exactly be a dramatic departure from your usual habits."

He stared at her for a moment, and then his mouth

curved slowly. "Very well, Miss Hilton, I give in. I only hope you do not come to regret your victory and think an ageing cynic like me a prize not worth the winning."

It was another warning, but it did nothing to dim her soaring relief. She knew that their flirtation would have to end at some point, but not just yet. It was the first real happiness she had felt since her arrival in England, the first time she had felt not quite so alone and as out of place as a square peg in a round hole.

"I should never make that mistake," she said a little too quickly to achieve the faintly mocking note she had intended. "And thirty-three or so is hardly what I should describe as ageing. You are only thirteen years older than me, Mr Lindsay."

"Maybe, but closer, I suspect, to a hundred in experience, Miss Hilton." He sighed.

She smiled sweetly and gave him what she hoped was a look of invitation. "That could be remedied, could it not?"

"Not here and now—" He laughed after a sharp intake of his breath, and gave her a small push into the marble-lined hall. "Behave, Miss Hilton, or I shall forget that I am a gentleman."

"Oh!" Janey came to a sudden halt and gasped as she looked around her at the gleaming hall. "I never realised this marble was pink-veined before—you have made such a difference to the house already."

"Not me," he said drily. "The improvements are all down to Brown and the servants. Brown regards dirt, dust and cobwebs as enemies to be vanquished at all costs. And, having done that, he is now badgering me for more servants."

"And will you be taking on more men?" Her carefully unconcerned question did not fool him for a moment, she realised, as he gave her a swift glance from beneath his dark lashes and smiled.

"I told you I have not made up my mind to stay yet. So don't start telling me which of the deserving poor I should employ."

"I am sorry, I did not mean to pry into your affairs," she apologised as the train of her habit slid unnoticed from her arm to pool upon the ground, and breathed an inward sigh of relief that he had not seemed to realise that her question had been based upon an entirely selfish desire to know whether or not he would be staying for some length of time.

"I need to think about it for a few more days, look at the quality of the land, the improvements needed," he said after a short silence. "There is no sense in throwing away money upon an estate that will never be profitable. That benefits no one in the long term."

"I did not think profit was so important to you," she said, without looking at him.

"There are a great many things you do not know about me." There was a warning note in his voice again which reminded her that he was right. She did not know him, not really. "And perhaps it is best you do not."

"Oh, there they are!" Annabel's trilling voice came drifting down the stairs. "I do hope you do not mind, Mr Lindsay, Lord Derwent has been showing me the ballroom. It is wonderful! A little gilt and paint and it would be as fine as any in London. How I should love to dance in it." She sighed as she reached the foot of the stairs. "I can imagine it now—'' she twirled a few graceful steps, and turned to smile up at Jonathan "—can't you?''

"Vividly. But I am sure the reality would be better than the imagination," Jonathan said drily. "Obviously, I must give a ball."

"Capital idea!" Lord Derwent said enthusiastically. "The Hoares over at Stourton would be sure to bring a party, and then there are the Morrisons from Fonthill and the people at Wilton—''

"Oh, all the county will come if Mr Lindsay invites them," Annabel said airily, posing gracefully with one elbow upon the newel post and giving Jonathan a flirtatious blue glance from beneath her eyelashes. "I know I should never refuse *any* of his invitations."

"Or anyone's," Janey muttered beneath her breath.

"What did you say, Miss Hilton?" Jonathan said mildly. "I did not quite catch it."

"I said—I said a ball would be—fun," Janey invented hastily, glowering at him, knowing as she saw the laughter in his blue eyes that he had heard her perfectly.

"Do you mean to come?" Annabel addressed her in astonished tones. "What of your leg? You have not danced since the accident."

"Then perhaps it is time I started. I shall certainly come—if I am invited?" Janey replied, throwing a faintly challenging glance at Jonathan.

"You are the first upon my list," he smiled at her.

"Then I shall be delighted to accept, Mr Lindsay." Her face lit up as, ignoring Annabel's coy glance of invitation, he stepped over to her and took her arm. When he touched her, she did not care what Annabel, Piers or the entire British aristocracy thought of her.

Piers, sprawled in a chair in the morning-room, a large glass of brandy in his hand, looked up as they all entered the morning room.

"Piers! What do you think! Mr Lindsay is going to give a grand ball," Annabel said excitedly, seating herself upon the chair Lord Derwent drew forward for her. "We are all invited. And even Jane has agreed to come."

"Is that true, Jane?" Piers frowned as he turned his head to look at Janey, who was laughing up at Jonathan Lindsay as he settled her upon the sofa and then sat down beside her.

"Yes, what of it?" Janey replied, her chin lifting as she met Piers's stare.

"Nothing, dear coz," Piers drawled. "I just wondered whether you are quite sure you are ready for society. It is, after all, scarcely a year since Grey died."

"It is *more* than a year, as your mother so kindly reminded me but the day before yesterday," Janey replied sweetly. "And since your parents have gone to every length to prevent me from having a season, I am sure they will not begrudge me attendance at one ball."

"Oh, of course not." Piers gave her a benign smile. "You do say the most extraordinary things, Jane. Mama and Papa only prevented you having a season because they were concerned, when you first came to this country, that you should not be made a laughing stock because of your lack of education and manners."

"A deficit that they have obviously more than compensated for since," Jonathan put in smoothly as he heard Janey's fierce intake of breath and saw the green glitter of anger in her hazel eyes. "But then I suppose they had had plenty of practice in improving manners with you, Filmore."

Piers's slack lips gaped like those of a landed fish and he went red with what Janey knew to be anger. Then he gave a ragged laugh. "If I did not know you were such a jester, Lindsay, I'd call you out for that."

"By all means," Jonathan voiced his invitation with a smile that made Janey think suddenly of a mountain lion she had seen once, lazing with deceptive tranquillity in the sun on a rocky ledge. "A jester like me will do anything for a little amusement."

Piers's colour changed from red to white. "Well, I would oblige you, of course," he spluttered, "but it's rather frowned on now, isn't it? And, what with you being a Member of Parliament..."

"Oh, pray don't let that stop you," Jonathan drawled, his smile wider. "It didn't stop Wellington, after all, and he was Prime Minister."

Annabel gave a small stifled moan and went as pale as her brother.

"Jono!" Lord Derwent said with uncustomary sharpness. "You will frighten the ladies with your teasing—Miss Filmore looks quite faint."

"My apologies," Jonathan said at once, his tone losing its edge. "Derwent is quite right, I was merely teasing, Miss Filmore. And you, Miss Hilton? I trust you are not feeling faint?"

He turned to Janey, his mouth curving slightly at the corners as he saw that she had been struggling to suppress laughter.

She swallowed. "Oh, no," she said with careful

sobriety. "It takes rather more than teasing to alarm me, Mr Lindsay."

"So I have observed," he drawled, his voice like velvet as his gaze travelled over her face and came to rest upon her mouth. "You seem to be quite fearless. Can I take it that you will not swoon into my arms at the sight of a mouse or spider, or the merest hint of thunderstorm?"

"You may depend upon it," she said firmly, determined that she would not rise to his bait like Piers. "But I am sure some lady will oblige you, should the occasion arise."

"Really, Jane!" Annabel gave a little gasp of shock. "You are as bad as—"

"Me?" Jonathan laughed as Annabel stopped in confusion. "I rather fear you are right, Miss Filmore. I think Miss Hilton and I are a well-matched pair, don't you?" he added carelessly.

He could not have shocked Annabel more if his choice of words had been deliberate, but perhaps they had been, Janey thought, biting her lip as she caught the gleam in his blue eyes. He was wicked. Quite wicked.

"I should not have said so," Annabel said tersely, "but then you are not so well acquainted with Miss Hilton as I am."

"A lack I look forward to remedying," he replied coolly, but his eyes were warm as they met Janey's gaze. "Where shall we begin, Miss Hilton?"

"I thought we had begun, when we met upon the downs," she returned blandly, deciding that two could play this game.

He smiled. A slow, slow smile that made her melt

and pool inside and want to hit him in the same moment. "The downs? Remind me?"

"Another time, perhaps—I should not wish to bore everyone else," she replied hastily, knowing she had just been outplayed and what was more, she was blushing and she never, ever blushed.

"Oh, neither would I," he replied innocently. "I have absolutely no desire to bore anyone else, Miss Hilton."

She caught her breath at the image his words brought to her mind. He was shameless, utterly shameless, and she was so far out of her depth that she was drowning. She stared at him helplessly, her lips faintly parted as she struggled to find a reply.

It was Lord Derwent who came to her rescue. "Awfully nice weather for the time of year, don't you think, Miss Hilton?"

"Yes. Almost springlike," she replied politely, glad that her voice was steady, even if her throat was dry and her pulse racing.

Jonathan shot Perry a glance and received a distinctly disapproving look in return, which startled him for a minute; then he smiled. No doubt Perry had just realised he was in severe danger of losing the wager and Triton. He leant back against the sofa, his smile broader as he let his hand fall to his side and brush Janey's fingers.

If Perry thought he could make him feel guilty with a few stern looks, he was mistaken. Even if Miss Janey Hilton was not quite so unshockable as she liked to appear, it was not as if she was some innocent,

protected miss, straight from the schoolroom, was it?
If he had had any doubts that she wanted him as much
as he did her they had disappeared as he felt her jolt
at his touch. Oh, no, he was going to enjoy winning
this wager...

Chapter Six

"Not quite the usual sort of girl," Lord Derwent observed as he and Jonathan drove back from Pettridges, having taken Janey home in the carriage. "Very pretty, though, and even my father could not complain at the size of her fortune."

"If you have an interest, say the word," Jonathan replied. "I should not care to stand in the way of Miss Hilton's lasting happiness."

"Me! Marry a Radical! And a millhand's daughter to boot!" Lord Derwent laughed. "The family would disown me in an instant. But you surprise me, Jono—I did not think you'd give her up so easily. I had begun to think—"

"What?" Jonathan interrupted harshly.

"Well—that you were over Susanna at last," Lord Derwent said tentatively.

"I was over Susanna the day she accepted that doddering old Duke's proposal," Jonathan said coldly.

"Really?" Lord Derwent snorted. "As far as I can see, she's had you wriggling on her hook these last six years. The minute you look twice at a marriageable girl, Susanna makes damned sure you don't look a third time. It's not just her husband she's made a fool of, you're not even the *only* one she deceives him with—"

"Enough, Perry!" Jonathan rasped.

Lord Derwent sighed. "Someone has to say it— you've been rattling round like a loose cannonball ever since she jilted you for her Duke, and leaving a trail of wreckage in your wake. There's half a dozen young women with broken hearts in Town who would agree with me."

"I have never misled any of the women you refer to. I told all of them I had no serious intentions. It is not my fault if they chose not to believe me!" Jonathan glowered and whipped up the horses to a faster pace.

"You're not exactly being as honest with Miss Hilton," Lord Derwent said, frowning. "It's obvious she's partial to you and when she finds out about the wager..."

"I see no reason why she should," Jonathan snapped. "Unless you are so unsporting as to tell her, Perry."

"It's more a question of conscience than being sporting," Lord Derwent said, sighing. "You know as well as I do, we should never have made that wager. Not that calling it off is likely to make a difference to your pursuit of her, I suppose?"

"None. Pursuing Miss Hilton is proving far too enjoyable to give up." Jonathan laughed. "And conscience be damned—you're just worried that you're going to lose Triton."

"Believe what you will. But I don't think I will be

the loser this time, Jono—" Lord Derwent shrugged "—I can always get another horse."

"Meaning?" Jonathan drawled, giving him a cool look as he hesitated.

"You might not find your self-respect so easy to regain," Lord Derwent said, after clearing his throat. "It's one thing to play games with the likes of Mrs Norton—she knows the rules—but Miss Hilton... Damn it, Jono, she's an unmarried woman and you could ruin her reputation."

"She is quite aware of the danger," Jonathan asserted with a smile, "and I assure you, Perry, she does know the rules—she simply chooses not to play by them. However much the lady Miss Hilton appears now, I can assure you that she is far from some sheltered innocent. In fact, I rather suspect she enjoys living dangerously."

"She will need to," Lord Derwent muttered grimly beneath his breath as Jonathan whipped up the horses and sent them speeding through the rather dilapidated gateposts at the end of Southbrook House's drive, "if she's foolish enough to fall in love with you."

Late the following afternoon as the light was fading, Janey hurried back towards Pettridges Hall. Her grey pelisse and gown were soaked right through from a short icy shower. It had been silly to think that he might decide to walk to the waterfall on such a dull, damp November evening, sillier still to do so herself just because there was a remote possibility of meeting him. Shivering and calling herself every kind of fool, she increased her pace to a near run and decided to take the shortest route across the stableyard.

"Miss! Miss Hilton! Could I have a word?"

She halted in response to the hail from the harness room and retraced her steps.

"Does it have to be now, Iggleston?" she asked the head groom as she stood at the harness-room door, her arms wrapped tightly about her for warmth. "I'm chilled to the bone."

"It's your saddle, miss, it got left at Southbrook yesterday. Mr Lindsay has just brought it back and said you ought to change your saddler. But it wasn't Hobson's fault, miss. Look…" He held out the girth of her side-saddle in his wizened, nut-brown hands.

Janey took it unseeingly, her heart and mood soaring, the cold forgotten as she wondered if he was as impatient to see her again as she was to see him. "Mr Lindsay is here?"

"Aye, and Lord Derwent. The master invited them to dine. I took the message over this morning, miss."

"Oh, I see," she said wryly. So *that* was why Mrs Filmore had been so insistent that she still looked peaky after her fall and should rest and dine in her own room. It was not the first time she had been relegated to her room when eligible bachelors had been invited to dine. The Filmores' efforts to prevent her marrying anyone except Piers before she was twenty-one had only been exceeded by their efforts to find a husband for Annabel.

Given the nature and character of the men the Filmores had considered desirable matches, she had usually been more than grateful not to have to endure their company at the dinner table. But if her guardians thought she was going to retreat gracefully tonight, they were mistaken. Her father had taught her that you had to be prepared to fight for what you wanted—and she wanted Jonathan Lindsay. Wanted to see him, hear him, and be kissed by him again...that thought sent a spiral of remembered warmth coiling through her insides.

"Look at it, miss—" with a start, she realised Iggleston was still talking about the girth "—a buckle might tear through after a lot of use—but both of 'em together—and new leather—" Iggleston shook his head in disbelief. "I've never seen that happen in fifty years, miss. And look how clean the edges are—that leather was scored, scored more than three-quarters through. And it weren't like that when I saddled up, miss, I swear it. No horse goes out of this yard with a girth I would not trust my own neck to."

"Are you saying someone deliberately cut the leather so the buckles would give?" Janey said, her attention caught now as she stared at the supple leather strap in her hands. "But who would do such a thing...?" Her words dwindled as the answer came. Piers!

Piers, who had brought Brutus round to the front of the house for her with unprecedented thoughtfulness. Piers! It would be just his idea of a jest to see her go flat upon her face in the mud. And he had chosen their route, had knowingly let her jump Wren's Dyke with a girth that could have broken at any moment. Some jest, she thought furiously. He could have killed her!

And that would probably have amused him, she thought grimly. Well, this time he had gone too far and she was going to tell him so! In the last month there had been a burr under her saddle, a dead rat in her bed and the disappearance of her brooch. Until now she had bitten her tongue, and let the matters go without comment, knowing that a reaction would only give him satisfaction. But this time she was not going to suffer in silence.

"I don't like it, miss, first that burr under your saddle, now this." The furrows on Iggleston's walnut face deepened. "Who'd do such a thing?"

"I think I can guess," Janey exhaled slowly as she struggled to control her growing anger. "And I suspect it was his idea of a jest."

"A jest! There's only one here who'd be that stupid!" Iggleston said disgustedly. "That burr were bad enough, but he's gone too far this time, and he needs telling so—if I were his father, I'd have taken a whip to him long ago. Do you want me to have a word with Mr Filmore?"

"No," said Janey resignedly, "he'd only blame you or me. I'll deal with it." One way or another, she added beneath her breath as she marched towards the house, her anger burning inside her like a flame. She had had enough of the Filmores! Had enough of their superiority, their pettiness and their constant denigration of her and her background! And, most of all, she had had enough of Piers's practical jokes.

Once in the house, she picked up her grey woollen skirts and ran across the hall and up the stairs, still clutching the girth.

"Whatever is it, miss?" her maid asked, starting up from darning some stockings as Janey threw open her bedchamber door, dropped the leather girth upon the carpet, tossed her bonnet onto the bed and began to unfasten her sodden pelisse. "No time for questions, Kate," Janey said breathlessly. "Can you get me some hot water to wash with, and get out the red silk dress? I have decided to dine downstairs after all."

"The red silk..." Kate's blue eyes widened for a moment, but then she smiled. "Yes, miss. It'll be good to see you out of those mourning clothes." Still smiling, she hastened away to do Janey's bidding.

Some fifteen minutes later, Janey checked her reflection in the looking glass. It did suit her, she thought, as she stared into the glass at the claret silk gown. She had ordered it especially for the dinner where her betrothal to Edward had been made public, drawing exactly what she had wanted for the dressmaker, remembering one of Lilian's simple cottons which she had always admired.

A frown furrowed her forehead. She had loved the gown from the first fitting—and Edward had been horrified by it. Edward had thought it made her look like a whore—though he had not said so in so many words. Unsuitable for an unmarried woman and even more unsuitable for a clergyman's wife, he had said in hushed tones. And then, seeing her disappointment, he had consoled her, telling her that she must not worry, in future he would assist her in the selection of her gowns.

That was the first time she had begun to wonder whether being married to Edward would be better than being the Filmores' ward. But by then it had been too late—Mr Filmore had risen to his feet and announced their engagement with stilted and wholly insincere words of congratulation.

She stared at her reflection in the mirror, wondering whether she should change into one of the more conventional frothy, frilly confections of pastel colours which Mrs Filmore had ordered for her when she first arrived in England.

She tugged a little at the deep pleated band of crimson silk which ran straight and very low across her breasts, leaving her throat and shoulders bare. She had forgotten this gown was quite so low, and, she thought with a tiny half-smile, how well it suited her.

Unrelieved by any contrasting colour, the glowing wine-coloured fabric set off her pale skin, making it look luminous and pearly, and enriched the soft gold of her hair which, with little time for curling tongs, Kate had caught up in a simple knot embellished with a pearl and tortoiseshell comb, leaving a few simple spiral curls to frame her face. No, she decided with a lift of her chin, she did not care what the Filmores or anyone else thought of the gown, she liked it and that was all that mattered.

After one last adjustment of the neck and twitching out the full skirt, which belled out from the tight waist which came down to a little point, she turned away from the mirror and went to her dressing table.

Opening her jewellery box, she put pearl drops in her ears, and then frowned as she found her pearl necklace missing. Not again, she thought with a grimace, her anger surging again. Surely Piers did not think she would fall for the same trick twice?

"Kate?" She turned to her maid. "Have you seen my pearls?"

"They're in their box, miss, I'm sure I saw you put them away last night," Kate said, her round face creasing into a frown. "Unless it was the night before?"

"They're not here now," Janey said, taking out a gold chain with a single pearl drop. "I must have put them down somewhere. Will you have a look for me while I am at dinner? I am late already. There—" she fastened the gold chain about her neck and turned a pirouette "—will I do, Kate?"

"You look beautiful, miss," Kate said approvingly.

"Thank you." Janey started for the door with smile and then hesitated. "You would not happen to know what Miss Filmore is wearing tonight?"

"Just about everything but the curtain swags, miss," Kate said with a wicked grin. "Her mother's diamonds, the white lace with the blue overskirt and the yellow bows, miss, and she has her hair curled and dressed with lace, a Swiss Bodkin and blue feathers. Jeanne says she's out to make an impression upon Mr Lindsay since, apparently, Lord Derwent is as good as spoken for by Lord Ishmay's daughter."

"I rather think she will succeed." Janey laughed as her eyes met Kate's. "I doubt he will have eyes for anyone else. Who else is dining tonight?"

"The Doctor and Mrs Hutton and the Reverend and Mrs Norris, I'm afraid," Kate replied, her voice heavy with sympathy.

Janey sighed. "Then I suppose I may look forward to a lecture upon the calming qualities of camomile tea and the inadvisability of concerning myself with matters outside the home from Mrs Norris, and Mrs Hutton speaking to me as if I have lost my wits."

"Least you'll have Mr Lindsay there," Kate said a little enviously. "From the way he handed you out of his carriage yesterday, I'd say you had an admirer there, miss.''

''Really, Kate!'' Janey said, going a little pink as she remembered exactly how Jonathan had lifted her down from the carriage, putting his hands upon her waist and letting her slide down the long lean length of his body, and holding her there far longer than was polite, until her breasts had grown tight and heavy, and her heart had begun to race. Just for a moment, an insane, glorious moment, she had known he had been tempted to throw all propriety to the winds and kiss her again in full view of Lord Derwent, the Filmores and the servants.

''Sorry, miss,'' Kate grinned. ''You'd better go, you're late already.''

''Yes.'' Janey turned for the door in a sweep of red silk and then swung back to stoop and pick up the girth.

''Whatever do you want that for?'' Kate said, her eyes widening in astonishment.

''A gift,'' said Janey with a grimace. ''A gift for Mr Piers.''

''They've already gone in, miss, the fish has just been served.'' Dawson, the butler, greeted Janey outside the dining-room door. ''Shall I take that for you?'' His impassive gaze dropped to the girth which Janey held at her side in one of her gloved hands.

''No, thank you, Dawson.'' Janey smiled at him blithely. ''Just open the door for me, if you would?''

He did as she asked, but she hesitated on the threshold momentarily, feeling as dazzled by the dining-room's grandeur as she had when she had first entered it as a seventeen-year-old girl who had never eaten a meal from anything but a deal table close to the kitchen range.

There was a part of her that would never get used to this, she thought wryly, as her gaze flicked from the green silk-hung walls to the great polished length of the mahogany table that was so laden with German porcelain, Irish crystal and English silver that there was barely any wood left to be seen, a part of her that would never belong in Jonathan Lindsay's world of luxury and privilege.

"Miss?"

She started, realising Dawson was still holding the door. Taking a deep breath, she swept into the room in a rustle of silk, determined that even if she felt like an interloper, she was not going to look like one. It was her house, she reminded herself firmly.

"Good evening," she said coolly and clearly as she was able, halting in front of the blazing log fire in the grate at the nearest end of the room.

Nine heads lifted and turned as one to look at her and all the men rose instantly to their feet. But there was no unison in their expressions. The Filmores looked annoyed, the Doctor and the Reverend and their respective spouses disapproving, Lord Derwent amused and Jonathan—

Far from the smile she had hoped for, Jonathan was simply staring at her, his eyes very dark in his frozen face, as if he had never seen her before, as if she were a creature from a different world. And to him she probably was, she thought, wondering if he thought her severe gown and simply arranged hair as unsuitable as Edward had.

She would never get things quite right, she thought despairingly. She did not belong. And for the first time since she had come to England, it mattered. It mattered because she wanted desperately to be a part of Jonathan Lindsay's world. But she never would— the Filmores had made that clear upon a thousand occasions. She might have money, but she would never be considered the equal of the people sat at this table, however hard she tried. She would always be the colonial, the millhand's daughter.

Jonathan exhaled the breath that had caught in his throat. He had become used to the way she hid her beauty beneath the dull grey and black gowns; now she had caught him as offguard as if she had drawn a blade from a scabbard. The dressmaker who had made that gown should be declared a danger to the public, he thought, as his gaze dropped from her face to the impossibly, wonderfully plain gown. If she wore it in town, it would set a new mode.

There was nothing to detract from the fierce beauty of her face, the surprising delicacy of her shoulders and arms. The tight bodice of glowing crimson silk highlighted the milky fairness of her skin, the darkness of her eyes and left scarcely anything to the imagination above her handspan waist. Feeling the distinct, uncomfortable stirrings of desire, he dragged his gaze upwards, trying to think of anything but the soft satiny swell of her breasts and how easy it would be to free them from the confines of that gown.

And then, as he caught her gaze again, he found himself startled by the bleakness in her dark eyes, a bleakness that puzzled him.

"This is very inconvenient, Jane. You will have to wait until another place has been laid."

It was Mrs Filmore's cold remark that brought understanding as he realised with a spurt of anger that neither of her guardians had any intention of making her late entry anything but embarrassing for her. They had not even made the slightest move to accommodate her at the table.

Janey's chin lifted. "If I had known we were to have guests, I should have been here earlier. Unfortunately, no one thought fit to tell me."

Her last remark hung in what seemed like endless silence as Mrs Filmore went a rather dull red.

"Oh, really, Jane," Annabel drawled sweetly. "I heard Mama tell you but two hours ago that we were to have guests."

"I recall nothing of the kind," Janey said tersely.

"No, no, of course you do not, you must not let it upset you, dear Jane, but perhaps it would be best if you dined in your room as you had intended. You do not look at all well." Annabel was all cooing concern. But Jonathan caught the sideways glance she exchanged with the doctor, the raised eyebrows and the brief tap of her finger to her forehead. Not for the first time, he wondered how someone of such good business sense as old Fenton had displayed so little judgement in the selection of guardians for his granddaughter.

And by the look of her pale face and the shimmering rage in her hazel eye, Miss Hilton was thinking much the same and, he feared, was about to say so, which would only lend substance to Annabel's nasty little innuendoes.

"I must disagree with you, Miss Filmore," he said lazily, just as Janey's lips parted to give voice to her anger. "I have never seen Miss Hilton look better, and I am certain she feels very well indeed."

Janey caught her breath as he smiled at her, the slanting, challenging smile that put an entirely different private meaning into his words. It was as well she was not over-given to blushing, she thought, as she smiled back at him and let her gaze drop to his lean whip-hard body before lifting it to meet his again.

"Thank you," she said demurely. "You are quite right, Mr Lindsay, I have rarely felt better." And then she had to bite her lip to stop herself from laughing as she saw that the "rarely" had struck home.

"I am gratified to hear it." There was a flash of laughter in his eyes as he inclined his head to her in the briefest of nods before turning to Mrs Filmore. "But perhaps Miss Hilton should not be kept standing. There is space for another chair beside me."

The hint of censure in his tone was barely perceptible, but it was there and it made her feel warm inside. It was wonderful not to feel utterly alone in this house that she had never come to think of as home.

"I suppose so," Mrs Filmore replied irritably. "Thomas—" she made an irritable gesture to the footman "—a chair for Miss Hilton and another place before the dinner goes entirely cold!"

Janey waited for Thomas to set the chair in place, and then walked slowly across the room towards Jonathan. At least he did not seem to disapprove of her gown, she thought, her spirits soaring as she felt his gaze follow her every step, every dip and sway of her hips beneath the rustling silk, every rise and fall of her breasts.

He was smiling at her, his eyes warm as she reached him. And then, as he drew out the chair the footman had placed beside him, he noticed the girth she held at her side, almost hidden amid the voluminous folds of the red silk skirt. His dark brows lifted in silent enquiry.

"After-dinner entertainment," she murmured as he helped her be seated and the rest of the gentlemen sat down.

"I did not know your tastes ran in that direction, Miss Hilton," he said with another lift of his brows as he glanced down at the leather strap again. "Though I understand a little gentle restraint can add to one's enjoyment."

For a moment she stared at him, not understanding. Then, as a memory of just why Lilian had thrown out one trapper into a rainstorm without so much as his shirt on came back to her, she felt a *frisson* of shock.

Which was exactly what he had intended, she realised, as she saw what was becoming a familiar teasing challenge in his blue eyes.

"That is not the sort of entertainment I had in mind," she said with a determinedly bland smile.

"Pity." He sighed in a tone that sent a melting heat through her body.

"And you should exercise a little gentle restraint upon your imagination, Mr Lindsay," she returned, stabbing a fork into the plate of fish that had just been laid before her as she tried to take her own advice and failed. He was so damnably handsome in his dark coat and snowy cravat, and so close to her she caught the spicy clean scent of his cologne. So close that, every time he moved, the soft wool cloth of his coat sleeve grazed the satiny skin of her shoulder like a caress, making her whole body prickle and grow tight.

"I'm trying but it's very difficult," he murmured, his breath warm against her ear, as he leant forward to pick up a glass. "That gown is decidedly stimulating—to the imagination," he added innocently, as she froze with the speared morsel of herring upon her fork.

"Are you utterly shameless, Mr Lindsay?" she said grittily as she lowered her fork to her plate.

"I don't know," he said, his eyes suddenly very dark and smoky as he held her stare. "Care to find out, Miss Hilton?"

Chapter Seven

It was more than teasing, she thought, her mouth and throat going quite dry. It was a most definite and improper invitation, and not one any gentleman should make to an unmarried lady at a dinner table before her guardians. The only response to it was to slap his face or laugh…or simply say yes.

She dropped her eyelids a fraction too late. She knew by the sudden fierceness in his face that he had read that last thought.

"Well?" he prompted silkily.

Janey laughed a little shakily. "I think you have just answered my question, Mr Lindsay. But should I require a fuller answer at some other time, I will be certain to let you know."

"Then I shall live in hope." He laughed goodnaturedly, dissolving the almost tangible tension that had flowed between them a moment before. "Which is more than poor Derwent looks likely to do," he added quietly. "One more toss of the beauteous Miss Filmore's head and he'll lose an eye to that Swiss Bodkin."

Janey glanced across the table and almost laughed aloud as Lord Derwent flinched from a particularly lethal toss of Annabel's over-ornamented head as she leant towards him confidingly.

"I am surprised she was not placed beside you," she said, turning back to Jonathan.

"I dare say Mrs Filmore could not resist the chance of an elder son, even if he is nearly spoken for," he whispered back. "A circumstance for which I am deeply grateful. Miss Filmore is not to my taste."

"Nor the fish, by the look of it," Janey said as she toyed with her own food. "Aren't you hungry?"

"The only appetite I have at this moment cannot really be indulged in upon a table," he said, as his gaze held hers. "At least, not in company—I doubt it would be considered polite."

"I doubt it would be comfortable."

He laughed, recognising her reference to their encounter upon the downs. "Comfort is important to you, Miss Hilton, is it not? I begin to think that, for all those rather puritan gowns and radical views, you are something of a sybarite at heart."

"Very probably," she agreed mildly. "I should do almost anything for crisp linen, French perfume, a goosedown bed, and hot water that I have not had to fetch and boil, Mr Lindsay. So would you, if you had spent any time on the trail in a wagon or in a cabin in the wilderness."

"Anything?" His eyes held hers. "That's a reckless offer, Miss Hilton. I might be tempted to purchase the contents of Bond Street tomorrow and throw them at your feet."

"*Almost* anything, I said, Mr Lindsay," she corrected him softly as the challenge and counter-challenge flowed between them again. "And I am not reckless."

"Aren't you?" His mouth curved as he studied her face intently. "I think you are a gambler, Miss Hilton. I should wager you are as fond of risk as I am. The more I know of you, the more I am convinced that we are two of kind."

"A well-matched pair?" There was an edge to her voice she could not quite suppress as she quoted his own words.

He frowned as he saw the bleakness in her eyes again.

"What is it?"

"Nothing." She gave a stiff smile and looked away. "I was just wishing—"

"Wishing what?" he asked.

That I was the Earl's daughter I could have been, a well-bred English lady, someone that you might consider for a wife instead of merely another conquest, she wanted to say, but couldn't. That was a cold truth she would face when she was alone, but not just yet. Just for now, she wanted to dream that there was more than desire in his eyes when he looked at her.

"Well?" he prompted softly as she stared unseeingly at her plate.

"I was wishing I was someone else," she said, barely audibly.

"Then that is a wish I would never grant you, even if I had the power," he replied softly in a tone that made her melt inside. "I would not change anything about you, Miss Hilton."

"Wouldn't you?" She turned her head to look at him again, her heart flipping over as he shook his head.

"No." He smiled and lifted his glass to her. "To perfection, Miss Hilton."

She stared at him, feeling as she were drowning in the blue warmth of his eyes as she met his gaze over the crystal glass. Don't, she wanted to say, don't make me fall in love with you. But what was the point? she thought with sudden wry self-honesty. It was too late—she already had. As Lilian had told her once, love was not a matter of choice, more like a horse bolting with you on its back: the only thing you could do was hang on for dear life and try and enjoy the ride before you got thrown off.

Why Jonathan Lindsay? she wondered, as she stared at his rakish face. Why did he have to be the man who could set her mind and body alight with a word, a touch, a smile…?

"Why aren't you wearing your pearls, Jane?"

She jolted at the sudden question from Annabel and put an uncertain hand to her throat. "My pearls?" she said blankly.

"The ones your grandfather gave you," Annabel said very markedly and slowly as if speaking to a child. "Don't you like them anymore?"

"Oh, no, it is just that I have mislaid them," she replied without thinking, too preoccupied to sense Annabel's trap.

"Mislaid!" Annabel said in horror. "They are worth a fortune. You must have the servants search for them as soon as we have dined. Really, Jane, you are becoming so forgetful. You would not believe how many things she has lost in the last month, Dr Hutton—we turned half the house upside down looking for a brooch that she had pinned to a shawl she was wearing!''

"And do these instances of absentmindedness occur often, Miss Hilton?" Dr Hutton asked her gravely.

"No," Janey said tersely, aware of Jonathan regarding her intently from beneath dark lashes and wondering if he was beginning to doubt her sanity—he certainly had more cause than the rest, given her attempt to rescue Jem and some of the outrageous conversations they had had. "And it was not absentmindedness; someone took the brooch out of my jewel case and pinned it to the inside of the shawl without my knowledge."

"Yes, yes, of course." Dr Hutton exchanged a glance with Annabel, which made Janey wish to stab him upon his large gouty nose with her fork. "You have not thought a change of air might do you good, Miss Hilton? Perhaps you are in need of rest."

"There is nothing wrong with me that will not be cured upon my twenty-first birthday," Janey said tightly, causing Jonathan to reflect with a smile that, while the Filmores might have the means to win the present battle, Miss Hilton was going to win the war, and meant them to know it.

"Which is some five months away, dearest coz," Piers smiled at her. "And, since this is England, not the colonies, you had best mind your manners until then, had you not?"

"And so had you, Filmore," Jonathan Lindsay said very softly, and very succinctly, his blue eyes as cold as the crystal glass of chilled champagne he held in his hand, "unless you would like to discuss the matter in a different manner."

Piers's wine-flushed cheeks went suddenly pale and Annabel gave a slight gasp.

"Jono—it's against the law," Lord Derwent groaned and then went very quiet as Jonathan's gaze flicked momentarily to him.

"Quite right, my lord," Piers blustered. "Much as I should like to take up your offer, Lindsay, duelling is frowned upon these days, especially by Members of Parliament."

"Who said anything about duelling?" Jonathan said with a tigerish smile. "I was thinking about a little boxing or horsewhipping, if you persist in treating Miss Hilton so ill-manneredly."

"I hardly see that how she is treated is your concern—" Piers began.

"Really, Lindsay," Mr Filmore broke in with forced cheerfulness, "we are all friends here, are we not? You must not think my son was in earnest— Miss Hilton and my son are the best of friends and she is quite used to his teasing, aren't you, my dear?"

His dear! Janey almost gaped, so unaccustomed was she to hearing an endearment from the lips of Mr Filmore. As for being the best of friends with Piers— words momentarily failed her.

"Perhaps she is," Jonathan answered before she could. "But I am not," he added in the same soft tones. "A fact that your son would be wise to remember."

There was an uncomfortable silence, filled only by the crackle of the fire, the scrape of silver against

porcelain and the clink of crystal glasses. A silence
in which Janey had to bite her lip to stop herself from
smiling like an idiot as she saw the utter astonishment
on the faces of the Filmores. They simply could not
understand why Jonathan should choose to defend
her.

Even the easy-going, kindly Lord Derwent looked
startled and, she thought with a faint sinking feeling,
more than a little disapproving. No doubt he thought
his friend had gone a little soft in the head himself to
defend a woman towards whom he had no obligation.

Lord Derwent cleared his throat and made a heroic
effort to put the conversation on safer ground. "Did
I hear you say that you are to bring in the new threshing machines this winter, Filmore?"

"Yes, within the fortnight. It'll save us a small fortune in wages," Mr Filmore said smugly. "I'll be
able to let ten men go at the end of the week."

Beside him, Jonathan heard Janey's sudden exhalation of breath, saw the outrage written upon her
face.

"Ten men!" Janey would have risen to her feet, if
it were not for Jonathan's arm suddenly gripping her
elbow, holding her down in her seat. "You have laid
off ten men at the beginning of winter! How could
you do such a thing?"

"Very easily," Mr Filmore said coldly. "You
should be thanking me for husbanding your funds so
carefully. Would you rather I paid men to be idle all
winter?"

"They need not be idle." She fought to sound cool,
controlled. "There are fields that need new drains,

hedges to be laid, copsing. The barn at Home Farm needs rethatching—''

"I do not need you to tell me how the estate is to be run," Mr Filmore said glacially.

"Please reconsider," she said pleadingly, struggling to control her temper. "Please—more than half the families in the village depend upon Pettridges for their livelihood and so many men are without work already."

"They are quite at liberty to look elsewhere for work," Dr Hutton said.

"Exactly," Mr Filmore agreed with a smile and lifted his glass.

"Where would you suggest they look?" Janey said desperately. "There is no work in the city mills or the factories these days because of the slump in trade and precious little in the country because of the enclosures and threshing machines."

"There is always work if a man is willing enough." Mr Filmore's lips pursed. "I am certain the men I lay off will find something to do."

"Undoubtedly," Jonathan agreed drily. "In Hampshire, I believe the labourers have taken up machine-breaking and rick-burning as a pastime."

"And they will be driven to the same here," Janey said fiercely, "if something is not done to help them."

"Then they will be punished," Mr Filmore said coldly. "Now, do be quiet, Jane, you are making yourself ridiculous as usual. Ladies understand nothing of these matters and nor should they wish to."

"I understand you will see women and children starve to death." Janey's hazel eyes blazed gold.

"Isn't it enough that you took away their common land, where they could at least keep a beast or two? Must you now take their livelihoods?"

"They can always apply for the poor relief," the Reverend said, dismissively setting down his wine glass and taking a large mouthful of salmon.

"The poor relief!" Janey looked at his rotund figure contemptuously. "I should like to see you live upon it for a week. A paltry pound or so of bread that does not even adequately feed one man for day, let alone a family for a week! I do not see how any man of intelligence can possibly regard it as an adequate substitute for a man's wages!"

"Oh, really, Jane, must you spout this Radical nonsense?" Annabel sighed. "You will spoil all our appetites."

"Quite," said Piers, who had already cleared his plate and was finishing his second glass of wine.

"You need not worry upon my account," Jonathan drawled, giving Janey a wicked sideways glance. "Miss Hilton could never spoil my appetite."

Janey found herself going pink, and looked down hastily at her plate.

"Nor mine," Lord Derwent put in gallantly.

"I never took you for a Radical," Jonathan said drily to his friend.

"I'm as much a one now as you are," Lord Derwent grinned back at him. "Who could fail to be converted when the cause has such a beautiful advocate?"

Far too many, thought Janey, as she saw the looks of disapproval exchanged by the Filmores with the Doctor and the Reverend.

"Oh, pray do not encourage her——" Annabel smiled lazily, winding one of her fat red curls about her finger as she glanced at Jonathan "——or she will be quoting Mr Lindsay's famous speech on behalf of the labouring poor next."

Beside her, Janey felt Jonathan go very still. She glanced at him, puzzled. "I doubt it." He smiled, but it did not reach his eyes as he met Annabel's challenging stare. "I hope Miss Hilton is far too sensible to take anything I say seriously. Isn't that so, Miss Hilton?"

"Yes." The monosyllable dragged out of her suddenly tight throat. It was a warning, as clear as a peal of bells rung from a church tower, that he was out of her reach and always would be. What there was between them was a flirtation, which would have no permanence, no importance—to him.

Suddenly miserable, she stared down at her Limoges plate, counting the petals upon the pale pink roses on the soft yellow ground as she half-listened to him conversing with Annabel, who was talking brightly and effortlessly about horses, hunting and the weather—all approved topics for a lady, according to the book of etiquette Mrs Filmore had given her upon her arrival in England.

"Don't." The sudden light touch of his fingers upon hers beneath the table made her head lift and her heart race.

"Don't what?"

"Worry so much," he smiled at her, his voice tender. "The men who are to be laid off will be well used to adversity; they will find a way through."

"I do not think anyone ever becomes used to

watching their children starve," she said, half-glad, half-guilty that he had mistaken the reason for her sudden depression. "I shall have to do something, I cannot simply let Mr Filmore turn those men off without trying to do something to prevent it."

"Whatever you choose to do," he said very quietly, as his hand closed over hers, "promise me that you will stay within the bounds of law this time? No more hare-brained conspiracies?"

"Very well." She sighed. "But my attempt to rescue Jem was not hare-brained—it was very carefully planned."

"So carefully planned that you would have been the one person easily identifiable," he said drily. "You must remember this is England, Miss Hilton, where the law will prevail, whether the cause is just or not."

"Sometimes," she said wistfully, "I wish my grandfather had never searched for me. Everything seemed much simpler in America."

"That's another wish you cannot expect me to share, since I should have been denied the pleasure of your acquaintance," he said gently.

"Is it really such a pleasure?" she asked a little distractedly, as he began to stroke her gloved hand with his fingers, tracing fine bones that seemed to become liquid at his touch. "By taking my side, you will not endear yourself to your new neighbours."

"You are the only neighbour whose opinion I care for and, I assure you, our acquaintance brings me nothing but pleasure," he whispered as he slipped his thumb into the small aperture beneath the lowest button which ran down the inner seam of her gloves from elbow to wrist and began to circle her palm.

"And not just that kind, either," he added with the flicker of a smile as he saw the sudden parting of her lips and the downward flutter of her eyelids at the shocking, startlingly intimate contact of their flesh. And then he laughed. "Do you know, Miss Hilton, I think that is the first time I have made you blush?"

"I suspect it will not be the last," she said a little shakily, wondering how so innocuous a caress could be so tantalising, so unendurable, that she drew her hand away abruptly.

"Oh, I think I can promise you that." His voice was husky as she raised her eyelids and met his gaze again.

"I am not so easily embarrassed," she retorted, more than a little cross with herself for being so transparently shocked by his remark.

"Embarrassment was not quite what I had in mind," he said, his eyes glinting with amusement.

"Why else should anyone blush?" she asked with such directness and clarity that several heads turned towards them.

He stared at her for a moment, wondering if she were being deliberately obtuse in order to embarrass him and get her own back, but there was nothing in her gaze but innocent and genuine enquiry.

He cleared his throat, aware of Perry's raised brows on the other side of the table, and Mrs Norris on his other side, straining to hear with her mouth open and eyes almost out of their sockets. "I really cannot imagine," he lied, giving Perry a murderous glare as

Lord Derwent clapped his napkin to his mouth in an apparent fit of coughing.

"And I was beginning to think you knew everything, Mr Lindsay." Janey smiled at him. She still did not know what he had meant, but she knew he had lied and could not resist teasing him.

"Not quite, and nor do you, Miss Hilton, I think," he replied slowly as he searched her mischievous, shining face with his gaze. For all her worldliness and unshockability, she was such an innocent in some ways. So passionate in her belief in fairness, truth and justice—and probably love, he thought with a sudden pang of conscience.

Perry was right—if he had an ounce of decency left, he ought to call the wager off and go back to town at the first opportunity before he hurt her, before things went beyond the point of no return. But then she smiled at him, her heart in her eyes and he knew it was already too late. What the devil, he thought with savage humour, as he reached out for his wine glass and drained it. He might as well be hung for a sheep as for a lamb.

"I trust you will not keep us too long, gentlemen," Mrs Filmore said after the dessert had been cleared. "Shall we withdraw, ladies? If you are too tired, Jane, you need not feel you must join us. You do become overtired so easily since your accident."

Overtired of you, Janey felt like retorting. For a moment she was almost tempted to accept the offer of escape. The dinner had been a torturous mixture of delight in Jonathan's company and frustration that they were not alone. Her whole body felt aching and heavy and as tight as an overwound clock spring. But if she retired early, she would not see him again this evening.

"Stay," he murmured softly as he pulled out her chair, making up her mind for her instantly. "I shall do my best to see the gentlemen do not stay at the port over-long."

"I am not in the least tired," she said brightly as Mrs Filmore frowned at Jonathan, "and I should not miss Annabel's new song for anything. She has practised it so very many times and at such very great length I swear I know every note by heart—and every wrong one, too," she finished with a fluttery little laugh that was so exact a mimicry of Miss Filmore's that Jonathan had to bite his lip in order not to laugh. Vulnerable! Innocent! he told himself wryly, she was about as vulnerable and innocent as Wellington behind his lines at Torres Vedras.

"And what will your contribution to the evening's entertainment be?" Piers sneered at Janey from across the table. "Nothing, I suppose, since you can neither sing properly nor play."

"Oh, I thought I should recount a few of the tricks you have played upon me of late, since you find them *so* amusing," Janey retorted.

"I don't know what you are talking about," Piers said and yawned.

"Then perhaps this will jog your memory?" She stooped suddenly to pick up the girth in both hands, and, stretching it out, she dropped it into the middle of the table.

The leather strap looked utterly incongruous lying amid the silver, crystal and porcelain. There was a faint gasp of surprise from the diners as they all looked from the girth to Janey, with expressions that ranged from horror to curiosity.

"What the deuce! You've spilt my wine and ruined my waistcoat!" Piers was the first to break the astonished silence.

"How very careless of me," Janey said, with a complete absence of regret. "You see——" she swept the table with a glance "——Piers thought it a great jest to score the leather so the buckles would break and I should fall from my horse. Is that not terribly amusing? He could have killed me, of course, but no doubt that would merely have added to his mirth."

"*What?*" Mr Filmore, having recovered from his initial shock, gave a roar of outrage at the same moment as Mrs Filmore gave a gasp of horror and sank back into her chair, demanding to know how Miss Hilton could possibly make such an accusation against her son, who worshipped the ground she stepped upon. Mrs Norris and Mrs Hutton scurried to her aid, muttering loudly about ingrates and ill-bred young women.

Jonathan's mouth curved momentarily as he took in the scene and saw the alarm upon Perry's face. Perry still had something to learn about Miss Hilton's remarkable directness and her disregard for convention. But then, as Mr Filmore continued to roar at Janey, he frowned.

"Take it back! Take it back at once!" Mr Filmore shouted, his moustache quivering so that it looked as if it were about to take flight from his face. "I have never heard such a nonsensical, insane suggestion in my life."

"Nonsensical?" Janey pointed to the girth. "Have

you ever seen buckles pull through new leather in such a way? It was cut—scored nearly through with a knife. Look, if you do not believe me.''

Mr Filmore glanced at the girth and then leant forward to snatch it up. "Ridiculous! It is bad leather and poor workmanship, that is all," he spluttered, coiling up the strap rapidly in his hands as he saw Jonathan staring at it closely. "Thomas—" he turned to the footman, who was trying hard to look busy clearing the sideboard "—take this away—see that it is destroyed at once so no one else is tempted to try and mend it—I shall have words with the saddler, of course.

"And you, Jane…" He shook his head in sudden, apparent grief after Thomas had taken the girth out of his hands. "Your fancies are becoming ever wilder. What reason would Piers have to harm you? He holds you in the highest regard."

"And pigs fly," Janey drawled in a biting tone that caused Mrs Norris to gasp and Jonathan and Lord Derwent to exchange an amused glance.

"Really!" Mr Filmore shook his head once more. "You see now for yourself, Dr Hutton, what I was speaking of."

"Indeed," Dr Hutton intoned gravely as he looked assessingly a Janey, who glared back at him. "A grave case, I fear…"

"A grave case of what?" Janey demanded, her American drawl pronounced as it always was when she was angry. "Honesty? Piers detests me and has done since I set foot in this house, and anyone who disputes that is suffering from terminal hypocrisy!"

"Now, now, my dear—" the Reverend Norris decided to intercede "—why don't you let my wife take you to your room? You are obviously overwrought."

"I am not going anywhere until Piers apologises," Janey said, fixing the Reverend with a glance that made the hand he had lifted to put upon her arm drop back to his side. "And I am not in the least over-wrought, I am merely angry and with good reason, as Mr Lindsay can vouch, since I fell off at his feet."

"Exactly so," Jonathan said coolly. "Miss Hilton has every reason to expect an apology for such a jest, if such an act can be considered a jest?"

There was sudden silence, then Dr Hutton laughed somewhat nervously. "As Mr Filmore says, it was just bad leather, Lindsay. No sane person would do such a thing as a jest."

"No sane person would even suggest such a thing!" Annabel said shrewishly, directing a stare at Janey.

"Are you suggesting I am losing my wits, Annabel?" Janey snapped in return, her hazel eyes glittering in her taut face.

"Hrrmph!" Mr Filmore cleared his throat and glanced at the doctor. "Better to humour her, perhaps?" he muttered.

"Yes, yes," Dr Hutton agreed with alacrity, giving Piers a very obvious wink. "Always better to humour the ladies, eh, Filmore?"

"But I didn't touch the blasted thing," Piers began sulkily, glaring at Janey. "If anyone's trying to murder you, it isn't me, though you make it tempting enough."

"Murder is hardly the right word, Piers." Mr Filmore gave a rather forced laugh as he saw Jonathan

Lindsay and Lord Derwent exchange a look. "My apologies to you all for this little domestic disagreement. This is all something of a storm in a teacup, gentlemen—but we must allow for these weaknesses in the fairer sex, especially in Miss Hilton's case."

"Oh, apologise to her, Piers, and then we might all get to enjoy our evening!" Annabel interposed with sudden vehemence.

"Very well," Piers said sullenly, giving his sister a glare before glancing up at Janey. "I apologise, dear coz, for whatever wrong, real or imagined, that I have done you. Will that do?"

"I suppose it will have to, since it is the closest you are likely to come to admitting the truth, dear coz," Janey said bitingly. Then, with an imperious nod to Mrs Norris, Mrs Hutton and Mrs Filmore, she said sweetly, "Shall we withdraw, ladies? I should not like to keep the gentlemen longer from their port."

"The ill-mannered, impertinent hussy!" she heard Mrs Filmore exclaim as she swept towards the door to the chorus of agreement from Mrs Norris and the others. "Behaving as if she were already mistress here!"

And carried it off like a duchess, Jonathan thought with a grin as he hastened to open the door for her.

"Well," he said as she glanced up into his face with more than a little uncertainty as she paused at the door, wondering if he might be thinking what the others were saying. "That was not quite the entertainment I had in mind, but it was very diverting, none the less."

"I am glad you found it amusing," she said with

more than a little defiance, "but do not expect me to
apologise for my behaviour. Piers is—"

"The most unpleasant young man I have ever had
the misfortune to meet," he interrupted her softly,
then, moving to screen her from the others with his
back, he touched a finger to her lips. A fleeting, devastating, tender gesture that rooted her to the spot. "I
am on your side, Miss Hilton—I'd scarcely dare to
be otherwise. And I shall come to your support in the
drawing-room as soon as I am able. I fear you are
going to be the subject of a concerted attack," he
added as Mrs Filmore began to advance, supported
by Mrs Norris, with Mrs Hutton and Annabel fluttering in their wake.

"I have survived worse." She smiled at him over
her shoulder, as she walked on through the door.
"Apaches and bears frighten me, Mr Lindsay, but not
Mrs Filmore and her cronies. What can they do? Lock
me up in my room like some errant child?"

They could do exactly that—or worse, he felt like
calling after her, as the nagging unease, which had
been growing since Janey had dropped the girth upon
the table, suddenly crystallised into a definite suspicion. He dragged his eyes from Janey's retreating
back and turned back to the others. No, he told himself, as he looked from the moustached Mr Filmore
to his overplump, silly wife, and then to Annabel and
Piers. He was becoming as wild in his imaginings as
that rustic.

The Filmores were just ill-mannered, narrow-
minded bigots who thought that anyone who did not
think or behave as they did was somehow weak in
the head. To think they might be deliberately trying

to make Janey look unbalanced and unfit to manage her affairs was to credit them with too much intelligence. And as for attempted murder—that was even more inconceivable. And what reason would they have? The Filmores had money enough, if rumour was to be believed. They did not need the Pettridges Estate badly enough to risk hanging for it.

But, none the less, he was not entirely reassured as he glanced after Janey and caught the flash of her red skirts as she disappeared into the drawing-room. He found himself wishing she were a little less fearless, a little more cautious in demonstrating her contempt for the Filmores—at least until she reached her majority. A great deal could happen in five months.

Chapter Eight

"Mr Filmore is engaged upon business and the rest of the family are not at home, sir," Dawson informed Jonathan the following afternoon.

That was something Jonathan already knew, having seen the Filmore siblings and their mama in their carriage heading down Southbrook's long drive towards the house from his bedroom window. Instructing Perry to detain them for as long as possible, he slipped out of the back door as they had rung at the front, taken his horse and headed for Pettridges Hall at all speed.

"And Miss Hilton?" he asked. "Is she at home?"

"I will enquire, sir." Dawson headed ponderously for the library, while Jonathan impatiently paced the hall; scanning the portraits upon the walls, he was not surprised to find that the brass plates on the frames identified them as Filmores. A gloomy-looking lot, he decided, all hanging judges and horse-faced women.

Where was that damned butler? He sighed fiercely, the minutes seeming like hours. He had to see her—he'd scarcely had the chance for so much as a word with her in the drawing-room last night, what with Miss Filmore's caterwauling of Italian songs, and Hutton's determination to recount every run the local hunt had had in the last twenty years. No, not see her, he amended, with wry self-honesty, he wanted to be alone with her, be able to touch her—as he had ached to do the previous night.

"Sir?" Dawson had returned and informed him that Miss Hilton was in the library, and he was to go in.

Old Fenton had obviously had a taste for books or display, Jonathan thought as the library doors were shut behind him. The room was lined from floor to ceiling with row upon row of leather-bound volumes. For a moment he could not see Janey, and then her bright "Good morning" caused him to look up to the very top of a rather unstable-looking library ladder, where she was bracing herself by her knees against the top rung as she flipped through a thick volume.

"Good morning." His gaze skated over her as he spoke, taking in everything about her, from the neat knot of coiled hair upon the crown of her head, to the kid slippers, peeping out from beneath the hem of her moss-green pelisse gown. The gown could scarcely have been a more modest contrast to one she had worn the previous night. The sleeves billowed from the shoulder, then tightened to fit closely at the wrist; the tightly fitting bodice buttoned from her narrow waist almost to the little winged collar that framed her long slender neck.

But it made no difference. The unsatisfied aching desire to hold her, which had kept him awake half the night, returned in an instant. He wanted to drag her off the ladder, put his lips to the little white V at the base of her throat, undo those buttons, one by one…

"I'll come down," she said, reaching up to replace the volume she was holding upon the top shelf.

A faint, barely audible groan came involuntarily from his throat as his eyes followed the lift and fall of her breasts beneath the constricting bodice.

Hearing him, she glanced down. The colour left her face. She had been aware of him watching her the previous evening, but then his hunger had been contained by the necessities of convention. This was different—they were alone, there was nothing to stop them—

"Oh!" she gasped as she trod upon the hem of her gown and her foot slipped.

"Miss Hilton!"

Grabbing at a shelf, she regained her balance as he lunged for the base of the swaying ladder and steadied it, amid a shower of pages from an old volume she had dislodged in the wild lunge to save herself.

He exhaled slowly with relief, leaning momentarily against the ladder, his forehead pressed against a rung, before he lifted his head to look at her again.

"Come down," he said almost wearily. "Please."

She descended slowly, carefully, holding up her skirts with one hand, the side of the ladder with the other. She was shaking inside, not because of her near fall, but because of the way she could feel his eyes on her, following every dip and sway of her hips, every movement.

She stepped on to the floor and turned to face him and found herself in the circle of his arms as he held either side of the ladder, and so close that the tips of her breasts grazed against his coat and became instantly hard. She drew in a rapid, audible breath and shrank back slightly against the ladder, something like the beginnings of panic fluttering in her stomach. It was one thing to tease, to dally with the idea of being his mistress, another to see the desire that flared like a flame in his dark eyes and know that they were alone and unlikely to be disturbed.

"You are very pale," he said, after a moment in which his gaze burned across her face. "Have you hurt yourself?"

"No. I—I did not sleep well last night," she said tightly. She had not slept for longing for him. Those secret dissatisfying caresses during last night's dinner had left her tossing and turning until dawn, longing to be in his arms again, longing to be alone with him. But now that she was—she was suddenly, inexplicably afraid of the intensity written in his face.

"Neither did I." There was a husky note in his voice that made her insides contract. "I could not sleep for thinking of you in that red silk gown—and out of it," he added, his mouth curving as he heard her faint, but sudden intake of breath.

She swallowed, her mouth and throat suddenly dry at the image his words conjured up in her mind, and wished that he would take her in his arms. When he held her, she forgot that she barely knew him, forgot that he did not love her, forgot that she could never hope to be more than his mistress.

"I was wondering if you might be able to think of any remedy for my insomnia?" he went on softly.

"Mrs Hutton swears by camomile tea—" she

blurted at, her nerve breaking suddenly. "You must be thirsty after your ride, I'll ring for some refreshment." She was babbling but could not help herself. "Some madeira—would you like—?"

"I do not want any madeira," he cut her off in mid-sentence, trapping her with his weight against the ladder. "Or camomile tea," he added thickly.

She lifted her gaze from the snowy folds of his cravat and looked up into his taut face, her heartbeat slowing to what seemed to her a deafening thump as his night-dark gaze held hers for a moment, before dropping to her slightly parted lips. She stared up at him, her back pressed to the ladder, her whole body unbearably tight with anticipation, with memory of his kisses, his touch.

"Well?" His voice was low, velvety, sending a shiver along her spine.

"Some brandy, perhaps?" she offered as a last-ditch defence with a wobbly smile. If he did not take her in his arms soon, if he did not touch her soon, she would scream—

"No," he said almost tenderly, his lips curving a fraction. "Just you."

She made a small ragged sound of relief as he caught her to him, and kissed her. Kissed her almost roughly, crushing her lips beneath his, thrusting into her mouth, demanding instant and absolute possession with a fierceness that was echoed by his hands as they swept over her, moulding her back, the narrowness of her waist, the curve of her hips, the fullness of her tight, swollen breasts...

She gasped, her head tilting back, as his fingers found their aching peaks, drawing her into a spiral of piercingly sweet and unsatisfying pleasure, a pleasure intensified to an unbearable anticipation as his lips moved from her mouth, along her jaw, down the length of her throat in hungry, rushed kisses that heated her skin and melted her inside. She reached for him clumsily, her hand sliding across his chest and shoulders, seeking a way to touch him, to give him the pleasure he was giving her, but finding nothing but frustrating layers of wool and brocade.

"You are wearing too much…" he groaned, echoing her own thought as he began to pull at the buttons of her bodice. "I want to touch you properly."

Her eyelids lifted and, with a mixture of shock and anticipation so sharp as to be almost painful, she watched his fingers move down, parting the buttons, so impatient, so male and hard against the satiny softness of the upper curve of her breasts, so brown and weathered against the translucent lawn of her chemise.

This was utter madness. And she did not care. She did not care about anything while he was touching her. Her heart began to race crazily as the last button parted at her waist and his fingers lifted to the neck of her chemise, tugged at the ribbon that fastened the gathered neck, then with almost rough haste at the soft folds.

"You are irresistible…" he growled as he slid a hand beneath the green wool on either side of her waist.

"Am I?" The words were half a gasp as the heat of his hands seemed to burn into her flesh and she shut her eyes.

"Yes." The word was hardly more than a low

noise in his throat as he bent his head and kissed her.
Kissed her throat, kissed the frantic beating pulse at
its base, kissed the tight, tight swell of her breasts.

Her breath came in a startled groan as his mouth
closed suddenly over an aching, coral peak. The rush
of heat, of pleasure was so overwhelming, so unex-
pectedly intense that she clutched at his shoulders, her
fingers curling into him as the floor seemed to sink
beneath her feet. She had thought she understood desire, understood what it was to be touched by him,
kissed by him, but this—this was almost frightening.
She did not know if she wanted him to stop or...

The thought was lost as he sucked her into a whirl-
pool of fiery, all-consuming and unfamiliar need that
had her reaching for his head, stabbing her fingers
into his hair, dragging his mouth up to hers as she
pressed against him, wanting to be closer, closer—

She made a sound of protest as he pulled back from
her suddenly with an oath.

"Janey—" his voice was low, urgent, demanding
her attention as she opened bemused hazel eyes
"—listen."

"Listen?" She looked at him blankly, her breath
still coming in shallow gasps, her pulse racing.
"What is it?"

"Your guardian—looking for you—" There was a
soft, almost despairing note in his voice as he looked
at her. There was no other exit from the room but the
one into the hall and, even if there had been time to
repair the damage to her dress, it would make no difference. One look at her shining eyes, her reddened
and swollen lips and her half-fallen-down hair tumbling about her glowing face, and any man with half

a brain would know exactly what they had been do-ing.

He swore beneath his breath. What had possessed him? He had come here to warn her to behave with discretion and had behaved like the most impetuous of fools. My God! This should amuse them at the club, Lindsay caught like the greenest of flats with an unmarried girl!

"My guardian?" she repeated slowly, still too drugged with desire to register anything except him.

"And, by the sound of it, Dr Hutton, in the hall..." He sighed as he reached out and pulled her sleeves back up onto her satiny shoulders and jerked the gap-ing edges of her bodice together with rough haste, trying and failing to find buttons and loops that matched.

"What?" She stared at him in horror as she real-ised the full extent of their predicament. "Filmore and Hutton?"

"I am afraid so," he said resignedly. "If you hap-pen to know of a secret door in the panelling, now would be a good time to tell me of it."

"No," she said as she fumbled frantically with her buttons, half of which were undone, half in the wrong loops, "but there is a perfectly good window. Come on!" She ran for one of the window-seats, knelt upon it and started to lift the heavy sash window. "Help me," she hissed at him as he stood staring at her.

"You can't get out of the window—it must be eight feet or more to the lawn," he said, shaking his head.

"I assure you I can," she said with some asperity.

"I've done far worse with an Indian upon my heels—now, come on!"

"Miss Hilton!" He dived for the window as she sat upon the sill and swung her legs out. "Wait! I am not entirely without honour, you don't have to—*Janey!*" He reached for her, but was a second too late to prevent her from launching herself off the sill.

He swore again as she landed in a somewhat untidy heap upon the lawn, and then vaulted out after her as the handle on the library door started to turn.

Janey was already sitting up when he landed beside her on his feet, as neatly as an Indian brave dropping from the branch of a tree. Jonathan Lindsay was a man of many talents, she thought wryly.

"Miss Hilton—are you all right?" His voice was thick with anxiety as he bent over her.

"Perfectly." She grinned at him as she scrambled to her feet and gathered up her skirts, displaying a most unladylike length of silk stocking-clad leg. "We'd better run before they come to close the window."

She set off without waiting to see if he was following, running as fast as her encumbering skirts would allow, down the length of the house, keeping close to the wall, and stooping now and again to avoid being seen through the lower set windows.

She wouldn't have looked out of place amongst the rifle boys in Spain, he thought with a half-smile, finding to his surprise that he had to exert himself a little to keep up with her.

"I think we are safe enough now," she said a few minutes later, as she halted and leant her back against the grey stone wall of the terrace, gasping in breaths of the raw November air.

"Thanks to you," he said as he slumped beside her. "You went down the side of the house like a professional skirmisher, Miss Hilton."

"And you came out of that window like one," she said with a slightly breathless laugh. "But then, you have had plenty of practice, no doubt, at escaping irate guardians and husbands."

"Now and then, in my ill-spent youth." A wry smile flickered across his mouth, then he sobered as he glanced sideways at her.

"And what about you, Miss Hilton, where did you acquire your skirmishing skills—escaping compromising situations with your lovers?"

"No, Indian raids," she said a little sharply.

"Indian raids!" He stared at her, his astonishment written upon his face. "You mean your settlement was attacked by natives?"

"All the frontier settlements were attacked from time to time." She shrugged. Sometimes, in this quiet part of civilised England, she found it difficult to believe as well. It had been a different world. "I shot my first Indian at thirteen…"

Her voice trailed off as the memory came back suddenly, sharp and horribly clear. Her father had been crouched against the wooden wall of the cabin, trying desperately to reload his musket; the Indian, a painted, snarling giant with an axe raised for the killing stroke, and then the blood blossoming across the Indian's chest as the recoil from her musket had sent her tumbling backwards.

"I had to do it," she said, more to herself than

him, "he would have killed my father." She turned her head slowly to look at him, wondering why she had blurted it out to him, when she had never spoken of such things to anyone else in England.

Her grandfather had made it very clear, on the long voyage home, that the less she said to anyone about her former life the better. He had told her that the people he expected her to mix with would simply not understand, and he had been right. It had caused consternation enough when she had inadvertently mentioned eating at the kitchen table.

"You had to fight—at thirteen—a girl?" His voice was shocked, but his eyes were dark, compassionate, as he held her gaze. "I saw women fight in Portugal—but I never imagined that you had had to do such things. Somehow, one always imagines America to be an extension of England…"

"You would lose that illusion the moment you stepped further west than Massachusetts," she said, her eyes dark as she remembered the endless trails she had travelled with her father and mother. Trails that had taken her through the forests of Kentucky, over stony mountains and desert and across the endless, buffalo-studded prairies. "No, it is not like England at all, Mr Lindsay. There are no fences, no walls, no boundaries—no one to tell you what you may or may not do—there are no limits except what a man imposes upon himself."

"You make it sound like some sort of egalitarian paradise," he said.

"Then I have not described it properly. The western frontier is more beautiful than you can possibly imagine, but it is also crueller—" She broke off again, remembering the extremes of heat and cold, the constant struggle to grow enough food for man and beast out of land that had never been cultivated.

"Your parents?" he asked tentatively as he saw the darkness in her eyes. "Was that an Indian raid?"

"No—" she shook her head "—they died of the smallpox, together with thirty-five out of our forty neighbours. It kills more settlers than the Indians ever have or will. I have never felt so helpless or so afraid in my life. Indians you could fight—but the smallpox, with no doctor in five hundred miles—" she shrugged "—it was hopeless."

"And then you went to live with Lilian?" he said, thinking that it was little wonder Mrs Filmore and her ilk held no terrors for her.

"Yes. With more than half the settlement dead, we decided it was best to go back to St Louis. Lilian had a little money put by and we set up the boarding house. We had no other means of making a living."

"That is where your grandfather found you? In Lilian's boarding house? It must have been very hard for you."

"In some ways, yes," she replied absently. "But Lilian protected me as if I were her own daughter. The trappers used to tease me about my book reading, my ladylike manners, and ask me if I were saving myself for some English lord—" She stopped, but a brief glance at his impassive face reassured her that he had not noticed her slip of the tongue. "But on the whole they were kind enough."

"And your plethora of lovers you told me about, were they kind enough?" he said mildly, watching her face.

"Lovers..." She looked away from him.

"Yes, lovers—tell me about them, Miss Hilton," he invited softly, and she knew that he had not missed that slip of the tongue after all.

"I—I can't—" she exhaled heavily "—there weren't any."

"I was beginning to wonder if you were going to wait until after I had seduced you to tell me that," he said with a half-smile. "You have not been playing entirely fair, Miss Hilton."

"If I was not playing fair, Mr Lindsay, I should not have jumped out of the library window so that you might be saved from having to make me an offer!" she retorted hotly.

"You did not have to do that," he replied gently. "I am not so devoid of honour as to have abandoned you to the gossips."

"I know," she said grittily. "Why do you think I jumped?"

His brows lifted. "Were you not in the least tempted to take advantage of the situation and net yourself an eminently eligible bachelor?"

"Oh, I was tempted—" she matched his mocking tone, but her eyes were dark, wistful, as she looked at him "—for a moment."

"A whole moment! Thank you for the compliment," he replied with a laugh and then sobered as his blue gaze met hers. "Did you think we should deal so ill together?"

"I could not see how we would do otherwise." She tried and failed to smile. "You have made it clear enough that your intentions towards me did not include marriage. I should not care to be a resented wife who had been forced upon you, Mr Lindsay.''

His eyelids dropped for a moment, and then lifted. ''No, you would not, would you?'' he said with a slow smile as he reached out to draw her to him. ''And yet you would be my mistress? Why is that?''

Because I could very easily love you, because I only feel alive when I am with you— The answer was in her eyes as she looked at him, but she forced a smile and shrugged her slender shoulders. ''The Filmores would probably say it is because I have lost my wits.''

''Then perhaps we are a pair,'' he murmured and kissed her briefly upon her parted lips. ''Do you know, I almost find myself regretting our escape from the matrimonial mousetrap?''

''Almost, is not entirely flattering,'' she said a little tersely.

''It is closer than I have come to considering marriage in a long time.'' He laughed softly as he brought her closer against him, and rested his chin against the top of her head.

''Then I suppose I should thank the Almighty for my lucky escape,'' she returned, her eyes sparking green fire as she tilted her head back to look up at him. He was playing with her, teasing when her heart was being twisted into a knot.

''Yes, you should.'' He was sober suddenly, the mockery fading from his eyes, leaving them dark, empty. ''I am not the man you think me, Janey. I have few principles and less conscience. You'd do better to find yourself another curate to fall in love with.''

"No." She shook her head. "I'd rather have a man with a few good principles than one with a great many bad ones and so much conscience he considered kissing me a sin to be atoned for."

"You are not making this easy, Janey. I am trying to do the honourable thing," he sighed.

"Why break the habit of a lifetime?" she said flippantly, though she felt like she was gambling for her life. "You seem to have survived well enough so far."

"True." He gave a gasp of laughter as she met his gaze with clear, challenging eyes. And then he hugged her to him, so close, so tight she thought her bones would crack. "But I am not sure I am going to survive a liaison with you, Miss Hilton, not at all sure…"

That made two of them, she thought, her heart racing beneath her ribs. But she did not care. So long as it was not over, she did not care. So long as she could be with him, she did not care about anything.

"But we are going to have to be a great deal more discreet." He sighed. "I am not sure you even ought to risk seeing me alone at all at present."

"Why?"

He hesitated for a moment. "Look, I know this sounds ridiculous—but I found myself wondering last night if Filmore might be trying to retain control of your fortune and estate after your majority."

"But how could he do that?" She stared at him.

"By having you declared unfit to manage your own affairs," he said slowly.

"You mean, by saying I am mad…?"

"The whole family seem to go out of their way to

try and give that impression. The business with the girth did not exactly help to counteract it.''

''No, I suppose not—'' she laughed ruefully ''—but I think you are reading much more into their maliciousness than there is. Piers always does something to make me look foolish every time we have a remotely eligible man to dine—the Filmores want us to marry, you see. And Mr Filmore seems to consider my fortune his son's birthright. I thought he would have apoplexy when my grandfather gave his blessing to my engagement to Edward. And now my year of mourning is over, he is trying to persuade me again.''

''So that's what they are about.'' He gave a stifled laugh. ''I should have guessed. I take it you are not co-operating in their scheme?''

She gave him a speaking look of disdain. ''I have made it perfectly clear to Piers that I should rather die than marry him—'' She broke off as he went very pale and still, his face frozen as he stared down at her.

''What is it? You look as if someone has just walked over your grave.''

''Nothing,'' he lied, her words conjuring up a vivid picture in his mind of her tumbling from the supposedly rotten staircase and of the severed girth. ''But...'' again he paused ''...I know this is none of my business, but what happens to your inheritance, if you were to die before you marry or reach your majority?''

''It all goes to a charitable trust for the good of the village—at least, that is what I asked my grandfather to specify in his will,'' she said after a moment of thought. ''So it would do Piers no good to murder me, Mr Lindsay,'' she added with a smile. ''Though I am sure there are moments when he would like to.''

''You are sure?'' He exhaled slowly with relief.

''Well, no,'' she confessed, ''I have never actually seen the entire will. But I assumed he did as I asked.''

''Find out,'' he said firmly, ''and do it discreetly—''

''Jane! Jane! Where are you, girl?'' Mr Filmore's shout from the other side of the house made them both start.

''Damnation!'' he swore softly as he caught her to him and pressed a swift kiss on her forehead before releasing her. ''The man is everywhere he is not wanted. You'd better go before he gets here. A few flowers in your hair and you'd pass for Ophelia in her mad scene—a fact that I am sure would not escape your guardian or be unwelcome to him.''

She laughed as she picked up her skirts. ''You make me feel like a heroine in one of Mrs Radcliffe's Gothics. You need not worry, I assure you I can defend myself from Piers Filmore and his father.''

''Yes, I suppose you can,'' he laughed, but his eyes were serious as they sought hers. ''But this is not the American frontier—battles are not won and lost with a musket here. You will bear in mind what I have said? At least until you are sure of the contents of the will?''

''I'll try,'' she replied blithely over her shoulder as she turned towards the terrace steps. The knowledge that he cared for her enough to be concerned had sent her heart soaring.

He watched her run up the terrace steps, a frown

upon his forehead. She was so damned fearless and, for all her experience of life at its rawest, so innocent.

"Lindsay!"

He turned slowly to see Mr Filmore and a tall, slightly seedy-looking man in a black coat, which was shiny at collar and cuff, approaching rapidly.

"Filmore." He returned the greeting easily and nodded to the stranger, waiting for the introduction that Mr Filmore neglected to make.

"What brings you here?" Mr Filmore demanded.

"A neighbourly call, that is all," Jonathan said coolly. "I gather I have had the misfortune to miss your wife and daughter, but your butler said I might find Miss Hilton in the garden."

"You have not seen her, then?" Mr Filmore said sullenly.

"No, have you lost her?" Jonathan enquired innocently.

"Yes, and that is not unusual," Mr Filmore huffed and turned to his companion. "As I told you, sir— her behaviour becomes wilder by the day. Between you and me, sir, I fear a complete breakdown of her sanity is imminent. Mr Lindsay will vouch for how she assaulted my son—and he was witness to her hysterical accusations last night—"

"Oh, I should call Miss Hilton's behaviour last night entirely reasonable in the circumstances and, as for her assault upon your son, I should swear upon oath it was nothing but self-defence," Jonathan drawled as he held the other man's gaze. "But if you are really concerned, you must let me recommend a friend of mine. He attended the King's late father in his youth and has made a study of such maladies ever since. I doubt there is a physician in the country more expert in such matters. He'll be down for the ball, I'll send him over—"

"Oh, I am sure there is no need to inconvenience you, sir," Mr Filmore said hastily.

"It will be no inconvenience—in fact, I shall insist." Jonathan smiled, but it did not reach his eyes. "I am sure you would not want people saying your ward received anything less than the best of care, Filmore. You know what ugly rumours can arise out of such things."

"Quite!" Mr Filmore said tersely. "But I fear Miss Hilton's beauty has caused you to look upon her behaviour with a far-too-indulgent eye. Now, if you will excuse me, sir, I have some business to attend to."

"Of course." Jonathan bowed. "My apologies to your wife and daughter—I am sorry I have missed them."

Janey flung open the ballroom doors that led off the terrace, shut them behind her, and then leant against them for a moment to catch her breath, her spirits higher than they had been since she had last galloped across the endless flower-bedecked prairie in the spring. He cared for her, she was suddenly sure of it. Her skirt in her hands, she waltzed her way across the polished floor, dancing with him in her imagination, reliving every touch, every kiss, every look from his blue, blue eyes, until she was dizzy and laughing, her hair flowing loose down her back.

"Jane! Whatever are you doing?" Mr Filmore's roar from the terrace door broke her daydream into pieces. "You look like—a—a wanton!"

Her heart plummeting, she skidded to a halt, and looked up to see Mr Filmore, Dr Hutton and a man she had never met before at the terrace door, staring at her in stony disapproval.

She drew herself up to her full height and pulled together the upper edges of her bodice as she saw the stranger's cold beady gaze drop and linger there.

"I am practising," she said coolly, "practising for the ball. It is so long since I have danced, I thought it would be wise."

"Practising! Half-naked!" Mr Filmore spluttered. "You are a—"

"Now, now, Mr Filmore, we must remember, Miss Hilton suffered a dreadful loss in that terrible tragedy. It is enough to disturb anyone's power of reason," Dr Hutton put in hastily.

Janie exhaled heavily. "Dr Hutton, I broke my leg last year, not my brain, and I should have thought even a physician of your calibre could tell the difference. My powers of reasoning are quite intact. My gown is unbuttoned because I became hot while dancing," she continued coolly, as Dr Hutton's mouth opened and no sound came out. "And now, if you will excuse me, I shall go and find some refreshment. Dancing is such thirsty work, is it not?"

Head high, she dropped them the most mocking curtsy she could manage and headed for the door.

"Come here! Come back here! Dr Pearson has come especially to see you," Mr Filmore shrilled after her.

"He need not have gone to the trouble, I am quite well," she said blithely over her shoulder, before shutting the door behind her with a satisfyingly final click.

"You see—what more evidence do you need, gentlemen?" Mr Filmore demanded triumphantly.

But Dr Hutton and Dr Pearson exchanged a doubtful look.

"I am not sure—not sure at all," Dr Pearson said. "Not now this Lindsay fellow is going to involve the King's physician—I have my reputation and my practice to think of."

"Your reputation, sir, is that you will do whatever is required for a sufficient fee," Mr Filmore snapped ill-temperedly. "But perhaps you are right—perhaps we had better wait a little until Lindsay has lost interest. By all I hear of him, it should not be long before he eschews the country life for Town."

"You are sure he will lose interest?" Dr Hutton said tentatively. "He seemed to be very taken with her last night. I do not think he would be a good man to make an enemy of, Filmore."

"Of course he will lose interest!" Mr Filmore snorted. "Lindsay and a millhand's daughter! I think we are safe enough there, Hutton, don't you?"

"I suppose so," Dr Hutton agreed without great enthusiasm.

Chapter Nine

"Well, you were right, Jono," Perry said as he strode into the drawing-room at Southbrook. "I took a quart or two at the local hostelry. That seedy-looking fellow you saw at Pettridges is a doctor—of a kind. He's from Town, apparently—and, the landlord's daughter tells me, Filmore is paying his bills."

"Ah, I was afraid of that," Jonathan sighed.

"You really think Filmore is trying to get her inheritance," Perry said, frowning.

"Yes, I do think so. I think he came up with this scheme for retaining control of her estate when it became clear that she would never consider marriage to the inimitable Piers."

"Hadn't we better do something about it?" Perry said.

"I think I may have done enough to stop him already. I made it clear enough to him that I suspected what he was about. If I know Filmore, he will not risk a scandal."

"Mmm," Perry said doubtfully as he dropped into a chair beside the fire, causing the spaniel that had been occupying it to give a muffled yelp and scrabble clear. "But if he's prepared to go that far to get her money—supposing he goes further, Jono?"

"Murder?" Jonathan grimaced. "It has crossed my mind, Perry, especially when I saw that damned girth and remembered what that rustic said. But I think Filmore was as surprised by the business of the girth as we were. And I cannot see Filmore risking his neck for her fortune, not when the family has money of its own."

"Perhaps he doesn't anymore," Perry said thoughtfully. "By all accounts, Master Filmore was playing very high last year at the tables—and losing a great deal more often than he won."

"Yes—you could be right. I think I shall look a little closer into Mr Filmore's affairs." Jonathan frowned as he stared into the fire. "And I think we will take a look at that staircase in the Tower. I'll ask Avery to come with us—he could probably tell if it had been tampered with."

"And Miss Hilton? Are you going to warn her?"

"I have hinted to her that Filmore might be trying to get her declared unfit to manage her affairs and she should be careful in her behaviour—but as for the possibility of murder? If I tell her that, she will probably confront Mr Filmore the next time she sees him. At best, such accusations would only increase his case about her mental state, and, at worst—"

"It might provoke him into acting," Perry finished heavily.

"Do I think Lindsay will make Annabel an offer?" Piers gave a derisive snort as he replied to his mother's hopeful question at the breakfast table the next day. "About as likely as snow in June, I'd say. He might be an arrogant swine, but he's not half-witted."

"Thank you kindly, brother dearest." Annabel gave him a withering glare.

"Don't fret, my dear..." Mrs Filmore beamed at her daughter "...I think Piers is quite wrong. What other reason would he have to call so soon after coming to dine?"

"Oh, for heaven's sake, Mother!" Piers groaned. "Can you not see? It is as plain as the nose upon your face—it is not Annabel he has taken an interest in—it's your delightful ward. Isn't it, my lovely coz? He never takes his eyes off her the whole time he is here."

Janey sighed and put down her fork. "If you say so, Piers, who am I to argue?"

"Who, indeed?" Mrs Filmore snapped. "As if Mr Lindsay would consider a match with Jane! Really, Piers, I think you have must have taken too much brandy last night."

"That would be nothing new," Annabel muttered.

"I did not say he meant to *marry* her." Piers directed a glance at Janey. "He probably knows he does not need to...since half her girlhood was spent in a brothel."

"Piers—" Annabel gave a stifled little splutter upon a mouthful of bacon "—you should not say such things."

"Why not?" He laughed and raised his wine glass to his lips. "It's true, ain't it, my beautiful cousin?"

Janey went white and put down her coffee cup with

a shaking hand as she fought back the impulse to hurl the hot liquid into Piers's mocking, sneering face. Piers had an unerring instinct for hitting upon her weakest point. But after Jonathan's warning about Mr Filmore's attempts to make her look unbalanced, she was not going to give him the satisfaction of seeing that he had done so, not if it killed her. She exhaled slowly, before looking up, and gave him her sweetest smile.

"No, it was a boarding house. But I should not expect you to appreciate the difference, Piers—that would require a mind capable of thought. And in the six months I *was* there, I was treated with greater respect and kindness than I have ever known in this house since my grandfather died. Now, if you will excuse me, I have an appointment to keep in Salisbury. I shall take the gig and Kate will come with me."

"Have you Papa's permission?" Annabel asked, her small pointed tongue flicking out of her mouth like a snake as she licked a crumb from her lip. "He said last night that none us must venture abroad until the unrest in the countryside has been quelled."

"Oh, I doubt he will mind my going." Janey smiled. "Do you think so?" Jonathan Lindsay had issued her the same warning, out of what she was sure was genuine concern for her safety, insisting she must not even think of walking to the waterfall on her own. A request she had agreed to reluctantly because it was their only opportunity to meet alone.

Annabel looked almost embarrassed for a moment and did not answer the question.

"And you'll miss Mr Lindsay, if he calls at his usual hour," Piers drawled.

"Good, then I shall have him all to myself," Annabel said archly. "Aren't you afraid I shall steal your admirer, Jane?"

Janey's gaze travelled slowly, from Annabel's over-curled and over-beribboned head to her pink silk gown, which was also decorated with ribbons, beads, lace and fringing. She shook her head and smiled, a slow, confident smile. "No," she said with a quiet certainty, "I am not at all afraid, Annabel, but by all means consider yourself at liberty to try, should Mr Lindsay call."

Mrs Filmore's gasps of incoherent outrage followed her out of the dining-room as she made her exit. Once outside the door, she laughed aloud. If war was what the Filmores wanted, war was what they were going to get!

"I don't like this," Kate said as Janey drove the gig smartly through the small town of Hindon. "It's too quiet. Where is everyone? There's no one in the fields, no children playing. And look at The Lamb—" she pointed to the coaching inn "—they've still got all the shutters on the windows. I think we ought to go back."

"I have to see my solicitors," Janey sighed. "It's the only way I might be able to stop the Pettridges men from being caught up in the disturbances. But if you don't want to come, Kate, you don't have to— your mother lives near here, doesn't she? Why don't you wait there for me?"

"You can't go to Salisbury on your own, miss, it's a good ten miles from here. And it's hardly light yet."

"Yes, I can," Janey said firmly. "Now let's go and ask your mother what is going on."

"Miss! Miss!" Kate came running out of her mother's small redbrick cottage some five minutes later, her round face white against her red hair, her blue eyes brimming. "They've gone to break the machines at Pyt House Farm, four hundred men, and they've got hammers, and pitchforks and iron bars, and my father's gone with them. But that's not the worst of it. My brother, Harry, he's run after him. He's only ten, miss—he'll get himself killed, I know he will. Mother says the squire has already sent to Hindon for the Yeomanry cavalry."

"Four hundred," Janey repeated. That had to be an exaggeration. But if it was anything like that number, she knew the authorities would react with a heavy hand, for fear of real insurrection.

"Yes, miss," Kate said tearfully. "And Harry's with them."

"How long ago did he leave?"

"A half-hour or so." Kate hiccuped.

"Then get in," said Janey, making an instant decision. "It's three miles to Pyt House. If we are quick, we might catch them before they get there, though how we're going to find Harry amongst four hundred, I don't know."

"He'll show up, miss—" Kate managed a watery smile "—his hair's the same colour as mine."

"Well, that's something." Janey tried to smile

back at her as she backed up the gig and flicked the whip over the pony's head. "We'll find him, Kate."

Jonathan reined in his horse in front of Pettridges Hall just as the sun broke through the early morning mist. He scanned the windows, hoping that he might see Janey and be able to signal to her to meet him at the stables without encountering the Filmores. A hope that was dashed as he saw a twitch of the yellow morning-room curtains, and the flash of Annabel Filmore's carrot-coloured curls.

He swore and sighed as a moment later the door opened. Fixing a polite smile upon his face, he dismounted. So much for getting to see Janey alone; now he would have to endure an hour of taking tea and Mrs Filmore's conversation. He sighed again. At least he would be able to see Janey, even if they could not really talk—or touch. Then he brightened. He could still suggest a ride, if the weather stayed fine. It shouldn't be too difficult for Janey and himself to lose Annabel and Piers Filmore.

Annabel came tripping down the steps to meet him in a frothing gown of pale lemon, bedecked with cerise ribbons, which also adorned her head. The overall effect was rather as if she had been dropped in a giant trifle, he thought uncharitably. But then, all women had looked grossly overdressed to him since he had met Janey. He reluctantly dragged his thoughts away from the direction of Janey in her clothes and out of them, and made his bow to Annabel.

"Why, Mr Lindsay, we did not expect to see you so early," Annabel trilled at him. "And it is such a cold morning. You must come in and take some refreshment. Dawson—'' she turned to the butler who was hovering at the open door ''—see that Mr Lindsay's horse is taken care of.''

Jonathan followed her into the morning room, making occasional answers to her observations about the weather and the progress upon the plans for the ball. His heart sank as he saw that only Mrs Filmore was in the room, netting a purse in a combination of particularly lurid colours that he suspected could only have been chosen by her daughter.

''Mr Lindsay! How lucky!'' Mrs Filmore greeted him. ''We've just been looking through my daughter's sketchbooks and were about to put them away, but now you will be able to see them—I shall ring for some tea, and then we will settle down to enjoy them. Annabel is so clever with her drawing.''

''And Miss Hilton?'' Jonathan asked casually, after some fifteen minutes of leafing through the leather-bound drawing-books of sketches that had long since become indistinguishable to him. ''What is she doing this morning?''

''Oh, she's gone to Salisbury—''

''I really don't know—''

Annabel and her mother spoke at the same moment.

''Salisbury?'' Jonathan stared at them. ''Then I presume Mr Filmore and Piers are with her?''

''No. They are out shooting,'' Annabel replied. ''Papa did tell us we must all stay at home, but Miss Hilton ignored him as I am afraid she usually does.''

''You mean she has gone alone!'' Jonathan stood up so abruptly he nearly knocked over the occasional table beside the sofa.

"Well, yes…" said Mrs Filmore uncertainly, as his blue eyes held her accusingly.

"And no one even tried to stop her, I suppose," he said bitingly. "Have none of you read the papers these last two days? The whole countryside is upon the edge of revolt. Anything could happen to her!"

"I do not see how we could have prevented her," Mrs Filmore said huffily.

"At the very least your husband and son could have gone after her—when did she leave?"

"About an hour ago," Annabel sighed.

"Then you will excuse me if I take my leave," he snapped, made his bow, and strode out of the room.

What optimism Janey had had about finding Harry died as they were forced to a halt in the village of Fonthill Gifford because the way was blocked by more men than Janey had ever seen gathered together in one place before. A murmuring, growling mass of ragged, angry men, clutching every kind of weapon from broom handles to pitchforks. In their midst, looking like a vessel afloat upon a stormy sea, was a prosperous-looking gentleman, standing upon a cart and struggling to make himself heard. She recognised him as John Benett, who owned the Pyt House estate and was the Member of Parliament for the county.

As she watched, wondering what to do next, one of the labourers was hoisted up upon the shoulders of his fellows.

"All we want is two shilling a day so we can feed our families. If we don't get it, we'll break your machines."

John Benett's response was to begin to read a

newly issued Royal Proclamation against rioting, which was received with derisive jeers. And not a man moved as he resorted to threats that the army would be used to stop them.

"We'll have broke the machines and gone before the Redcoats get here," the labourers' self-appointed spokesman shouted at Benett.

There was a roar of agreement and the mob began to move.

"Wait!" John Benett shouted. "I'll give five hundred pounds to any man of you who will inform upon ten others! You may have it now, this very moment!"

If he was prepared to part with five hundred pounds, why not give them their two shillings a day for an honest day's work? Janey felt like asking him.

"Don't you mean thirty pieces of silver, Benett?" the spokesman returned fiercely. "You keep yer five hundred, you'll find no Judases here!"

There was another roar of agreement from the crowd as they began to flood away in the direction of the farm.

"I can't see him, or Dad, anywhere." Kate sighed as she scanned the fast-thinning crowd.

"No," Janey said. "What a fool that man is! He could not have said anything more guaranteed to make them angry than to offer them money to inform against their own."

"Aye!" Kate's pretty face contorted with dislike. "Just because we're poor, the gentry think we have no honour or feelings!" And then, glancing at Janey, she added hastily, "I know you're not like that, miss. You're different."

"Well..." Janey sighed "...the Filmores would

probably tell you that's because I'll never pass for the gentry, and,'' she added, glancing at the furious and red-faced John Benett, who was striding up and down his cart barking orders at his agent, ''I can't say I particularly wish to, if he is an example of it.''

''Miss! There he is!'' Kate stood up suddenly in the gig and pointed. ''I saw him—Harry!''

''Come on, quick, before we lose him.'' Janey leapt down and knotted the reins about a gatepost.

Clinging to each other, they tried to push their way to where they had glimpsed Harry, but the weight of men behind them carried them the wrong way.

''Out the way, you two,'' a burly man said without rancour as he pushed them to one side, ''you'll get hurt here—'' Then he swore. ''Kate, what in the good Lord's name are you doing here? You get yourself home at once!''

''But, Dad—''

Janey, glimpsing Harry a few yards away, left Kate to make the explanations. Picking up her skirts, she began to run.

''Harry!'' she shouted, but knew the boy had not a chance of hearing her amid the general clamour. And, no matter how hard she tried, he remained a little ahead of her, his bright red head bobbing amid the now-running crowd. Why did women have to wear skirts? she thought fiercely as she hoisted hers up further to try and get more speed, and then she tripped and fell on the cobbles. By the time a kindly shepherd had hauled her to her feet, she had lost sight of Harry and Kate and lost her hat.

The mob swept her forward again, out of the village and down the track to the farm. It was impossible to turn back down the narrow, thickly hedged lane—there was no choice but to go forward.

"Harry!" she shouted again, hopelessly, as she caught sight of the boy.

And then all was bedlam as the crowd swept into the yard, breaking down the locked gate, climbing the walls. Janey pressed herself into the corner of a wall, for lack of anywhere else to go. The expressions on the faces of the men breaking into the barns with their iron bars scared her. This was no peaceable protest, this was months of suppressed anger and fear spilling out.

"That's broken the blasted machines!" someone shouted minutes later. "That'll show Benett what we think of his wages!"

"And about time!" A man whom Janey took for a quarryman, judging by the dust upon his clothes, agreed noisily beside her. "Tuppence a day! That's what they want us to work for! Tuppence!"

"Aye, and it'll not be long before that's all he wants to pay us!" a smocked labourer said, pushing a stave into the quarryman's hand as there was a crackling that Janey recognised as musket fire.

She stood up from where she had been crouching. "Get out of here!" she shouted at the quarryman and the labourer, who both stared at her as if she were a ghost. "That's musket fire. The Yeomanry are here—and they'll have you in this yard like rats in a trap."

The labourer turned his grey head. "She's right—they'll catch us here like we had the French at Hougemount—"

"The woods," Janey said desperately. "Tell everyone to head for the woods—"

She broke off and lunged forward, catching Harry's arm as he came skittering across the yard.

"Hey, let go of me!" Harry struggled and wriggled.

"No!" Janey said, hauling him almost off his feet. "Your sister is looking for you, and if we don't get out of here, we are very like to be hurt. So do as I say."

"She's right, lad." The labourer took Harry's other arm. "Come on, miss, I'll help. Let's get into those woods—that's the only chance we've got against the mounted boys."

Somehow, despite her hampering skirts, Janey managed to follow Harry and the labourer as they scrambled over a grey stone wall.

The first screams came as they began to run across the ploughed field that stretched between the farm and the wood. She glanced behind her. There were mounted men in the lane, slicing at the labourers with sabres, some using the flat of the blade, others the edge.

"Come on, Harry!" She increased her pace, cursing the heavy chalky soil that clung to her boots and petticoats, slowing her down, as she half-carried, half-dragged the frightened boy towards the shelter of the beech wood.

Glancing behind her, she saw men were streaming from the yard, running for the woods like herself, pausing now and again to shout defiance at the mounted men who had ridden into their midst, wielding swords against pitchforks, firing muskets at men armed with nothing but stones.

If she had not seen it with her own eyes, she would

not have thought it possible in England, she thought, as the keen air began to knife into her labouring lungs as she and Harry plunged on across the furrows.

"We'll give 'em a run for their money," the grey-haired labourer greeted her from behind a beech tree as she threw herself and Harry flat upon the mossy ground at the edge of the wood as a musket ball whistled over her head. "Horses won't be so much advantage to them here."

"No, but—muskets will," Janey said breathlessly, lifting her head to see men cantering across the ploughed field towards them, some waving sabres, and some whooping as if they were in the hunting field.

Her heart sank. There could not be a better recipe for disaster than frightened and angry labourers who did not have the sense to run away, and half the local young gentlemen out to play soldier.

The nearest horseman, in a scarlet and gold officer's uniform, was a good-looking young man, in a fair and florid way. She recognised him with a groan. Captain Crowne, late of the Horseguards, and one of Annabel's admirers. He had dined often enough at Pettridges. And his solution to any complaints by the poor was to "hang 'em or flog 'em". Mercy was not among his more noticeable qualities and she doubted he would stop to distinguish between woman, child or labourer.

"Harry—" she caught the shivering boy's hand "—when I say go, I want you to get up and run with me as far into the woods as we can. We'll find our way through and get out the other side. Ready?" she asked him.

Harry nodded.

A second later they were running, ducking and diving between the trees as the first cavalrymen began to crash into the woods.

She ran almost blindly, her head ducked against the brambles and twigs that tugged at her hair and clothes.

Harry kept with her, keeping pace as she slithered down a bank and splashed across a small stream but, as they climbed up the far bank, he began to flag.

"Got a stitch in me side, miss," he gasped. "I got to stop for a bit."

"You can't," she gasped back, dragging him on. Behind she could hear the pounding of a horse's hooves, the splashing of its feet as it came through the stream.

But then Harry stumbled, and she knew it was useless. They could not outrun a horse.

Putting Harry behind her, she bent and snatched up a fallen bough. She knew enough of fighting to know that a sharp blow upon the horse's nose would cause it to shy away and spoil the rider's aim. The bough held high, she wheeled to face the horseman. And then, as she recognised him, a relief that was so intense that it made her weak at the knees swept through her.

"Mr Lindsay—oh, thank God!" She sat down abruptly upon the damp muddy ground beside Harry and tossed aside the bough.

"No," he said, his voice as taut with anger as his white face. "Thank Kate. She at least had the sense to do as her father told her. I found her sat in your gig, and she told me what you were about—that, I take it, is her errant brother?'' He glanced down at Harry's small crouched figure.

She nodded, then, as the thought struck her like cold water, lifted her head. ''What are you doing here? You have not joined the Yeomanry in murdering defenceless men?''

''No!'' he snapped as he swung down from his horse. ''Though I could easily be persuaded to do murder upon you!''

''Why?'' She looked at him blankly.

''Why?'' The air left his lungs with the rush of an explosion. ''Shall I tell you what I am doing here, Miss Hilton? I called early at Pettridges to see if you wished to ride and discovered that you, in your infinite wisdom, had decided to travel to Salisbury unescorted on a day when half the countryside is in revolt! And that the blasted Filmores had done nothing to stop you!

''I came after you as far as Hindon, where I was told by an ostler that you had turned back for Fonthill Gifford—and having followed you there I find you have run willy-nilly into the middle of bloodbath after some damn fool boy! And next I see you climbing over a wall and being chased across a ploughed field by that bloodthirsty hothead, Crowne!''

''Oh.'' She got slowly to her feet and began to dust herself down. ''There is no need to shout. You are frightening Harry.''

''No need to shout!'' he repeated heavily. ''That's the worst mêlée I've seen since Waterloo. There is a man lying dead back there, another with half his arm gone—I thought you were going to get yourself maimed or killed!''

"It would have saved you the trouble of murdering me," she said tentatively. She had never seen a man quite as angry before, or as worried about her safety, she thought, her eyes very soft and dark as they sought his.

"True." He exhaled audibly. And there was the merest glimmer of a smile upon his lips and a slight warming of his blue gaze as he looked at her. "But don't tempt me, Janey Hilton."

"You're not going to murder 'er! I won't let you!" Harry piped up suddenly, brandishing Janey's discarded bough.

"I'll give you sixpence if you are quiet," he said, fixing Harry with a glare.

"All right." Harry dropped the bough with alacrity. "I won't say nothing." He held out his grubby hand.

Jonathan fished in his blue coat pocket and dropped the silver coin into it.

"Sold for sixpence. You're not very good at choosing your knight errants, are you, Miss Hilton?" he said drily as their eyes met over Harry's head.

"Oh, I do not think I chose so very badly, Mr Lindsay," she returned with equal dryness. "You are a little late, but you are here."

"I told you I am no damned Galahad," he growled. "Come on, let's get out of here before Crowne arrives and recognises you—or some other amateur soldier shoots us by accident. You look like a hoyden," he added as his gaze travelled over her loosened hair hanging to her waist, and her muddied and torn grey pelisse.

"Then I suppose I had better behave like one," she

said mildly and, stepping forward, reached up to kiss him briefly upon his cheek. "Thank you for coming to find me."

"If you think to get around me like that, you won't, not this time," he growled. And then, as her hazel eyes continued to hold his gaze steadily, he turned away suddenly to pick up Harry and dump him unceremoniously upon the saddle of his sweating grey and took the reins over its head so he could lead it.

"But," he added, his stern face cracking suddenly into a grin, "you may feel at liberty to try to do so upon another occasion, Miss Hilton."

And then, as there was the crack of a musket and a scream of pain nearby, he sobered again. "Come on—the sooner you are safely home, the better I shall like it."

"So why this sudden desire to go to Salisbury?" he asked a little later when, the sounds of the fighting fading behind them, they slowed from a half-run to a walk, the grey plodding patiently behind them with Harry pretending to be a soldier upon its back.

"I wanted to see my solicitors, to ask if there was anything I could do to prevent Mr Filmore laying off men when it is so close to the time when I shall have control of the estate."

"I see..." He sighed as his arm curled about her waist. "You do not think this fracas might make him change his mind about using the threshing machines?"

"No. He thinks only of profit and nothing else." Janey sighed.

"Then write to your solicitors," he suggested. "I

will deliver it by hand for you tomorrow and wait for their answer.''

"You would do that for me?" She turned her head to look him in the eyes.

"I should do almost anything for you, Miss Hilton." He smiled down at her, and her heart seemed to skip a beat. "I thought you might have realised that by now."

They walked on in silence and she let her head rest against his shoulder. It did not matter that she was muddy, cold and tired—even the riot did not seem to matter. She had never felt so happy in her life as she did at this moment with his arm about her, knowing he cared for her.

Chapter Ten

But as she stepped into the kitchen of Will Avery's grey stone cottage late the following evening, her spirits were far from buoyant. And her heart sank further as the ten men packed into the tiny room snatched off their caps as she greeted them, and she saw the hope in their eyes. A hope that died as she gave the smallest shake of her head.

"No luck then, miss?" Will Avery said heavily as he offered her the carved oak chair, black with age, which stood beside the fire.

"I am afraid not, Will," she said as she sat down. "I have just got an answer back from my solicitors. There is nothing I can do until I am twenty-one. I am so sorry," she added as she saw the hopeless, desperate expressions upon the faces of the ten men Mr Filmore had let go. "I have tried every argument I could think of to change Mr Filmore's mind, to no avail. And he says if any try and prevent him using the machines by violence he will have the Yeomanry out as they did yesterday at Pyt House."

"Tha's it, then, I'll break their bloody machines—

like they did yesterday and in Ansty,'' one man said, his voice raw with anger. "I'll break 'em into pieces and anyone who tries to stop me—and I don't care if I swing for it. What bloody difference is it going to make? I'd rather hang than watch Bess and the little 'uns starve—''

"Adam, there's a lady 'ere—'' a grey-haired man muttered, shuffling his boots on the slate floor.

"It's all right, I quite understand,'' Janey said quickly. "If I were in your position, I know I should feel the same. But please, I beg you to do nothing to endanger yourselves—again—'' she added. There were one or two familiar faces she had glimpsed in the mob the previous day. "As soon as I inherit, I promise that you will have your old employment back and better wages.''

"We know that, miss, but what do we eat for the next five months?'' another man said hopelessly. "Wiltshire wages have always bin worse than Kent and the like, but lately it's bin even worse. None of us has got so much as a farthing put by, the children be half starved as it is.''

"I know,'' she said despairingly, "but there is nothing else I can do unless I marry before my birthday.''

"And there's not much chance of that, with your fiancé dead a twelvemonth,'' a young man with dark brown curls said bluntly, "unless that Lindsay fellow makes you an offer. Will said he's supposed to be the friend to the poor-speaking for us in the Parliament. Can't you persuade him, miss, tell him what good he'd be doing if he wed you?''

Janey stared at him, her heart skipping a beat.

Marry Jonathan! She had not even allowed herself to think of it. He had made it clear enough his intentions towards her were hardly the honourable kind. And she had lived long enough in England to know that the sons of Earls did not marry the daughters of mill-hands, no matter how wealthy, unless they were in desperate need of funds, which Jonathan certainly was not.

And yet—after yesterday she was beginning to believe that he cared for her as well as desired her. So why not, why not ask him? She had not loved Edward, but she had been prepared to marry him to get control of the estate. So, could she not find the courage to ask a man whom she did love if he would marry her? What was there to lose if he refused?

"Tha's enough, Jethro," Will put in sharply. "None of this is Miss Hilton's fault, she's a lady, not one of your flibbertigibbets. You've no right to suggest anything of the kind. You make your apology right now."

"It does not matter, Will—" Janey said, staring unseeingly at the black iron kettle which hissed gently as it hung upon its hook over the flames of the fire. There was everything to lose if she asked him and he refused, she thought sickly. It would be an end to their friendship, an end to her deepest, most secret hopes and dreams.

"It does," said Will, giving Jethro a black look. "Though it would help matters if we knew whether Mr Lindsay intends staying on at Southbrook— there's bound to be work if he does."

"I know," Janey replied, pulling herself out of her reverie. "I shall be seeing Mr Lindsay on Saturday evening—if he is to stay on at Southbrook, I am sure he will want to take on some men. The threshing machines are not due at Pettridges Farm until Monday week. Please do nothing before then—I might be able to do something for the family men, at least.''

"Oh, yeah,'' Jethro, the blunt young man, said sourly. "Wait so you can get the Yeomanry out to stop us doing anything. Like sticks to like, especially when there be money in it.''

"That is unfair!'' Janey replied fiercely. "I do not think violence is the answer, but I should not betray you, or act against you. I have known what it is to be hungry, and what it is to watch your family die and be helpless to prevent it!''

"I'll believe that when I see you breaking one of their machines,'' Jethro muttered. "Playing Lady Bountiful is one thing—but risking your neck is another. You go back to your gentry friends, Miss Hilton, you don't belong 'ere.''

"Tha's enough, Jethro,'' Will growled. "Miss Hilton was at Pyt House yesterday, trying to stop Kate Cowley's brother from getting hurt. She's only trying to help us. She's never been anything but a friend to this village and you know it. You apologise to her now and treat her with the respect she deserves or you'll find yourself out of the door before those boots of yours touch the ground.''

"It does not matter, Will.'' Janey sighed and stood up. "Jethro is right in a way. If you are considering violent action, it is better I do not know of it. I had better go.''

Will showed her to the door and closed it behind them. "Don't take what Jethro says too much to heart, miss. His sweetheart's in the family way; now her father's demanding to know how he's going to support her and the baby since he's got no place.''

''I know. Kate told me of his circumstances.'' Janey sighed.

''Did her father get home safe, yesterday?'' Will asked.

''Yes, thank heaven,'' Janey said with feeling.

''Not like that poor devil Hardy, shot him dead like a dog they did—''

''Yes, poor man.'' She frowned. ''If—if anything does happen, you will take care, won't you, Will?''

''I'll do me best, Miss Hilton,'' he said. ''And don't you go risking yourself again any other way,'' he added somberly. ''After that business at Pyt House yesterday, men are angry. It's not just Southbrook, things are bad everywhere. Half the men in the Knoyles, the Deverills and Mere aren't making enough to feed their families, either—and then there's this talk of bringing in cheap labour from the cities. Tha's making even those men who still have work unsettled. They can't feed their families on what they get now. If wages go any lower—'' He broke off with an expressive shrug.

''I cannot think there is any truth in that rumour at least.'' Janey sighed. ''Not even Mr Filmore would consider replacing a cowman or shepherd with a factory hand who does not know a cow's nose from its tail or the difference between a sheep and a ram, no matter what the saving. But you will try and stop them from doing anything too rash?'' she added as they reached the gate at the end of the brick path.

''I'll try, but I can't promise,'' Will said. ''Some

of 'em are beyond reason..." He paused, his face splitting into a sudden unexpected grin as he opened the gate for her. "But perhaps things aren't quite as hopeless as we think—looks like you got yourself an escort home again, miss. Afternoon, sir!" he called out cheerfully before turning away. Janey stared at the man upon the grey horse beside her gig, her heart skipping and leaping beneath her ribs as their gazes met and held.

She stood staring at him helplessly, something inside her melting as he swung down from his saddle, all lithe, lean grace, and came towards her.

"What are you doing here?" she said.

"I rather think that is my question," he said a little tersely. "I thought you promised me this afternoon you would go nowhere alone again."

"I am not alone, Kate is with me," she said glancing towards the gig and smiling a little as Kate, whose eyes had been out upon stalks, hastily looked away and pretended uninterest.

"Two women are little better than one." He sighed. "I cannot think what the Filmores were about to let you out again."

"None of the local people would hurt me," she replied with a half-smile, as she wondered what he would think if he knew how she had ridden across prairie and through forest with little more than her horse's surefootedness and speed as her protection from wild animal and Indian alike.

"It's not the local labourers that worry me," he said as he reached out and tucked a stray strand of her honey-coloured hair into her bonnet.

She went still as his fingertip grazed her cheek.

"You—you don't believe this nonsense they are spouting about agents provocateurs?" she said a little unsteadily as his hand dropped back to his side and his blue gaze burned into her eyes. "It is obvious why men are rioting—the machines are taking away their already meagre livelihood and forcing wages down further."

"You are probably right." He frowned. "But as a favour to me, please do not go about alone? Not until—not until things are settled again. Promise me, Janey?"

"Very well," she conceded with a smile, the way he said her name, and the concern in his eyes, warming her through like a flame.

He did care for her, he did—she was almost sure of it—almost sure enough to risk asking him if he would marry her. She took a deep breath, feeling herself start to shake inside at the thought.

"You're shivering," he observed instantly. "It is time you were home."

Before she could even begin to frame the question in her own mind, he had taken her arm and handed her up into the gig and the moment was lost.

"I take it the news from the solicitors was not good?" he asked as he handed her the reins.

"No," she said heavily. "And I hate to think what will happen when the machines arrive at Pettridges Home Farm—"

"So do I." He frowned again. "This business is getting out of hand. There have been disturbances at forty places in the county within the last two days. And, I hear, at dozens of places in Hampshire and Dorset."

"The whole thing could be stopped in a day or two, if only they would improve the wages a little and the provision for the poor." Janey sighed as she picked up her whip.

"Perhaps," he said as he remounted. "I am not so sure. If the discontent reaches the towns, the government might find itself with a full-scale insurrection upon its hands." He looked at her, as she was silent. "Miss Hilton, if you hear of any plans for mischief, promise me you will tell me. If disciplined troops are brought in before anything happens, it can prevent people getting hurt."

"I know." She released the brake and flicked the whip over the skewbald pony's head. "But I don't think the men trust even me enough to tell me of any plans, not any more, not after yesterday."

"Well, whatever happens, promise me you will not get involved. I might not be there to rescue you next time."

"I am hardly your responsibility," she reminded him with a sideways glance.

"No?" His dark brows lifted as he met her gaze. "Someone has to look after you, Miss Hilton; as the Filmores do not seem to consider it their duty, I see no alternative but to make it mine."

"I am quite capable of looking after myself, Mr Lindsay," she replied a little sharply, aware of Kate hanging upon every word. "And you have no duty to me at all."

"I suppose you are right, Miss Hilton," he replied with a smile from his saddle. "But won't you indulge me, just a little?"

"I rather thought I already had," she muttered as

she flicked the whip over the horse's head, and sent the gig rattling forward down the stony lane.

"Not nearly enough." He grinned at her as he brought his horse alongside.

And, as his wicked, laughing gaze met hers, she knew with sudden absolute certainty that this was the only man she wanted to spend her life with, the only man she would ever want.

Then suddenly, as he stared at her, his expression sobered. "What did your solicitors say about the will? Who does get your fortune if you die before you inherit or before you marry?"

"They would not tell me," she said. "Apparently, my grandfather left express instructions that that part of his will was to remain secret unless it was required. I think he meant to protect me from adventurers."

"So no one but the solicitors know who would inherit if something happened to you." He sighed with relief.

"Yes," she said, and then laughed as she looked at him. "You're not still thinking Piers is out to murder me, are you?"

"No." He gave a slightly forced laugh. "Of course not."

"You're so lucky, miss." Kate sighed as she helped Janey out of her many-caped green pelisse coat. "Having a man like Mr Lindsay in love with you—"

Janey gave a mirthless chuckle. "I am not at all sure he is in love with me, Kate."

"Oh, miss, it's as plain as a pikestaff." Kate hung up the coat to dry, ready for brushing. "He's that

smitten, he'd jump off a cliff if you told him to—
riding all that way to Salisbury and back.'' She said
enviously, ''There's nothing he wouldn't do for you.
I wish my Tom was half as keen.''

''I wish I was as sure of Mr Lindsay's affections
as you are,'' Janey said as she sat down in the chair
beside her bedroom window. ''If I was sure of
that…'' The rest of the thought remained unvoiced as
she stared out across the dusky park and saw the
mounted figure cantering through the thickening mist.
The horse, the rider in the dark coat and broad-
brimmed hat, were totally familiar to her…

''No!'' The word dragged out of her throat and she
shut her eyes.

''Miss! Miss!'' Kate came running across to her.
''What is it? You're white as a sheet—'' She stopped
and blanched as she also looked out of the window.

''Mr Grey!'' she gasped.

''You saw him, too?'' Janey gave a sigh of relief
and steeled herself to look out of the window again
and saw only the empty park. ''I saw him as well.''

''It was his ghost!'' Kate was aghast.

''No, don't be silly,'' Janey said briskly, pulling
herself together. ''It was nothing but a trick of the
mist and the light. And please, Kate, don't mention it
to anyone else—Mr and Mrs Filmore seem to think
me weak in the head as it is.''

''Yes, and it would suit them all too well if you
were,'' Kate said, frowning as she looked out of the
window into the mist. ''Yours wouldn't be the first
fortune got that way, miss.''

''Not you as well, Kate,'' Janey said in despair.

"Mr Lindsay is half-convinced the Filmores are plotting to have me 'put away', if not worse."

"You should take heed of him, miss. Did you never hear of that poor Henrietta Harcourt, miss? It were in all the papers. But I suppose it were just before you came," Kate said. "Her uncle bribed some doctors and had her put into the asylum so they might keep her money for themselves. It was only when her sister came back from India that the uncle was found out and she was released."

"It sounds like something out of a novel, Kate." Janey laughed.

"Maybe, but it happened, miss," said Kate weightily. "And I think you should be careful it don't happen to you."

"I'll do my best," Janey said placatingly as her maid returned a little huffily to her tasks. "I shall do my best to behave with absolute decorum next time the good Doctor comes to dine." Then, as a thought struck her, she turned. "Get your cloak, Kate, we're going outside."

Ten minutes later she and Kate stood staring at the soft turf of the park.

"That's the heaviest ghost I've ever heard of, Kate," Janey said, frowning as she stared at the fresh hoofprints.

"Yes," Kate agreed. "Do you know what I think, miss? Someone is trying to frighten you out of your wits. Now I think of it, it wasn't Mr Grey I saw, it was a hat like his, a horse like his—"

"But who would do that—?" Janey began to say, shivering and pulling her hood closer about her face against the raw air.

They both spoke at once as they looked at each other.

"Piers!"

"Master Filmore!"

"I think the best thing to do is to ignore it," Janey said after a moment. "We'll let him think we did not see him. He'll probably try again tomorrow—"

"And the next day," Kate chuckled.

"And the next." Janey laughed. "Let's hope for inclement weather, shall we, Kate?"

On Saturday evening, Janey stared into her pier glass, her stomach so full of butterflies that she felt sick. Preparations for the ball had meant that she had not seen Jonathan for three days. And the confidence she had begun to have about his feelings towards her had diminished beneath the barrage of Annabel's gossip about his past conquests, and the number of broken hearts he had left strewn in his wake.

If he had disdained to marry the daughters of Earls and Dukes alike, why would he consider plain Miss Hilton? A question Annabel had not hesitated to taunt her with every time Jonathan Lindsay called.

She took in a breath, and lifted her chin. Nothing ventured, nothing gained, she told herself, as she surveyed herself critically. Her gown was a foaming confection of white silk gauze and lace, with short puffed sleeves which began at the top of her arm, in line with the low heart-shaped neckline, leaving her throat and shoulders bare. The uppermost layer of gauze had scattered embroideries of gold thread that shimmered and glistened in the candlelight.

"Don't forget this, miss." Kate came forward and

fastened a wide white silk ribbon stitched to a pearl-encrusted buckle about the tiny waist, tying the two ends at the back in a bow.

"You don't think we have made it too short?" Janey said, smoothing back the front of the full rustling skirt to peer at the toes of her gold satin slippers, which she was unaccustomed to seeing.

"No, miss," Kate assured her. "Madame Tovee said it's the fashion now for the hem to sit upon the ankle. Now, if you'll just let me finish your hair."

Janie stood patiently as Kate wound and pinned the knot of heavy gold on top of her head with pins decorated with delicate pearl flowers, and then carefully arranged a fall of loose ringlets at either side of her slender face.

"There," said Kate happily, "now you look like a princess in a fairy tale, miss."

But I don't feel like one, thought Janey, as Kate carefully arranged a grey silk brocade cloak about her shoulders. Her reflection might look cool, remote, but inside she was shaking with nerves. How did you go about asking a man to marry you? Especially a man like Jonathan Lindsay—

"That's the carriage coming round, miss," Kate said from the window. "You'd better go down."

"Yes." Crossing the room to her tester bed, she picked up the gold and white reticule from where it lay upon the red counterpane and made her way slowly out of the room.

"Oh, do come on, Jane," Annabel said tartly as Janey stepped off the last step of the flight of stairs into the panelled hall, where the Filmores were gathered in all their imposing finery. "We've all been waiting for you, though I do not know why you are coming—you can hardly be expecting to dance when you are so lame.''

"Annabel," Mrs Filmore said reprovingly with a toss of her scarlet and black plumed coiffure, which reminded Janey of the undertaker's horses. "I am sure Jane will be far too sensible to make a spectacle of herself again. Now, come along, girls, into the carriage and do be careful not to crush your skirts, and you had better be careful of your hair when you are getting in, Annabel."

Janey glanced at Annabel's hair, which was an elaborate arrangement of curls, false pieces and what looked like half a shrubbery of pink silk flowers and green leaves, adding at least four inches to Annabel's diminutive height.

"You should have borrowed Annabel's maid," Mrs Filmore said as she followed Janey's awestruck gaze. "The French are so clever with their hands. That girl of yours always manages to turn you out with a touch of the country convent about you."

"What is it that makes women think they look attractive with half an ostrich, a ton of horsehair and a garden upon their head?" Jonathan said to Lord Derwent after they had greeted the Morrisons and the party from Fonthill and ushered them into the already-full ballroom.

"Don't ask me—most of 'em would wear a water pail if they thought it was the latest mode," Lord Derwent said with a grin. And then, as he glanced down over the gilt balustrade into the hall, he smiled.

"Course, there are some who have more sense, like Miss Hilton."

"She's here?" Jonathan's expression of bored indifference changed to a smile as he, too, looked down over the balustrade and saw Janey begin to climb the stairs in the Filmores' wake, several steps behind them, tall, slender and shimmering in her white and gold gown.

"Gets better-looking every time you see her, that one," said Lord Derwent. "There's something about her that you just can't help watching—moves like a thoroughbred."

"If you have no serious intentions towards her, I should take it kindly if you would watch someone else," Jonathan said quietly. "She's mine, Perry."

"Glad you realise it," Lord Derwent murmured, then put on a bright smile as he greeted Mrs Filmore and Annabel effusively.

Janey climbed the last of the stairs at an ever slower pace, her knuckles white as her face as she gripped her reticule. After one snatched glance from the hall, she had not dared look at Jonathan.

She was not going to be able to do it, she thought. She could not just walk up to him and ask him to marry her.

"Oh—" She gave a gasp as she tripped upon the top step and all but fell.

But then her arm was caught, held, and she regained her balance.

"I knew it. I knew she would show us up," Annabel muttered audibly to her mother.

But Janey barely heard her, as she found herself

staring at Jonathan's snowy cravat and felt the warmth of his hand upon her arm, burning her skin.

"You really must stop prostrating yourself at my feet," he said, his voice so warm, so affectionate, that she found the courage to look up.

He smiled down at her, and then his dark brows knit as he saw how pale she was, and felt how she was trembling.

"Are you all right? You did not hurt yourself?"

"No." Her voice was a whisper.

"You're shaking."

"I am nervous," she stammered. "I am not used to these occasions—I am not often invited."

"I think you soon will be," he said softly. "Half the men here are already looking at you, so be sure to save me the first dance. You have no idea how much I have missed you these last three days—"

"Have you?" she said a little breathlessly, as the hope began to grow inside her that it would be all right after all.

"Jono! Look who we have with us! Is she not a sight for sore eyes?" a male voice said loudly from behind Janey.

Jonathan's hand clenched so suddenly and violently upon her arm that she had to bite back an exclamation. And then she saw the colour drain from his face, leaving his blue eyes blazing, brilliant.

"Susanna!" The name was hardly more than an exhalation.

Her insides turning to ice, Janey turned her head as his hand dropped abruptly from her arm. Staring back at Jonathan from the midst of Sir Richard Hoare's party was a tall, queenly-looking woman, with pale green eyes, jet-black curls and a warm smile on her voluptuous mouth.

From her other side, Janey heard Lord Derwent swear softly beneath his breath.

"Well, Jono, have you forgotten me entirely?" The woman stepped forward in a rustle of purple silk, her hand outstretched, confident of her reception. "You have not written to me in weeks."

"I could never forget you, your grace." There was an edge to Jonathan's voice that Janey had never heard before. She found herself staring as he picked up the languid white fingers and raised them slowly to his lips. And then, without knowing how, she knew quite suddenly, without any doubt at all, that he and this woman had been lovers, perhaps still were. She remained transfixed, stunned by a pain that was almost physical as she watched Jonathan's mouth curve into a smile.

The brunette's pale green eyes left Jonathan's face and flicked to Janey, and one finely plucked black brow lifted in amusement.

"I do not want to distract you from your guests."

Jonathan turned slowly, and looked at Janey blankly.

He had forgotten her, Janey thought, forgotten her from the moment he had set eyes upon this elegant aristocratic woman, who was so obviously his perfect counterpart. She wheeled, a sudden lump in her throat that threatened to choke her as she fled into the noise and light of the ballroom.

There were people everywhere. A rippling churning sea of pale silks, lace, taffeta and glittering cut stones, with the dark coats of the men standing out like black rocks in the foam.

And not a single face she recognised. She could not even see the Filmores. At a signal from someone, the orchestra began to play a waltz. The floor around her emptied and she found herself standing alone in its centre. People were staring at her, wondering why she was alone. She walked hastily to the side, acutely conscious of the barely discernible limp that made her skirt dip and sway as she walked.

"Excuse me, excuse me—" Somehow she made her way through the press and found a chair against the wall beside two gossiping dowagers. She sat down, wishing she could sink into the floor as curious glances followed her.

"Susanna Spencer always was shameless," the elderly woman nearest to her said. "To have the nerve to come here tonight after she jilted him for old Sutton—well!"

"Quite," the other woman agreed with a nod of her plumed head. "Just look at her now! You would think it was him she was wed to."

"I thank God daily that she is not," said the first dowager. "And I'd have thought Jonathan did, too, after six years."

"I heard he still means to marry her, the moment Sutton is dead and she is free."

"Piffle!" said the first dowager. "Jonathan would never be such a fool, not even if he still loved her."

"I should not be so sure," the other said. "Susanna Spencer came out of her cradle knowing how to turn any man's head."

Feeling sick, Janey followed the direction of their

gaze. The brunette was laughing, her beautiful head thrown back, emphasising the lushness of her white breasts, which were barely contained by the purple silk gown. And her elegant white hand lay possessively upon Jonathan's arm as they entered the ballroom. She looked away, staring down at her reticule. She had been so stupid, so full of foolish dreams and hopes—

"Lost your admirer, Jane?" Annabel's voice made her start. "You did not really think that he would have eyes for anyone else now Susanna Spencer is here, did you? She is the only woman ever to touch his heart, everyone knows that."

Everyone but me, Janey wanted to say. But she knew if she opened her mouth she would cry and make a complete fool of herself.

"Mama wishes you to join her upon the sofa at the far end," Annabel continued. "You'll have plenty of company—it's where all the wallflowers sit."

"I'd rather stay here," Janey forced out of her constricted throat.

"Oh, why can you never do as you are told!" Annabel snapped.

"Leave her," the dowager snapped back at Annabel. "You're not doing her any good. It is obvious she is out of sorts. Now, Miss—" She paused, glancing at Janey.

"Hilton," supplied Annabel.

"Miss Hilton will be quite safe with us, will she not, Hermione? No doubt she is feeling a little shy," the dowager said, snapping out her finely carved bone and lace fan and beginning to waft it to and fro.

"Are we going to dance or not?" The chinless young man standing behind Annabel sighed.

"I suppose so, come along." Annabel flounced away in a flutter of white and pink taffeta and blue lace.

"Thank you," Janey said after a few minutes in which she struggled to regain her self-control.

"Think nothing of it," the dowager said grandly. "Never could stand the Filmores—unpleasant people, very unpleasant. Got some bad blood in them somewhere, I'll warrant. Now, lift that pretty chin up, m'dear. You're not the first heart to be broken by my grandson."

"Your grandson?" Janey said, startled.

"Yes—" the dowager's wrinkled face split into a wicked grin "—I'm Lady Stalbridge and this is my sister, Lady Merwell. Now, do tell us all about yourself and how you know my grandson."

Somewhat to her surprise, Janey found herself doing so. Even the circumstances of her first meeting with him amused Lady Stalbridge greatly.

"Yes, he can be quite the most arrogant of men at times, just like his grandfather—" she laughed "—but I don't think you could quite accuse him of being a dandy, his hair is always a little too unruly. And he saved your little arsonist, you say?"

"Yes."

"He always was kind," Lady Stalbridge said confidingly. "Tries hard to hide it, of course, but I remember him taking on four stable lads once who were twice his size, all because they had kicked a stray dog. In tears, he was—"

"Thank you, Grandmama." Janey went very still

at the dry voice and found herself staring at the buttons upon Jonathan's dark blue coat.

"What d'you want here?" Lady Stalbridge asked. "Thought you'd be dancing with that Spencer hussy."

"If you are referring to the Duchess of Sutton, she is dancing with Lord Bath."

"Dropped you for a title again," his grandmother replied with a snort. "That does not surprise me."

"For your information, Grandmama, Miss Hilton has already promised me this dance."

"Developing some taste at last," Lady Stalbridge said. "About time, boy."

After a frosty glare at his grandmother, Jonathan extended his hand to Janey. "Miss Hilton? Will you do me the pleasure?"

He was cool, aloof, formal, as he held out his hand to her. She did not know him like this, Janey thought, she did not know him at all.

"Will you do me the pleasure?" he repeated.

"I don't dance," she said stiffly. She did not want to be in his arms. Did not want him to touch her and know that it meant nothing because he had only ever loved this Susanna Spencer and so obviously still did. "I can't."

"Nonsense," said Lady Stalbridge, after glancing from her to her grandson. "Anyone who moves as gracefully as you can dance. You go with him, m'dear, and give that woman a taste of her own medicine. That's what you've got in mind, Jono, ain't it?"

"You don't understand," Janey began helplessly. "My leg—I have not danced in a year."

"I don't care," Jonathan said, stooping to take her

hands and pulling her unceremoniously to her feet. "You are going to dance with me if I have to carry you around the floor."

"All that money gone upon his education and he still forgets his manners." His grandmother sighed heavily, earning herself a another furious glare from her grandson as he propelled Janey to the dance floor.

"Janey," he said exasperatedly a few seconds later, "we cannot dance if you insist on trying to be a sword's length away from me. Come here and tell me what the devil is wrong with you this evening."

"There's nothing wrong with me," she said miserably, her treacherous body melting and slipping into perfect step with his as he brought her closer.

"There is, I can feel it," he said. "Lord Derwent has not said anything to you?"

"Lord Derwent?" She looked up at him blankly. "About what?"

"Nothing." His expression relaxed. "I would not hurt you for the world. You know that, don't you?"

"And the Duchess of Sutton—I suppose you would not hurt her either?" she said bitterly.

"So that's it—!" He laughed with relief. "Feeling a little green about the gills, Janey?"

"Yes!" she said fiercely—the last thing she could bear at this moment was his teasing.

"You need not be."

"No?" She tossed her head. "You love her, you still want to marry her. But you would not marry me, not even if I asked you, would you?" Her voice faltered on the last two words, which had come out wistful rather than angry, as she met his gaze, and hoped against hope that he would tell her she was wrong.

"Is that a proposal, Janey?" He chuckled. "I suppose I should have expected that you were the one woman who would not wait to be asked. This is very sudden, considering the alacrity with which you jumped out of the window last week. Has my grandmother put you up to it? I confess I am flattered, even if she did."

He had not even taken her seriously, she thought with a mixture of rage and despair. But then, why should that surprise her? He had never had serious intentions towards her—never wanted to marry her as he had this Susanna Spencer!

"You need not be flattered," she returned sharply. "It is just that my lawyers said there was nothing I could do to prevent Mr Filmore bringing in the machines until either I am of age or I marry."

"I see." He laughed aloud. "Only you, my sweet radical, would think you would persuade me to marry you on the grounds that it would keep men in employment."

"That's not the only reason," she said thickly. "It is just that I thought, given the speech you made and the way you helped Jem, you might consider—"

"Sacrificing myself for the greater good." His mouth twisted into a smile that did not reach his eyes. "You've got the wrong man, Janey. The speech was a sham from beginning to end!" He sighed as he swung her around the corner of the floor. "Something which I have been meaning to tell you for some time. I made it merely for a wager."

"A wager! Upon such a subject!" She lifted disbelieving eyes to his face as she understood with sudden clarity Annabel and Piers's disdainful laughter.

"You mean the whole thing was a lie. How could you?"

"Probably because I am an unprincipled wretch who cares only for his own pleasure," he said wryly, not meeting her gaze. "I did try to warn you I am no Galahad, Miss Hilton."

"I see," she said flatly. "And kissing me like you did, was that for a wager, too?"

He missed a step. "Janey—"

"Oh, no." She stopped dead as she read the answer in his eyes, heard it in his voice. "It was, wasn't it? You—" Her voice cracked suddenly upon the last word and she tried to pull out of his grasp. "It has all been a game to you."

"Janey, Miss Hilton!" he hissed at her as he jerked her back into step. "Filmore is watching us. Do you want to give him more evidence to suggest your mind is unbalanced?"

"What more evidence does he need when I have been stupid enough to believe you actually liked me—wanted me? Tell me, did they all know? Annabel, Piers—how they must have laughed."

"No one knows—at least, only Perry, with whom I made the wager, and he will not tell anyone. In fact, he wished to call it off almost as soon as it was made—"

"And I am supposed to be grateful for that!" she snapped, the gold flecks in her hazel eyes blazing as brightly as the gold thread upon her dress in the candlelight.

"Janey, listen to me. I do like you." He dragged her closer. "A very great deal—it might have begun as a wager, but it was far more than that from the first moment I touched you. You must believe that.''

''I don't know what to believe,'' she said bitterly. ''I thought you were different from the rest! I thought you cared about things—people—I thought perhaps you lo—'' Her voice trailed off. She had to get away before she made a complete fool of herself.

She twisted out of his grasp, picked up her skirts and ran. Ran through the other dancers, out of the ballroom and down the broad sweep of stairs, past startled servants, across the hall and out of the house. Jonathan's spaniel, which had somehow found its way out of the gun room, followed her, barking at her heels, thinking it was a game.

She ran and ran, across the wet lawns, along the drive to the stable block.

''My carriage, please,'' she blurted out to the first groom she encountered. ''The blue barouche with the bays—I want to go home.''

''Well,'' said Lord Derwent as he stood upon the front steps of Southbrook House beside Jonathan and watched the lanterns of the barouche disappearing along the drive into the darkness, ''looks like you have just lost the wager, Jono.''

''It would seem so,'' Jonathan said grittily.

''Oh, well, I don't suppose it matters now Susanna is here,'' Lord Derwent said carefully. ''I gather old Sutton is on his deathbed and she will soon be free. That must be some consolation for losing Miss Hilton's affections.''

''Oh, yes,'' Jonathan said with a ragged laugh. ''I have the undying devotion of a woman who left me at the altar, and who is willing to throw herself at me while her husband is upon his deathbed, by all accounts. My perfect match, wouldn't you say, Perry?''

''I did try to warn you,'' Lord Derwent said with a sigh. ''And as for Susanna, I never thought she was the perfect match for you, nor did any of your friends.''

''Or your family,'' Lady Stalbridge said crisply from behind, making them both wheel around. ''Now, tell me about Miss Hilton. I understand she is your neighbour. What's her background?''

''She is the granddaughter of an industrialist; her mother ran away with a millhand to the colonies,'' Jonathan said tersely. ''Her grandfather brought her back to live upon the neighbouring estate after her parents' death.''

''Oh, what a pity,'' Lady Stalbridge replied. ''I rather liked the look of her. Not such a simpering ninny as most of the young women one gets nowadays. But, of course, that makes her quite out of the question for you, Jonathan.''

''Out of the question for what?'' her grandson asked belligerently.

''Marriage,'' Lady Stalbridge replied blithely. ''You know the rules, Jonathan. Lindsays don't marry trade, never have.''

''I do not give a damn for the rules, Grandmother,'' Jonathan declared. ''And who said anything about marriage?''

''Such passion, Jonathan,'' his grandmother said reprovingly. ''You'd almost think you were in love with her.''

"I assure you I am not. I gave up such sentimental notions a long time ago."

Lady Stalbridge and Lord Derwent exchanged glances as Jonathan stalked away.

"How is it that someone as intelligent as Jonathan can be such a dolt when it comes to his own feelings?" Lady Stalbridge shook her head.

"He never does think straight when Susanna is around," Lord Derwent said, offering Lady Stalbridge his arm. "A pity she had to arrive just now."

"Yes," said Lady Stalbridge, "I rather think it is. Tell me, what do you think of this Miss Hilton?"

Chapter Eleven

"How nice," Mrs Filmore announced happily at breakfast upon the Sunday morning. "We are all invited to dine at Southbrook tomorrow evening. I knew you had made an impression upon Mr Lindsay, Annabel."

"He only danced with me once, Mama," Annabel said sourly. "He had eyes for no one but Susanna Spencer. And, when he was with me, he kept making the most outrageous remarks about my hair."

"If you ask me, he was so drunk he didn't know who he was dancing with half the time," Piers drawled. "Something, or perhaps I should say someone, seemed to have put him quite out of sorts."

He glanced across the table at Janey, who was concentrating upon spreading the butter to the very corners of her toast. "Shall you be coming to Southbrook to dine, my dearest coz? Or are you still suffering from the mysterious malady which caused your departure from the ball?"

"No. I am perfectly well, thank you, Piers," Janey said coolly, determined that Annabel and Piers should never know how much Jonathan Lindsay had hurt her. "Of course I shall go, if I am invited."

"Oh, you are, my dear," said Mrs Filmore, a note of incredulity in her voice as she read further in the note. "Lady Stalbridge has specifically requested the pleasure of your company."

"How kind of her," Janey said woodenly. "Are we to walk to church or ride this morning? It is such a bright morning—I rather think I shall walk."

"Must we?" Annabel groaned. "I have such a headache."

"Shouldn't have let Captain Crowne fetch you quite so much 'lemonade', should you?" her brother sneered.

"Shut up, Piers," Annabel snapped. "Or I will tell."

"Oh, I shouldn't start revealing secrets, sis, dearest." Piers gave his sister an unpleasant smile. "You never know what might come out."

"I am a trifle fatigued as well," Mrs Filmore said. "We will take the carriage. You may do as you wish, Jane."

"Then I shall walk," Janey said.

"Which way are you going?" Annabel asked.

"Through the lower meadow," Janey answered.

"Oh, I should take the upper path," Annabel suggested. "The lower meadow is still very muddy."

"But that means going through the covert—" Piers began to say.

"I am sure Jane will not mind that, she has such a penchant for walking through woods." Annabel cut him off with a look.

"Thank you," said Janey, more than a little startled by both brother and sister's helpfulness, "I will."

"Are you sure this is the right way, miss?" Kate asked Janey an hour or so later. "It's ever so overgrown, you can hardly see where to put your feet."

"I know," Janey said, as she struggled to disentangle the billowing leg-of-mutton sleeve of her pelisse coat from a hawthorn twig. "I think the going is easier over there to the left—Miss Filmore said her brother had said to be sure to keep to the left of the fallen ash."

Freeing her sleeve, she plunged through the long dead grass and ferns. She had almost reached the shorter grass, which had been cropped by sheep, when there was a wrench upon her skirts and a bruising bang against her shins that brought her sprawling to the ground.

Kate, who was but a step or two behind her, screamed.

"What on earth—?" Janey began struggling to sit up and then her voice dwindled as she saw that what had snagged a great swathe of her skirts and brought her down was a gin trap.

She stared at the vicious iron jaws, the blood draining from her face, her mouth and throat going dry, and for a second she could not move for fear of the pain she expected to follow.

"It's a trap, miss, a mantrap," Kate said shakily. "Are you hurt, miss?"

Janey swallowed and forced herself to move her constricted legs. "No, I can feel the iron against my skin, but it is only my skirts it has caught, not my legs.''

''Oh, thank the Lord,'' said Kate, who had gone quite ashen. ''If it had been your leg—''

''Well, it wasn't,'' Janey said with determined brightness, knowing she had come within an inch of disaster. The trap, which had bitten through layers of woollen pelisse coat and gown and cotton petticoats, would have sliced just as easily through flesh and bone. ''Now, see if you can help me get it apart.''

The two of them wrestled in vain with the jaws of the rusty trap for several minutes.

''It's no good,'' Janey said breathlessly. ''We're just not strong enough to move it.''

''We're nearer to church than home. I'll get someone,'' Kate said, getting to her feet. ''I'll be quick as I can.''

''Thank you,'' Janey said, trying to shift herself into a more comfortable position upon the damp ground. ''But for the love of God, Kate, be careful where you step until you are on open ground, in case there are more of them.''

''Don't worry, miss, I will be,'' Kate assured her. ''My grandfather bled to death in one of these accursed things.''

''Sir! Sir!''

Jonathan's horse went up upon its hind legs as Kate, bonnet flying on strings, and shawl flapping like a goose's wings, threw herself over a stile and on to the bridle path along which he was riding with Lord Derwent, Lady Stalbridge and the Duchess of Sutton.

"What the devil are you playing at?" Jonathan snapped.

"It's Miss Hilton," Kate blurted out, her face almost as red as her hair from running. "She's caught in a trap, sir, a mantrap. We were walking—"

"What?" The blood left Jonathan's face. "Where?"

"Over the hill, sir, beyond those trees, but she's not—"

"Get help, Perry, the doctor—" Jonathan did not wait for the rest of Kate's explanation. Turning his horse's head, he backed it up against the other hedge that lined the narrow bridleway and then sent it forward in two bounding canter strides to jump the stile.

"While I go for Dr Hutton, can you find some men to get a hurdle or a gate?" Lord Derwent said to Lady Stalbridge and the Duchess as he kicked his horse forward.

"But she's not hurt, sir," Kate said, catching at his rein. "I was just about to tell him it was only her clothes that was caught. But the trap's so rusted we can't budge it."

"Thank God for that," Perry said with a sigh of relief, reining in again.

"Amen," said Lady Stalbridge with a smile as she watched Jonathan's grey galloping at full stretch across the field. "I think we'll leave him to it then, shall we, Derwent?"

"Perhaps we should go and offer assistance," the Duchess drawled.

"Oh, no, there is no need for the rest of us to miss church, I am sure," Lady Stalbridge said firmly. "Jonathan will manage well enough, I am certain."

"Yes, I dare say you are right," the Duchess agreed a little acidly as she stared after the galloping grey. "If he does not break his own neck in his haste to get to her."

The bright sunshine of the early morning had given way to ominous-looking dark clouds. Huddled into her dark green pelisse coat, Janey drew up her knees as far as her constricted skirts would allow. It was, she thought, as she wrapped her arms about herself and let her head rest upon her knees, the last time she would listen to one of Annabel's helpful suggestions.

The rapid drumming of a horse's hooves made her lift her head a few minutes later.

She barely had time to recognise the rider as Jonathan before he had flung himself down from the back of his blowing and sweating horse and was beside her.

"Janey! Where are you hurt?" He was breathless, frantic almost, as he stripped off his riding gloves and tall hat and flung them aside. "You must not move," he said as he knelt down next to her and she twisted to look at him.

"I'm not hurt," she said through chattering teeth. "It's just my skirts and petticoats that are caught."

"You're not hurt—" The breath left his lungs in an audible rush and the haggard look left his face. "Thank God! You do not know what has gone through my head these last few minutes. I was expecting to find you bleeding to death with your leg smashed."

"I'm just stuck, and cold," she said, feeling a flicker of happiness amid the numbness she had felt inside since the previous night as she saw the relief in his eyes and upon his face. He *had* cared for her a little, then, she thought. It had not all been pretence. "If you could get a branch or something, you can probably pry the jaws apart."

"Of course—here—" he stripped off his topcoat and put it about her shoulders "—I won't be long."

A few minutes later, after considerable effort on his part, she was free.

"Are you sure you are all right?" he asked as he helped her to her feet and drew her away from the gaping jaws of the trap.

"Perfectly—apart from a bruise or two," she said, pulling her hands out of his. "And just a little cold and wet. But the walk home will warm me soon enough. Please do not let me keep you longer from church."

"Don't be silly. You cannot possibly think I should let you walk back alone after this. Come here." He wrapped his top coat more closely about her shoulders, his hands lingering upon its edges as he drew it close under the small point of her chin. "I know you are angry with me, and with every reason. But can we not be friends again? I shall not deceive you again, not upon any subject."

"Friends?" Her voice quavered as his fingers brushed her jaw and they both went still for a moment. "I am not sure that is possible."

"No." His eyes darkened as her gaze met with his. "I suppose it would not be possible for you to forgive me for the wager?"

"No. And I understand the Duchess's husband is not expected to live more than a month," she said, after a short silence in which they stared at one another without moving.

"So people say." His hands lifted from the collar of the coat to cup her face.

"She is very beautiful," she said thickly as his head bent beneath the broad brim of her black straw hat, which was beginning to soften in the rain.

"Yes," he agreed as his mouth brushed over hers, featherlight.

"And you are still in love with her," she blurted desperately against his cheek, wishing she had the strength, the will to pull away.

"So people tell me," he murmured absently and kissed her again. A brief tender kiss that sent slivers of warmth through her chilled body.

"And she loves you," she said raggedly as his mouth lifted from hers and his hands dropped to her shoulders and then her waist, drawing her closer.

"Perhaps," he said slowly. "One can never tell with Susanna, she does not wear her heart upon her sleeve as you do."

"I don't!" she protested fiercely.

"I am afraid you do." He sighed softly. "Your feelings are always in your eyes—you'll never be able to play the game like Susanna and her kind."

"I know that!" Her face crumpled suddenly beneath his gaze and for want of anywhere else to hide it, she buried her head upon his shoulder. "I hate you!" she muttered against his waistcoat. "I wish I had never met you, never touched you—"

"Oh, Janey, what am I do with you...?" he groaned and held her closer, neither of them noticing as his top coat slid off her narrow shoulders to the ground.

Love me, she wanted to say. Love me as I could

so easily love you. But if she did, he would only
laugh at her, laugh at her as he had when she had
asked him to marry her.

"I am truly sorry about last night, Janey," he said
softly. "I did not mean to be so brutal with my con-
fessions. It was a shock seeing Susanna walk in
through the door—"

"I don't want to know. Take me home, please."
She lifted her head, the brim of her hat catching upon
his jaw as she did so. "Now."

"Only if you promise you will come to Southbrook
tomorrow?" he said, distentangling himself from the
hat and peering beneath its brim at her shadowed face.

"Anything. Just take me home, please."

Without another word he picked her up and carried
her over to his horse and lifted her on to the saddle.
After a considerable amount of wrestling with her
torn skirts and petticoats, which displayed rather more
than was seemly of her pantaloons, she seated herself
comfortably astride.

"Can you manage like that?" His brows lifted.

"I rode this way for the first sixteen years of my
life, Mr Lindsay. There are not many horses broken
to side-saddle on the frontier."

"I suppose not." He frowned as he glanced up at
the darkening sky. "I fear we are going to get rather
wet."

"If you get up behind me, we might be quicker,"
she suggested. "If you think your horse will survive
the double load."

"Oh, he'll stand it," he said with a half-laugh.
"Whether I will," he added a little raggedly as he
picked up his coat, "is another matter."

Janey did not understand quite what he meant until he swung up behind her. There was only just room for the two of them in the saddle. She could feel his rock-hard body behind her from shoulder to ankle, his chest against her back, the front of his thighs to the back of hers beneath her rucked-up skirts. They could scarcely have been closer if they had been spoons in a drawer.

"You'll have to take your hat off, or it will poke my eyes out," he said as he reached around her to pick up the reins and she remained utterly rigid and still.

"Oh, sorry." She lifted her hands to her head, and unpinned the hat from her hair, which promptly slid out of its heavy knot to tumble down her back. "Is that better?"

"Much," he said, shifting the reins into one hand and rearranging the back of her skirts to his satisfaction. "Comfortable?" he asked as he slipped his left arm loosely about her waist.

"Yes. Thank you." She tried to remain rigid, tried to hold herself away from him as the horse began to walk. But it was hopeless. Her body had a will of its own, seeming to soften and merge into his lean hardness with every stride of the horse.

"You have beautiful hair," he said after they had ridden in silence for a few minutes.

"Do I?" There was the faintest of tremors in her voice as she felt him rest his cheek against the back of her head. She wanted to turn. Turn and touch her lips to his skin, wanted it so much that it hurt physically.

"Yes. It is like silk—like your skin," he said

against her ear, the warmth of his breath making her skin prickle upon the nape of her neck. "And it smells of lavender," he said thickly a moment later.

"Does it?" She exhaled unevenly, her hands clenching upon the brim of her hat. "You had best be careful—the trap is there," she added in a rush.

"Yes," he said, as he steered the grey carefully past the mantrap. "You will not walk here again, will you?" he asked as he glanced down at the rusty metal and shuddered. "The damned things should be outlawed."

"Yes. I should not have come this way if Miss Filmore had not suggested it," she agreed numbly, wondering how it was that she could make conversation when she felt as if it was her heart that had been crushed in the savage jaws of the trap. Last night she had been so certain she despised him, so certain she could give him up. And now—now, as he held her close, she was utterly confused...

"Miss Filmore suggested it?" His voice was as grim as the expression upon his face as his arm tightened about her waist. "And no one objected? Surely Piers Filmore or his father must have known the keeper had set traps up here?"

"I doubt it. Neither Piers nor his father really take much interest in the running of the estate—" Her last word was a half-gasp as his hand slipped into the deep V-neck of her pelisse and his fingers fanned out over her ribs and she felt the warmth of his hand begin to seep through the fine wool of her gown.

"Don't they?" he said almost absently as his fingers began to stroke the soft undercurve of her breast. "According to Richard Hoare, who was your grandfather's banker, Piers has been taking a great deal of interest in the affairs of the estate, or at least the financial arrangements.''

''I think he still hopes I will marry him when I have been upon the shelf long enough,'' she answered breathlessly, her head tilting back against his shoulder as his fingers feathered upwards and he cupped her breast, circling its hardening tip with his thumb, sending ripple after ripple of liquid melting heat through her limbs.

''If he thinks you are likely to be left on the shelf, he's a fool, Janey,'' he whispered softly, his lips nuzzling aside a tress of hair and finding the little hollow behind her ear. ''But this is one accident too many. Something which I am going to make very clear indeed to Master Filmore and his father. And you, you are going to promise me that from now on you will take care never to be alone, never ride without checking your harness, and do not eat from any dish until someone else has...''

''I shall do more than that.'' Her voice quavered a little as he reinforced the instruction by biting softly into her throat. ''My father gave me a pair of sleeve pistols on my fifteenth birthday, I'll keep them with me—''

''Sleeve pistols?'' She heard the slight catch of his breath and then he laughed. ''You are a constant surprise, my love, do you know that?''

''I am not your love,'' she said raggedly as his lips kissed a path up the length of her neck to the point of her jawbone and her hat dropped unnoticed from her suddenly nerveless hands to be pulped beneath the grey's hooves. "That was clear enough last night."

"So clear that you asked me to marry you?"

"Like you said last night, we all make mis-takes." Her voice caught and rose as his finger and thumb tightened upon the hardened nipple of her breast.

He laughed softly as a shudder went through her. "Yes, I suppose we do. And I am beginning to think meeting you, Miss Hilton, was one of mine. My life was so much simpler before I saw you standing at that gate in the lane. I never used to think about anyone but myself."

"I have not noticed the change." She sighed, her eyes shutting as reality seemed to spiral down to the feel of his lips against her skin, the clever teasing caresses of his fingers.

"I saved Jem for you, did I not?" he murmured against her ear, nipping gently at its lobe.

"For the wrong reasons. It was to help you win your wager—wasn't it?" She struggled to hold on to reason.

"I lost the wager."

"Lost it?" The words were little more than a whisper. "But you got your kiss—"

"It wasn't just for a kiss," he said succinctly.

For a moment she didn't understand. And then realisation dawned. She jerked upright, her eyes wide open.

"The wager was to seduce me!" She gasped in disbelief. "Have you no—no shame—?"

"Not much." She did not need to see his face, she heard the smile in his voice. "About as much as you, I should say."

"You—you—" She twisted half around to try and strike him but, as her gaze caught and clashed with his, she was lost. She did not even try and move as his mouth captured hers, did not even notice that the grey had come to halt, or that the clouds broke, and the rain soaked them within seconds. There was nothing but this—nothing but the bittersweet knowledge that he still wanted her, and she wanted him, even if he did love his beautiful Duchess.

It was the restiveness of the horse that brought them both to the realisation of the stinging rain that was running down their faces, their necks, even between their lips.

"You are the wickedest man I know," she said breathlessly as he released her.

"Good," he said unconcernedly, pulling her back against him again as he sent the grey forward again into a canter. "Because I should hate to think what would happen to you if you met someone with fewer scruples than I."

"I cannot think he exists," she said with feeling. And then, after a minute or two, "Just out of curiosity, what would you have won if—?"

"The full brother of last year's Derby winner." He laughed. "And he's almost certain to win next year. Why the devil I had to be afflicted with a conscience that morning upon the downs, I really don't know."

"Are you sure it is not a temporary condition?" she asked, on some impulse which she did not entirely understand.

"If it was, we would not have passed that barn over there," he said grittily, taking the reins in both hands again and exhaling heavily.

"I don't see what conscience has to do with sheltering from the rain," she said with deadpan innocence.

"Janey, if you and I were alone in that barn, we would not be sheltering from the rain."

"No?" She smiled at the tightness in his voice.

"No. And the first time I make love to you, it is not going to be some rushed tumble in a barn," he said shortly.

"You are so sure of me?" she said with a slightly choked laugh.

"Yes. I knew you would be mine the first time I touched you. I've never wanted any woman as much as I want you."

"Not even your Duchess?" she said wearily as she leant into his body, and let her head tip back against his shoulder again, not caring about the rain falling upon her face.

"No. I wanted Susanna because every other man I knew did. That is how it began—the desire to compete and win. And then, after she jilted me, it was a matter of pride to win her back from her husband."

"And now?" she asked unsteadily, knowing her happiness hinged upon his answer.

"Now—I just don't know," he sighed. "For six years I have been sure that she was the only woman I really wanted—and then I met you. And since then, I have been sure of nothing. I can't promise you anything, Janey, not yet—"

"I have not asked you for any promises."

"Not in words, no," he said softly, holding her closer to him. "But you do with your eyes, Janey, every time you look at me."

"I cannot help it," she said, as she shut her eyes against the stinging rain.

"I know." He dropped a kiss at the corner of her eyelid. "No more than I can help wanting you."

They rode the rest of the way to Pettridges in silence.

"Will you come in and get dry?" she asked tentatively as he brought his horse to a halt, not wanting to part from him.

"No, I must be getting back to Southbrook. Several people stayed over after the ball."

"And the Duchess was one of them?"

"Yes," he said, after a fractional hesitation. "She was."

"Oh, I see."

"Do you?" He sighed as he swung down from the grey's back and lifted her after him. "I very much doubt it. I am not at all sure I understand it myself. And if you are wondering, she slept in the east wing, and I slept in the west."

"Oh."

"Oh," he mocked her softly.

"I had better go in," she said awkwardly as he let go of her waist.

"Yes." He gathered up his reins and put a foot in his near stirrup, and then turned to look at her again over his shoulder. "Janey—"

"What?"

"Nothing," he said, after a moment. "But will you promise me that for the next week or so you will not take unnecessary risks of any kind—nothing that would give anyone an opportunity to harm you? There are a great many desperate men who, given sufficient incentive, might be persuaded to strike at anything or anyone whom they blame for their condition.''

''I told you, none of the local men would hurt me.''

''They might not be local—'' he said soberly.

''If Captain Swing raises his head here, it will be because of landlords like Mr Filmore, not because of any outsiders.'' Janey sighed. ''But don't worry, I am not about to take up machine breaking, even if my sympathies lie with the labourers.''

''I am relieved to hear it.'' He laughed as he mounted the grey. ''You will come tomorrow, won't you?''

''Yes,'' she said simply, knowing that neither wild horses nor the Duchess of Sutton would keep her away.

''Miss, whatever have you been up to?'' Mary, the housemaid, greeted Janey in the hall.

''I had an accident with a gin trap,'' Janey said surveying her reflection ruefully in one of the hall mirrors. Wet, her hair was the colour of dark treacle, flowing down her back, and her eyes looked enormous and dark in her pale face. Her lips were swollen. She lifted a hand and touched them, caught for a moment in a memory that made warmth flow through her.

''A gin trap!'' Mary looked at her horrified. ''Are you all right?''

''Perfectly.'' Janey's smile widened. ''It was only my clothes that got damaged. Mr Lindsay came to my rescue and brought me home, but we got caught in the rain.''

''Oh,'' Mary said, in sudden understanding of the

dreamy look in Janey's eyes. "Shall I have a hot bath drawn for you, miss?"

"Please," Janey said, her thoughts still on Jonathan and what he had said about the Duchess. No promises, he had said, *yet*. Her dreams hung on that one little word.

"Miss?"

"Yes, Mary?"

"I don't know quite how to say this, but Will was wondering if you had had any success with Mr Lindsay?"

"Not yet," she replied slowly. "Ask him to persuade the others to be patient just a little longer."

"It's not going to be easy, miss," Mary said worriedly. "There's all sorts of wild rumours flying. They're even saying that men are going to be brought down from the mill towns in the Midlands to do the work at half the wages our lads were getting."

"I am sure that's not true." Janey shook her head. "Weavers will never make shepherds and stockmen. But I'm doing my best, Mary," she added with a slight wry smile. "I promise you that."

"So there you are, Jono," Susanna said as she swept into the library at Southbrook and found Jonathan sitting in what was becoming his favourite leather chair, with his slippered feet resting upon the fender, and the liver and white spaniel upon his lap. "I am beginning to think you are avoiding me." She smiled at him, her ringleted head tilted prettily.

"Oh, pray, don't get up," she said acidly after a moment in which he remained staring into the flames of the fire. "I can see the morning's little adventure of playing Sir Lancelot to your colonial friend has quite tired you out.''

''What?'' Jonathan started as Tess raised her head and gave a muffled possessive growl. ''Sorry, Susanna, I was miles away, wool gathering.''

''So I saw.'' Susanna sighed as she sat down in the opposite chair, and arranged the primrose yellow silk skirt of her gown gracefully. She frowned slightly as her gaze travelled from his tousled hair, to his loosely tied cravat, over his unbuttoned waistcoat and down to his slippered feet. ''You are becoming positively rusticated, Jono. You always used to be so well turned-out. That dog is moulting—''

''And you are as beautiful, as perfect as ever, Susanna,'' he interrupted her, letting his eyes travel slowly downwards from the immaculate glossy black ringlets to the gown that clung to her full breasts and narrow waist. ''I thought marriage to such an old man might have changed you, but he has not made so much as scratch upon you, has he? But then, perhaps you have left your mark upon him—you always were something of a cat when roused.''

''That's enough, Jonathan!'' The brunette got to her feet and strode to the fireplace. ''I endured your bitterness, your infantile attempt to make me jealous last night, because you were drunk—but now you do not even have that excuse!'' Her voice had dropped a tone, become husky as she leant upon the mantel. ''Do you wish to make me unhappy?'' There was the slightest of catches in her voice, a hint of a sob as she turned her head to glance at him over her shoulder with her slanted green eyes.

''Of course not.'' He sighed.

"Then come here, tell me so." She held out her arms to him.

"Susanna, you are married," he said wearily as he stood up and took her hands.

"That has never proved an obstacle to you before, has it?" She smiled at him archly.

"People change."

"I have not." She moved closer to him, looking up from beneath long black lashes. "And he does not care that we have been lovers—he never has, so long as we are discreet."

"No," he said succinctly, "you have not changed. But I have. I have wasted six years of my life, waiting for you to decide that you had made an error of judgement—and now I know that I was the one who made the error."

"But, Jono, he's ill—another month or two and I will be free! We can do all the things we had planned: go to Paris or Venice and live as man and wife until my year of mourning is up. Then we can come back here and marry—"

"Those were the things you planned," he said quietly. "I am not sure they were ever what I wanted."

"You want to marry me, don't you?" She pouted at him, then she laughed. "You know, I've never expected you to be a monk, Jonathan. Take the colonial girl to bed if it makes you happy, I shall not mind."

His hands tightened on her wrist. "That, Susanna, is exactly the problem. You really would not mind."

"Oh, so I suppose you would rather I flew into a jealous rage like your virginal colonial friend did last night?" She laughed again and would have come close against him if he had not kept her at arm's length.

"Yes," he said slowly, as he stared at her fashionably pale, discreetly powdered face, her darkened lips, and found himself remembering suddenly that Janey had freckles across the fine bridge of her nose and that her lips had tasted only of rain. And that when Janey looked at him, her eyes went soft and dark, not hard and glittering like two cut emeralds. "I think I would prefer that—then I might be able to believe that you actually cared for me once, Susanna." He released her wrists abruptly.

"You know I care for you—"

"But not enough to have my child—"

She went ashen. "How did you—?"

"Your husband wrote to me. He wanted me to know that it had been your decision alone to get rid of it, that he had not pressed you in any way. In fact, he would have been glad to acknowledge it as his heir. He thought I had a right to know—which is more, apparently, than you did!"

"It was the wrong time, Jono—I could not face the Season looking like a brood mare—we had Royalty to entertain."

"Spare me the excuses, Susanna. Please. I do not think there is any more to say upon the subject—you have said it all. My carriage is at your disposal, whenever you wish to use it. I am sure Lord Bath would be delighted to have your company, if you cannot bring yourself to do your duty by your sick husband."

"Jono—" the colour drained from Susanna's face "—are you sending me away?"

"I think that would be best, don't you?" he said

coldly. "Goodbye, Susanna. Please convey my wishes for his recovery to your husband, and my apologies. You have made fools of both of us."

"Brown," said Lord Derwent in a whisper, as the butler passed him in the hall carrying the tea tray, "that carriage, that was that—?"

"The Duchess of Sutton, m'lord," said Brown, his bland face impassive.

"And when is she expected back?" Lady Stalbridge asked with a lot less reticence.

"Not for a very long time—" Brown paused for maximum effect "—if ever, I should say, m'lady."

"Got rid of the hussy at last!" Lady Stalbridge gave Lord Derwent a slap upon the back which made Perry flinch. "Now all we have to do, Derwent, is find him a suitable wife. He cannot, of course, be allowed to marry that colonial Miss Nobody!"

Lord Derwent and Brown both made involuntary shushing noises. "The library door is open, my lady," Lord Derwent said urgently.

"So!" Lady Stalbridge continued at full volume. "My grandson knows that I should never permit him to marry trade, no matter how rich or pretty."

"She is not pretty, she is beautiful," Jonathan announced from the threshold of the library. "And I have no plans to marry anyone, Grandmother. Is that clear?"

"Absolutely, dear boy," Lady Stalbridge said, looking down her long hooked nose.

"I suppose you must be fretting to get back to Town?" Jonathan said hopefully. "Lord Stalbridge will be missing you, no doubt."

"Your grandfather will be at White's, swilling brandy and playing cards till dawn," his grandmother snorted. "I doubt he has even noticed my absence yet. And I have no immediate plans to return to Town, I rather like it here. It's so peaceful."

"Was," Jonathan muttered darkly beneath his breath.

"Might not be for long," Lord Derwent said after exchanging a glance with Jonathan. "The riots could well spread here, you know. Perhaps you would be better in Town."

"My dear boy, I was visiting a cousin at Versailles when it was stormed by the mob in '89, so you do not think a few ploughboys with too much cider in 'em are going to frighten me, do you?" Lady Stalbridge sighed heavily. "Oh, and by the way, Jonathan, I have invited Diana and her mother down for a few days. I knew Derwent would be pleased to see her. They'll arrive tomorrow."

"Diana—" Perry groaned. "She will expect me to propose."

"Then you had better start practising pretty speeches or running, hadn't you, boy," Lady Stalbridge said blithely. "Now, Jono, what've you got in the stables that I can ride? I want to have a better look at this place of yours now it's stopped raining again."

"I don't like this business of Miss Hilton and the Filmores," Lord Derwent said to Jonathan as they strolled along the row of loose boxes, looking at the horses after Lady Stalbridge had ridden off with one of the grooms. "The way they went on about Miss Hilton this morning at church, you'd have thought she threw herself into the trap on purpose. Not one of 'em showed an ounce of concern for her. And I almost got the impression they were disappointed she had survived it.''

"I do not like it either," Jonathan said, "but I have no firm evidence of any wrongdoing, Perry. Filmore seems to have stopped his intimations about her sanity since I warned him off. The girth, the trap can all be put down as accidents—"

"Like the collapse of the staircase in the Tower?" Perry's fair brows lifted. "Three accidents in the space of a year?"

"Yes," Jonathan frowned. "The first of which removed an inconvenient fiancé."

"But surely they would not risk murder? Not the Filmores—I mean, they are one of the old families, they have money and land enough of their own," Perry said.

"Not any more, according to Richard Hoare," Jonathan replied as he stroked the nose of a bay mare absently. "Apparently, old Filmore made some foolish investments and their Northumberland estate is mortgaged up to the hilt, and the young one has accumulated so many gambling debts, he dare not show his face in Town this Season."

"I see." Lord Derwent's frown increased as they walked on down the line of loose boxes. "So what will you do? Go to the local magistrate?"

"He's a friend of Filmore." Jonathan sighed and put out a hand to rub the nose of his grey as it whickered a greeting. "He'll not act without firm evidence."

"Mmm," Perry agreed, "I think the sooner we

look at that Tower the better. Have to do it on the
quiet, of course, since it's on Filmore's land.''

"Yes—perhaps next Sunday morning, while everyone is at church. I'll speak to Avery," Jonathan said.
"And in the meantime, I intend to spend as much
time in Miss Hilton's company as is possible. I want
to try and keep the Filmores late at the table tonight—
and then I'll press them to stay over. By the look of
it there should be more rain tonight, so they'll probably accept."

"Well, just make sure Miss Filmore's in the opposite wing to me," Perry said gloomily. "That
young woman frightens me, and as for her mother—"

"Oh, don't worry, Diana will see them off." Jonathan laughed.

"True." Perry brightened. "I suppose she should
be here soon. Wonder if she'll let me have a ride on
that new bay of hers?"

"Probably." Jonathan grinned at him. "I had the
distinct impression she bought it as a wedding gift for
you."

Chapter Twelve

As Janey walked into the drawing-room at Southbrook Jonathan, who had had his back to her, turned. She stood quite still as his gaze blazed over her, from the coronet of braids upon the top of her head, to her bronze silk slippers, and then came back to her face, knowing with some deep female instinct that he would come to her, that he could not stay away, any more than she could from him.

"Miss Hilton." He bowed over her hand, holding her fingers to his lips a moment longer than was strictly polite. "I hope you are quite recovered from your soaking?"

"From the soaking, yes," she said after a moment. "I trust you did not suffer any ill effects?"

"Nothing but a sleepless night. I could not stop thinking about what might have happened."

"I did not sleep well either," she said, a faint colour rising in her cheeks.

"Do I take it camomile tea was not entirely efficacious?" he drawled, his tone sending a flood of heat racing through her body. "We shall have to think of another remedy."

"I have always thought camomile tea quite sufficient for unmarried women," Lady Stalbridge said drily from behind Janey's shoulder. "Now, my dear, do tell me where you got that bronze taffeta. It suits you so well—and I wish to make a present of a dress length to a niece who is fair like you."

It was only then that Janey realised Jonathan still had hold of her hand, and that the others were all staring at them. Hastily she pulled her fingers out of his and turned in a rustle of tawny silk to meet Lady Stalbridge's amused bright blue gaze

"She's gone," said Lady Stalbridge succinctly, correctly interrupting Janey's surreptitious glance about the drawing-room as they made polite conversation about dress lengths. "He sent her packing yesterday afternoon."

Janey did not even try to pretend she did not know what the old lady was talking about. "He sent the Duchess away," she said slowly, her gaze flicking to Jonathan, who was greeting Mrs Filmore and Annabel politely.

"For ever, I think," Lady Stalbridge said happily.

"For ever," Janey echoed as Jonathan looked up and smiled at her.

"Thought that piece of news would bring some colour to your face." Lady Stalbridge chuckled.

"Ah—you haven't met Lady Diana Patterson, have you?" she said as a chestnut-haired young woman, who was a little taller than Janey, strode into the room, a pair of fluffy grey puppies with enormous feet gambolling at her heels. Heels which Janey could not quite help noticing appeared to be somewhat incongruously encased in riding boots beneath the elegant blue silk gown.

''Knew I'd forgotten something,'' Lady Diana said unconcernedly as she caught the direction of Janey's stare. ''Mama will have a fit. She was cross enough that I was late—I was trying to get Perry to use his legs properly on the bay—he's the laziest rider I know—''

''Lady Diana—Miss Hilton.'' Lady Stalbridge made the introductions with a slight sigh, and then turned away, muttering something about being born in a stable, to answer an enquiry from Mrs Filmore.

''So, you're Miss Hilton. Perry wrote me all about you, says you'd have us all in a tumbril given half a chance.'' Lady Diana grinned at Janey. ''Can't say I'd blame you. Oh—bad boy!'' She tugged the hem of her gown out of one of the puppies' mouths, which then promptly turned its attention to the flounce on Janey's skirt.

''Just clout him if he's too much of a nuisance,'' Lady Diana said blithely as Janey bent to disengage her skirt from the puppy's jaws.

''I trust you were referring to the puppy,'' Jonathan said, as Janey straightened, holding the squirming puppy in her arms.

She smiled, feeling that instant jolt of her heart, her body that she had come to expect whenever he was close to her.

''Give the beast to me.'' He took the puppy from her, his hand brushing the softness of her breasts as he did so, sending desire shearing through her with such force that she paled.

"Depends on who's being the nuisance, Jono."
Lady Diana's brown eyes sparkled as she glanced
from Jonathan to Janey. "From what Derwent told
me, Miss Hilton should set about you with a horse-
whip. Where is he, by the way? Hiding again, I suppose?"

"No," said Lord Derwent huffily from behind her.
"Good evening, Lady Diana."

"Derwent." Lady Diana's glossy chestnut head
was inclined in a careless nod. "I'd be really grateful
if we could get this marriage nonsense out of the way.
There's a sale on at Tattersall's at the end of the week
that I really want to go to and Mama's not going to
let me go back to Town until you've proposed."

"Tiresome of her," Perry replied. "What's in the
sale?"

"Russell's greys and that bay of Wellesley's."

"Begad! Wouldn't mind that myself. I'll come
with you—if you'd like me to, that is?"

"Course I would, idiot." Lady Diana sighed.
"Now, are you going to marry me, Perry?"

"Yes."

"Good," said Diana briskly. "Let's go and tell
Mama, shall we?"

"You really mean it?" Lord Derwent's face lit.

"Come on," Jonathan said shortly to Janey, who
was feeling somewhat embarrassed at being witness
to what should, she felt, have been a rather more private moment. And more than a little envious of Diana's easy confidence. "Help me get these damned
dogs shut up, before their mother comes looking for
them. Here, you take this one."

"Their mother?" Her brows arched in enquiry.

"Diana's blasted wolfhound," Jonathan explained as he steered Janey out of the drawing-room with his free hand. "It's the size of a small horse and she takes it everywhere with her—ah—Brown, take these up to Lady Diana's room, will you?"

Taking the other puppy from Janey, he dumped the writhing pair unceremoniously in the unimpressed Brown's arms.

"I rather like Lady Diana," Janey said as Brown carried the puppies away, his stiff back expressing the measure of his disapproval.

"Diana?" He smiled as, after a glance over his shoulder into the drawing-room, he drew her to one side of the door. "Yes, I thought you would like her. She's another woman who does and says exactly what she wishes."

"Do you think I do?" she said in surprise.

"Yes," he said, lifting a hand and smoothing a stray golden ringlet back into place upon her temple. "For instance, just now, you have decided that you want to kiss me."

"Have I?" Her mouth curved upwards at the corners and her heartbeat quickened.

"Yes," he said as he put a hand upon her waist.

"Someone might see us," she said as she tilted her face up to his.

"I don't care," he said as their lips met. "I do not care about anything but you..."

And neither do I, neither do I, Janey thought as she opened her mouth to his kiss and let her fingers slide into his silky black hair, holding him to her. The Duchess had gone and he was hers, at least for a little while and just maybe, for ever.

"Ahem!" It was a loud cough from Brown which brought them jerking apart some minutes later. "Sir, there is a Captain Crowne requesting to see you and the other gentlemen. Apparently, the Yeomanry is to be called out—they fear another riot at Bourton Farm, on the Zeals road."

"Oh, no," said Janey, a cold sense of dread sweeping over her.

"Show him into the drawing-room," Jonathan said brusquely, and then, taking Janey's arm, his voice softened. "Come on, Miss Hilton, let us find out what your precious labourers are up to."

"You may have your dinner, gentlemen, and there is no cause for alarm ladies," Captain Crowne assured them a few minutes later as he stood beside the drawing-room fire, a glass of claret in his hand. "The mob will take an hour or so to collect and another hour or two to walk the distance—"

"Then why do you not intervene now and prevent them from going?" Janey asked sharply.

"Because we want to catch them in the act and make an example, Miss Hilton."

"Like you did at Pyt House, I suppose!" Janey said, ignoring the warning touch of Jonathan's fingertips upon her bare shoulder as he leant upon the back of the yellow silk sofa where she sat next to Lady Diana.

"Exactly! Give them a taste of a sabre and shot," Captain Crowne said, smiling at her, oblivious to her disapproval. "And take a few prisoners, of course, so they can be tried and properly punished. Then we should not get any more trouble in the district. And with luck there'll be a few less mouths for the parish to feed, what!" He laughed and looked about him, as if expecting approbation.

"Here, here," intoned Mr Filmore.

"Sabres and muskets seems a bit much," put in Lady Diana. "I'd have thought a few cracks of a hunting whip would send 'em home fast enough. It's not as if they're likely to be armed, is it? And half the ones I've seen about here don't look as if they've the strength to be much trouble."

"And exactly where has this mob come from?" Piers asked.

"All about, the Knoyles, Mere, Semley, even, I believe, some disaffected men from your own estate, Mr Filmore."

"My estate," Janey muttered.

"Yes," Piers sneered at her. "And now you see what gratitude you get for your cosseting of them."

Janey ignored him, her attention focused upon Captain Crowne. "You seem very well informed about their intentions, Captain. How do you know that it is not a peaceable protest?"

"Men do not go about peaceable protest upon an autumn midnight, Miss Hilton," Captain Crowne replied. "Now, you ladies must not worry your pretty heads about it. It will all be sorted out by morning."

"You mean that men might be dead and injured by morning," Janey retorted. "Something which you could prevent if you wished it!"

"Dead!" Mrs Filmore groaned. "I do believe I feel quite faint. We could all be murdered in our beds."

"I doubt it," Lady Stalbridge muttered derisively.

"Time to start worrying when they set up the guillotine upon the village green."

"Quite." Captain Crowne tossed off the rest of his wine. "So, I can count upon all of you gentlemen? I know you and Lord Derwent are not members of the militia, Mr Lindsay, but may I count upon your assistance?"

"Of course. Be good to do a bit of sabre rattling again, won't it, Jono?" Lord Derwent said cheerfully.

"Yes," Jonathan agreed after a moment's hesitation. "Eleven o'clock at the Red Lion, you say?"

"Yes, we do not want them to know we are aware of their intentions," Captain Crowne said. "They should be well on their way by then."

"How could you?" Janey said to Jonathan furiously, as he led her in to dine a few minutes later. "How could you agree to be part of it? They are planning to send soldiers against men who have at most fired a rick or broken a machine—in all the riots in Hampshire, not one farmer or landowner has been touched, only property—can property really be worth more than lives?"

"In the eyes of the law, yes. In mine, no," he replied tersely. "Which is why I agreed, because if I am there, there is just a chance I might persuade them to avoid bloodshed. Though I don't hold out much hope," he said grimly, "not with hotheads like Crowne in charge. There are moments when I wish old Boney was still about—he'd have blunted that young man's ardour for killing."

"I'm sorry," she said. "It is just that it makes me so angry because it is all so unnecessary. If people were just a little less greedy, less bent upon imposing progress on others at any cost—"

"You cannot turn back the clock." He sighed as he pulled out her chair for her. "The machines are here to stay, Janey. For every one that is broken, another ten will be made because there is money in it. Money for the manufacturers, money saved by the farmers."

"I know," she said bleakly. "But, at the very least, the poor relief should be increased while men look for other work."

"Speaking of which," he said as he sat down beside her, "I am thinking of restoring the old cotton mill at the edge of the estate.

"Hincks Mill?" She gave him a puzzled look. "There is no money in cotton at present."

"I'm going to convert it for silk. I understand there is a healthy market for ribbons. Miss Filmore alone should keep it going for a decade."

She smiled, knowing he was making an effort to lift her spirits.

"You have decided to stay at Southbrook?"

"Yes. I intend to start taking on men next week. I wish now I had made the decision earlier. It might have prevented some of your people from being dragged into this affair tonight."

"There has to be some way to stop it," she said, sighing. "There have been riots and protests since October. You would have thought the government would have stepped in by now with a solution."

"The government has only one thing upon its mind and that is political reform. They are desperate to get the landowners upon their side at present and will do nothing to offend them.''

''I wish they would put as much effort into reforming the poor law,'' she said bitterly. ''Representation for Birmingham will not feed men this winter!''

''No, but it might in time,'' he said. ''The broader the representation, the more likely it is that the dominance of the landowners in Parliament will come to an end and there will be better conditions for both labourers and factory workers.''

''But it will be too late.'' She bit her lip.

''It might not turn out as badly as you think.''

''You don't believe that, do you?'' she said as she looked at him.

''No,'' he said after a moment. ''I think it is going to be a unpleasant mess and people on both sides are likely to get hurt.''

''You will take care,'' Janey said later that evening as she stood upon the lantern-lit steps of Southbrook House, waiting for the carriage to be brought round.

''Don't worry.'' Jonathan smiled at her as he adjusted his sword belt. ''I can't think the Almighty let me survive Waterloo to meet my doom in a rural brawl.''

''I suppose not.'' She tried to smile back, but it did not reach her eyes.

''And you—I should have been happier if your party had agreed to stay here the night,'' he said softly. ''You will make sure all the doors at Pettridges are locked and tell your horseman to keep watch at the stables.''

"Yes," she said, "but I cannot think they will come there."

"Promise," he said sternly. "You can never be sure what a mob will do."

"I promise I will see that all the doors are locked and the stables have a watchman," she said, thinking that it was not a lie. She would see to it that all the doors were locked, it was just that she did not intend to be inside Pettridges Hall once they were.

The long case clock in the hall of Pettridges struck eleven as the door was opened to them.

"I think I shall take a glass of madeira before I retire," Mrs Filmore said. "It will help me sleep."

"I will join you, Mama," Annabel said, following her mother into the drawing room. "Did you see what Lady Diana was wearing upon her feet! I think she is as crack-pated as Jane."

Janey exhaled with relief that they had not invited her to join them. Picking up her skirts, she sped up the stairs to her bedchamber.

Kate, sitting in a chair beside the fire with mending in her lap, started and got to her feet as Janey entered.

"You need not have waited up," Janey said. "Go to bed, Kate, you look tired."

"I could not sleep, miss. It's my father, I am so afraid he will get into trouble, miss." Kate's good-natured face crumpled.

"Has he gone to Bourton House Farm?" Janey asked.

"Yes. How did you know, miss?" Kate said in alarm. "It is supposed to be a secret."

"It's about as secret as the names of Harriet Wilson's lovers!'' Janey said tersely. ''Help me off with this, Kate, then find me my old riding clothes I brought with me from America.''

''What are you going to do, miss?'' Kate said as she helped with the hooks of the bronze gown.

''I don't know,'' Janey said. ''But I have to try and do something.''

Within a few minutes she was in the stables, dressed in a jacket and divided skirt of soft brushed leather, supple as cloth from much use. Snatching up a stable boy's discarded cap, she stuffed the long heavy braid of her hair into it, and led out Mr Filmore's fastest chaser.

''Here, you!'' She heard Iggleston's shout as she leapt from mounting block to saddle. There was no time to stop and explain, not if she was to get to Bourton House before the Yeomanry. She brought her legs against the chaser's side and sent it flying forward out of the yard.

''Stop!'' Iggleston's angry voice followed her. Janey ignored him, and uttered a small prayer of thanks that there was a full moon that lit the ground almost as well as daylight as she galloped across the park, bent low upon the chaser's neck. ''I hope you can jump,'' she muttered as they came up to the first hedge.

The horse steadied itself, and soared over, and she breathed a sigh of relief. To go at this speed in this light was dangerous enough on a good horse, but on a bad one it would have been suicidal.

Field after field, hedge, ditch, wall passed in a silvery blur as she concentrated simply on keeping the chaser going as fast as was possible. For the last stretch, she risked taking the road, aware all the time of the distant drumming of the hooves of the Yeomanry clattering behind her.

At the entrance to the yard of the home farm, she reined in, slipped off the chaser's back and tethered it to the gatepost. No one noticed her arrival. The yard was packed with men, just as it had been at Pyt House. A heaving, murmuring mass of men, carrying staves, hammers and torches, whose faces were fierce and haggard in the flickering light of torches and lanterns.

Their attention was focused upon the men at the front, who were in heated discussion with the men who worked the Bourton House Farm and the tenant farmer, Mr Coward, who by the sound of it had no intention of making any concessions at all to the labourers.

Glancing about her, Janey could not see a single face she recognised. And for the first time, she felt afraid. A physical fear that made her want to turn and run. But she couldn't. She had to at least warn them that the Yeomanry were coming.

If she could only reach their leaders or find Will or one of the others she knew—tentatively, she began to push her way through the crowd. By the time she had lost her cap, been pushed back, and jostled roughly out of the way a dozen times, she knew it was hopeless. She was never going to get to the men at the front in time. A dark-haired man beside her frowned at her as she was caught in a pool of light from a lantern he carried. "Be off with you, lass, this be no place for women——'' He broke off, staring at her. ''Miss Hilton! What the devil do you be doing here?''

''John!'' She recognised Will Avery's brother, the village cobbler, with a flood of relief, knowing he was an intelligent, level-headed man like his brother. ''The Yeomanry cavalry from Hindon are coming——'' she blurted out. ''They will be here in minutes and are intent upon using force.''

''The Yeomanry——'' John repeated and then swore.

''Perhaps soldiers, too, from Warminster,'' Janey said despairingly. ''Listen. You can hear the hooves——''

''God save us! Get up there!'' Picking her up in his great hands, he boosted her halfway up the side of one of the tall haystacks. Janey scrabbled and clawed her way over its sloping top to crouch at its summit. A moment later John was beside her, standing up, his feet planted firmly apart as if he stood upon solid ground. Silhouetted against the great silver disc of the moon, he cupped his hands to his mouth.

''Lads! Run, lads, run——the Yeomanry's out for blood again,'' he shouted. Faces began to turn, to look up and there was a growing murmur of anger, alarm. ''Get out of here! Spread out, lads!''

There was a single crack like a whip, John's hands dropped suddenly from his face, reached out in an odd helpless gesture, and then he pitched forward liked a felled oak. He rolled once, twice, down the face of the stack and then plummeted to the ground. His body made a dull sickening thud as it crashed upon the cobbles, face down.

''No...'' The moan came from Janey's mouth without her even being aware she had uttered it. "Oh, no!"

For a fraction of a second there was absolute silence, a silence that was broken by the hiss of steel being drawn and an agonised bellow of fear and rage from the men in the yard. And then all was chaos. Crouched at the top of the stack, Janey could not bring herself to look as shouts and screams and the sound of musket fire filled the air.

She did not know how long she lay with her body pressed against the hay, her eyes shut—seconds? Minutes? She could not tell, or when she first realised something was burning.

She opened her eyes and lifted her head. Showers of red and orange sparks were shooting upwards into the star-studded blackness of the sky. And then, with a surge of panic, she realised the rick had been set alight.

She scrambled to her feet, coughing as the smoke bit into her lungs. She had to get down and quickly. She turned from one side to the other, seeking an escape, but the rick was ringed with flames now, crackling, roaring flames that leapt hungrily upwards.

It was some instinct, rather than hearing her scream, that made Jonathan look upward. Not believing what he saw, he rubbed his eyes with the back of his wrist, and then looked again at the blazing rick of hay.

And then he was running, running, pushing men aside, dodging horses and panic-stricken oxen alike. Snatching up a bill hook, he scrambled up a short ladder propped against the nearest rick to the one in flames.

Anchoring himself with one hand with the bill hook, he edged as near to the edge of the stack as he dared.

Janey didn't see him. She had lost him in the crowd and was turning helplessly, looking for a way down through the rising ring of flame. She would have to jump, jump onto the cobbles some twenty feet below—

"Janey!"

His shout brought her to a halt. She could barely discern his tall dark shape beyond the wall of flame leaping up before her eyes.

"Janey! You will have to jump across!"

"I can't," she sobbed hoarsely, "it's too far—too hot—"

"It isn't! I'll catch you! *Come on!*" he roared hoarsely as she hesitated. "I'll catch you! Jump! Janey!"

It was the anguish in his voice as he screamed her name that cut through her terror; she gathered herself, took one running stride into the flames, and flung herself towards his outstretched hands.

She landed, her body half on the sloping roof of the other rick. She was slipping, slipping down into nothing... She opened her mouth to scream and then she felt the back of her buckskin jacket caught, and he was hauling her up by sheer brute strength. And then his arm was around her, holding her so tightly she thought her ribs would crack.

His feet slipped suddenly and, with an oath, he threw himself backwards upon the slope of hay, taking her with him. Grabbing the bill hook with his free hand, he arrested their downward slide.

For several seconds she lay with her head against his chest, aware of nothing but the vital, thudding beat of his heart beneath her. Aware, only, that she was safe and that she loved him. Loved him more than anything, more than life, more than she feared fire or death.

"Janey," he said raggedly, breathlessly, as he struggled into a sitting position. "We must move, this one will go next—come on."

Somehow, with the aid of the bill hook and his sheer strength, they slithered and scrambled down the steep sides of the rick until they reached the top of the short ladder.

He caught as her as she almost fell off the last rung.

"Janey! Are you all right?" he demanded as he hugged her close.

"Yes," she lied. She felt sick and dizzy as she stared down at John's body, which lay horribly still at the base of the burning stack.

"He's dead—"

"Yes," he said bleakly. "There is nothing we can do for him or half a dozen others, I fear. Come on— let us get away from here before anyone sees you. If Filmore sees you here like this, that will be all the evidence he needs to suggest that you are not fit to take control of your own affairs."

He did not wait to say more, but ran across the yard, dragging her after him.

"Sir! Sir!" A lad of about fourteen accosted them, tears streaming down his smoke-darkened face. "Please help me, sir, *please.*"

"Jake? What is it?" Janey recognised him as Mr Coward's ploughboy.

"It's the horses—Old Bess and Cassie and the rest of the team, they're in the barn and it's on fire and they won't come out. I've got to get them out, sir—Mr Coward's getting the cattle out of the byre."

"Show me," Jonathan said.

Jake pointed to a long, low, brick building whose roof was alight at one end, sending sparks shooting up into the star-studded blackness of the sky.

"Janey—get on my horse and stay out of trouble," Jonathan said brusquely. "Jake, you come with me."

Janey watched him run across the yard, stripping off his coat as he sped towards the open barn doors from which smoke was already billowing.

Then taking off her jacket, she followed. The barn roof was alight, the beams blazing, and the smoke so dense it was almost impossible to see.

It was only the shrill screaming of the terrified horses that gave her the courage to go into the barn at all. She took a deep breath of the harsh night air and headed for the stalls, guided by the sound of stamping hooves and Jonathan's voice as he urged the horses out of their stalls.

A huge black shire came cantering out of the smoke, almost running her down, then another. Then she saw Jonathan, coughing, gagging, as he half-led, half-dragged out two more, their great heads blind-folded with his coat and shirt.

"Take these and get out of here!" he gasped at her. "I'll help Jake with the others."

She did as he said, thrusting her coat into his hands and grabbing the halters of the horses he held.

Somehow, by dint of bullying and coaxing, she got them to the door, where they needed no urging to get away from the barn, and jerked out of her hold to go careering across the yard and jump the gate like hunters, scattering men before them.

A moment later two more horses surged out, then Jake, his feet hardly touching the ground as the two horses he was leading reared and plunged, desperate to escape the crackling, roaring blaze behind them.

"Mr Lindsay," she said to Jake, her heart turning to ice, "where is he?"

"Went back for the missus's cob and the donkey," Jake spluttered.

"Jonathan—no!" Her voice was a cracked whisper, not a scream, as she heard the crash of a beam falling, and half the roof fell in with an explosion of flame.

But then, a second later, out of the rolling clouds of smoke, she saw him leading a fat grey cob in one hand, a small, ancient-looking donkey in the other.

She ran to him, dodging the milling men, cattle and oxen that surged this way and that about the yard.

"I thought you were dead! If you ever do that to me again," she croaked at him from her hoarse throat as she skidded to a halt in front of him, "I will—I will—"

"Do what?" he rasped back as he released his charges. "Shake me until my teeth rattle? That's exactly what I wanted to do to you when I saw you on that rick and then in that barn! Now perhaps you know how I feel when you persist in putting yourself in danger!"

The anger drained from her as she stared at him. She had not realised until this moment that he cared for her so much.

"I am sorry," she whispered and put her arms about his neck, and kissed his smoke-blackened cheek. "I will not be so foolish again."

"Neither will I," he growled as his arms closed about her and brought her close against his bare chest. "I think I must be going insane, risking my life for a donkey, of all things. And it's your fault! A month or so ago I had a very well-ordered life. Morning calls, cards, the odd wager—never risking as much as a finger for anyone but myself and now—since I have met you—"

"I have caused you nothing but trouble," she murmured as she rested her head against his shoulder, and luxuriated in his warmth, his strength. He was like a rock, she thought, her own particular rock in the midst of the swirling, milling maelstrom about them.

"Exactly." He sighed and touched his lips to her smoky hair. "But since you have the ill judgement to love me, I might forgive you."

She went still. What point was there in denying it, when it was true?

"Come on," he said softly. "We're going home before we freeze to death and someone recognises you. Where the devil's my horse?"

Ten minutes later they were both up upon the grey, careering out of the mêlée away from the flames into the cool, welcome darkness.

"The horse I came on—" she began as they passed the gate where the chaser had been tethered but was no longer.

"Leave it, it is probably upon its way home by now."

"I will not be able to get in for some hours," she

said. "Mrs Filmore has the place locked up like a fortress—I shall have to wait for the kitchen maid to open the back door."

"Then you had better come to Southbrook," he said after a fractional hesitation. "I am beginning to think that some fates cannot be avoided..."

Neither of them spoke again on the long cold ride back to Southbrook.

But she could feel the tension, the anticipation growing between them with each step of the grey, each contact between his smoky skin and the thin silk of her habit shirt.

"You could have been killed tonight—" he said as he lifted her down off the grey before Southbrook House.

"So might you." She swayed forward, letting her forehead drop against his bare chest. He smelt of smoke and sweat, a quintessential male scent that made her want to put her lips to his cool, chilled skin.

His grip upon her shoulders softened and slid down to her elbows.

"You must be cold," she said after a moment of utter stillness.

"Not when you touch me..." He breathed against her smoky hair. "Never when you touch me—"

He caught her up suddenly in his arms, and she let her head fall against his shoulder as he carried her up the shallow white stone steps to the tall double doors. They would become lovers. It was inevitable...had been inevitable from the first moment they had touched.

The knowledge was there in the wide dark eyes of her reflection as they entered the candlelit hall and were greeted by their images, mirrored in the great gilt framed glasses which adorned the walls. And it was in his face, dark with smoke as he looked down at her, before his eyes too lifted to their entwined image in the glass.

"Zeus! Look at us. We look like savages!"

"Yes." She stared at their reflection. There was something astonishingly intimate about seeing herself held in his bare arms, her smoke-darkened hair rippling over his shoulder. She had not realised until this moment quite how muscled his body was, how different to her own.

"If I was an honourable man, I should wake my grandmother and put you into her care," he said slowly.

"And I suppose if I were a perfect lady, I should demand that you do exactly that," she replied, a half-smile curving her mouth.

"Are you going to?" His eyes were almost as dark as the smoke that stained his face as he held her gaze in the glass.

"No." Her quiet monosyllable seemed to echo to the very ceiling of the marble-lined hall.

He smiled. A slow, tender smile as he looked down into her eyes.

"You're determined to ruin my reputation, aren't you, Miss Hilton?"

"Yes." She smiled back at him.

Shifting her weight in his arms, he carried her across the hall and up the two flights of blue-carpeted stairs, and into his dressing room, where he set her down gently upon a couch and picked up a folded rug from its foot and wrapped it around her. Picking up a bottle of brandy from the table beside her, he poured it into a glass and handed it to her.

"Drink it, you look exhausted," he said as he pulled open an oak closet and took out a shirt and coat. Then, catching the surprised glance she gave him, he smiled. "My horse—I can't leave him standing, much as I should like to—" he added, as he bent and kissed her briefly upon the mouth. "I won't be long, I promise you."

He was right. She was exhausted. The hectic ride across country, the horror of the scene in the farmyard, had left her utterly drained. She sipped her brandy, staring into the embers of the fire. It was shock, she supposed, that made the horrifying images of the night hover at the corners of her mind, refusing to be clarified, or put in any order. The only thing that she could remember with clarity was Jonathan's hands reaching out to her upon the other side of the flames. The note in his voice when he had shouted her name, the relief as his arms had closed around her—and the moment when she thought the roof of the barn had collapsed upon him. She had never been so afraid in her life, not even in the Tower—

It was on that thought that her eyes closed and the brandy glass tilted in her hand.

Chapter Thirteen

The dream began as it always did, with her walking along the track which led to the Tower at sunset. The sky was red and orange, vivid as flame behind the black bulk of the Tower. She did not want to go any further, did not want to go into the darkness of the Tower, but her feet kept rising and falling on the muddy, rutted track, carrying her up the hill, past Will Avery leading a plough team down to the village and his forge.

She stared at him, stared at the great grey horses, their manes and tails rippling in the breeze like seafoam. Help me, she wanted to say, but her mouth would not open, her tongue would not work. She could only walk. On and on, up the hill.

And then he was gone and there was her grandfather, standing beside the folly. He smiled at her and said something. Something she could not hear, but she knew he was wishing her luck for her wedding on the morrow. Except that he could not be there, because he was dead. He had died the week after her engagement was announced. She knew that, and yet she reached out to him, begging him for help. But then he was gone and her hand found only the door of the Tower.

The iron key was cold in her hand as she turned it in the lock. The door swung inward, pulling her into the near-total darkness. She felt for the wall; it was cool and damp beneath her hand as she began to climb, keeping her hand upon it as the staircase spiralled up and up, seeming to go on forever. And then at last she was at the top door; she pushed it and stepped out on to the top of the Tower.

And there was all Pettridges spread out before her: field after field, some ploughed, some fallow; the sweep of the woods, the trees turned to fire by the last rays of the setting sun; a sprinkling of cottages and a network of lanes, like silver ribbons leading away to the gentle slopes of the downs which nestled along the horizon like sleeping dogs.

It was beautiful. It was hers. And it did nothing to lift the weight from her heart, nothing to stop the cold creeping fear that swept over her even as the November mist rolled in and blotted out the horizon, rolled over her wet and cold. She could not see. She could only hear the voices.

Edward's voice and *hers*...laughing, murmuring, in the mist. She had to see, she had to—she leant over the parapet. They were there at the base of the Tower.

Edward. Edward in his sombre black coat and wide-brimmed hat. Edward, who had said he loved her. Edward and a woman, heavily cloaked, but so dreadfully familiar. She watched, her stomach churning as he embraced the woman passionately and she knew in an instant that he had never cared for her as he did this woman, never—it had all been lies.

Edward! She shouted but there was no sound. But he looked up. She saw his face contort with horror as she snatched off the pearl ring he had given her and sent it spinning and glittering down to the feet of the hooded woman.

"No!" His shout echoed all around her as she turned away and sought the door that led back into the Tower. It would not open. She tugged and tugged but it would not open. She could hear Edward's footsteps on the flagged floor of the tower, hear his frantic shouts.

"Jane! What are you doing here? Stay there!" His shouts echoed through the Tower as the door suddenly gave.

"Jane! *Stay there!*" He was almost screaming as she stepped on to the landing and put her hand upon the banister rail and looked down. He was staring up at her—his hands lifted as if in supplication, his face white in the last rays of the sun that arrowed through the open door.

"No!" he screamed.

And her scream merged with his, as the entire landing seemed suddenly to give way and she went plummeting down into the stairwell. Something hit her head, her leg and then there was such a jerk to her body that she thought she had hit the ground. Why wasn't she dead? She opened her eyes, not understanding.

And then she realised—what had seemed eternity had been no more than a split second. Her skirts had caught upon a broken creaking timber, slowing her fall, and she was hanging over another jagged timber like a rag doll. Edward was spreadeagled upon the floor below, pinned to the flagged floor by a vast oak beam, as neatly as one of the butterflies that he so liked to collect was fastened to a board.

He was dead. She knew that instinctively. And she did not care. She could not feel anything except terror of the void beneath her. She could not even scream for help as she watched the woman bend over him, pull off her gloves and throw to one side as she shook him in a frantic, useless attempt to rouse him.

She had been right, she thought dully. It was her. She knew it even before the woman finally lifted her head, her hood falling back from her silly, pretty face, which was contorted with rage. Rage, not grief.

"Help me." The words were a whisper, as the blood trickled from the wound on her head into her mouth, and the numbness in her leg gave way to agonising pain.

"Why?" The woman's voice sliced upwards like a blade. "Why did you have to come today and not Sunday? You have ruined everything! You always do!"

And then she was gone and the door was slammed, leaving her in the darkness.

The empty darkness in which there was no noise but the creak of the timber.

The timber beneath her waist gave suddenly and fell with a bang and she jerked down, only to be stopped at the extent of her skirts, hanging like a puppet from a string.

It was then that she screamed. And screamed until she was hoarse and no sound came from her throat.

Today, not Sunday. Why did that matter? How long before the fabric in her skirt tore? How long before someone would look for her? Today, not Sunday? The questions turned in her pain-clouded mind as she hung over the void. Her head hurt, her leg hurt. She did not want to think. She dare not think about the creaking beam, or the thinness of the fabrics that made up her skirt and petticoats, or the unforgiving flagged floor so many feet below.

Today, not Sunday—the words revolved in her mind like a windmill. And then the answer came with bleak clarity as she drifted on the edge of consciousness. By Sunday she would have been Edward's wife—and he would have inherited everything. Edward had known the stairs were unsafe. Edward had known she came here every Sunday. He had meant her to die—all the time, he had meant her to die, and so had *she*.

She had always known inside that Edward had not loved her, known that *she* had despised her, but to think they had meant to kill her was like taking a step into an abyss. She shut her eyes, retreating into inner darkness. A darkness that was punctuated by men's shouts, and shearing pain. And then there was Will's kindly face, telling her she would be all right, and Piers saying she was a damned fool.

And then she was in her room, Kate fussing over her, ashen-faced, and then Kate was gone, and it was Annabel bending over her, smiling—offering a spoon—a spoon that Piers dashed out of Annabel's hand, his face scarlet with rage.

"Janey—Janey!"

She opened her eyes to find Jonathan kneeling beside her. "You were having a nightmare."

"Was I?" The dream had gone, back to the edges of her mind where she could not quite reach it.

"About the riot?" he asked softly, as he picked up the empty brandy glass that had fallen from her fingers, and placed it upon a table.

"No." She frowned and shivered, the dream leaving her, as it always did, with a nagging unease. "It was about the Tower—I know I have dreamed it before, but I can remember so little of it when I wake."

"It doesn't matter, you're safe now," he said gently as he held out his arms to her. "Come on, your bath is ready."

"I think you are in greater need of one," she said wryly as he helped her to her feet and she looked up into his distinctly grimy face.

"I thought we might share it." He smiled at her, a slow tender smile that sent her pulse racing. "I knew you would not wish to impose too much extra work upon the servants at this hour."

"No, of course not." She laughed a little shakily as he put his arm about her waist and led her through another door into a bedchamber, which was softly lit with candles and a blazing fire, in front of which was a large wooden bath, lined with linen and steaming with fragrant warm water.

She swallowed as he halted her beside the fire, her mouth and throat suddenly dry as he began very gently to unbutton her soft shirt, his gaze never leaving hers as she stood absolutely still, her body so taut it hurt.

He slid the shirt from her shoulders, gliding it off

her slender bare arms as if she were as fragile as porcelain and might break if he touched her too roughly. The soft silk pooled noiselessly upon the rug, as did her leather skirt.

"You are beautiful, Janey Hilton, so soft, so perfect," he said. She looked at him a little uncertainly as his gaze burnt over her, heating her bare skin as much as the flames from the fire.

"So are you," she said thickly, as he stripped off his breeches and she saw how lean he was, how honed and male. "Perfect, I mean—not soft—"

"I should hope not," he said drily with a lift of his black brows as her gaze dropped and then fled hastily upwards again.

"I don't know what I mean," she said flusteredly, her cheeks burning with a heat that had nothing to do with her proximity to the fire. "And I don't know what to do—well, not exactly—"

"Didn't they have baths on the frontier?" he teased and scooped her up in his arms, and before she had time even to react to the shocking contact of her skin against his, she found herself lying on top of him in the warm water.

"Not like this—mostly it was a cold river," she said breathlessly as he began to sponge the smoke from her face, with the utmost gentleness. "And you know I was not talking about baths."

"Ah." He smiled. "Did you mean this?"

"Yes." She sighed and shut her eyes as he kissed her, giving herself up to his mouth and hands and body without reservation. Nothing in her life had felt as right as this...

Or this, she thought later as they lay in his tester

bed, wearing nothing but the candlelight, with her head upon his chest, and the warm weight of his arm wrapped about her waist. This was where she belonged.

She stretched lazily; her body ached in places, but her skin felt like satin against the crisp linen sheets and she felt beautiful and loved. So loved...even if he had not said it in so many words. And so safe...

"No regrets, Janey?" he asked softly, his black lashes lifting from his cheek.

"No." She sighed as he shifted onto his side and began to stroke the curve of her hip. She would never regret this, not even if she never saw him again.

"Was this from the accident in the Tower?" he asked as he traced the faint silvery scar on her thigh with a fingertip.

"Yes."

He hugged her closer. "Will Avery told me something of it. You must have been terrified."

"I cannot remember much of it. Just fragments here and there, like Will saying Edward was dead..." Her voice thinned, as she reached into the blackness at the edge of her mind where she was usually too afraid to go. "They told me he was dead and all I felt was relief that I should not have to marry him."

"You did not want to marry him?"

"No."

"Then why did you agree to the betrothal?" he said, as he touched his lips to her throat and kissed her.

"I never really did," she said slowly. "Edward told me that my grandfather was ill, and that his dearest wish was to see me settled before he died. He said

that to put Grandfather's mind at rest, it was the least
I could do for him in exchange for everything he had
given me. And then Edward explained how much
good we could do for the village if we were married...and that if I were his wife I should not have to
endure Mr Filmore as my guardian when my grandfather died.

"It seemed a good idea at first, but then I began to
have doubts...sometimes, when Edward did not know
I was there, he would say things that made me wonder
if he thought any differently of me than the Filmores
did—and although he said he loved me, I never felt
he meant it. That's why I went to the Tower the evening before the wedding. I thought seeing the estate
and knowing I could prevent Mr Filmore managing it
might take away the doubts.''

"And did it?''

"No. It made no difference. When I thought of him
kissing me, touching me—when he did not love me,
nor I him—I knew I could not go through with it.''

"You did not go there to meet him?'' His hand
stilled upon her waist.

"No—'' She shivered suddenly. "He—he came
later—I can't remember.''

"Good,'' he growled gently against her ear as he
held her close. "Because I intend to make you forget
Edward Grey ever existed.''

"You were going to take me home,'' she reminded
him even as her body melted into his. "It must be
nearly dawn—''

"Not yet.'' He sighed and kissed her. "Not yet,
Janey.''

* * *

It was long past dawn when he woke to find her sleeping in his arms. He swore softly, thought for a moment of waking her and then decided against it. There were some fates which he had no desire to fight.

"Hello." He smiled at her as she woke an hour or so later and looked at him with drowsy eyes.

"Mr Lindsay!"

"Yes." He laughed at her momentary confusion. "I think after last night you might call me Jonathan?"

"I might be persuaded." She smiled, knowing from the tenderness in his eyes that nothing had changed. He still wanted her. Perhaps even loved her... She touched her lips to his stubbled chin, enjoying the rough texture, and his salty, male taste.

"Like this." He turned his head and captured her mouth.

"Jono! Jono! Wake up!" Lord Derwent crashed into the room like a thunderbolt. "Filmore is downstairs—says Miss Hilton is missing from her bed—"

His voice died and he went scarlet as Jonathan and Janey sat up, Janey clutching the sheet to her chin.

"Ah—Perry, you must be the first to congratulate us," Jonathan drawled as he put his arm about Janey's shoulders, as cool, as collected as if they had been in the drawing-room. "Miss Hilton has done me the honour of agreeing to become my wife."

"Have I?" Janey stared at him. "Jonathan, you don't have to do this."

"Oh, yes, he does," Perry said brightly. "That's wonderful news, Miss Hilton—Lady Diana will be delighted. Sees you as a kindred spirit, you know."

"Yes, well—you can kiss the bride later," Jonathan said drily. "Out, Perry—and not a word or—" He made a graphic gesture across his throat. "I'll be down to see Filmore as soon as I am dressed."

"You don't have to marry me," Janey repeated as the door shut behind Perry and Jonathan pulled on his dressing-gown.

"Yes, I do." He smiled at her and bent to drop a kiss upon her forehead. "There is simply no alternative, given the circumstances—Perry is right. Besides which, I love you—didn't I tell you that last night?"

"No." She gave a half-exasperated laugh as she looked at him and knew with a surge of joy he was telling the truth. "Not in so many words."

"Then I suppose I had better make amends." He smiled at her and, dropping on to his knees, caught her hand and lifted it to his lips. "I love you, Miss Hilton, I think I have loved you from the moment I first saw you, or at least the moment you stopped looking at me as if you wished to consign me to the guillotine. So, will you marry me?"

"Yes," she answered, her face glowing. "But are you sure? My father would have been the first to tell you he was no gentleman."

"I do not give a damn what your father was. If he produced a daughter like you, Janey, then he was a gentleman in the only way that matters." He leant forward to kiss her again. "So the only obstacle I see is explaining to your guardian exactly what you are doing here."

"We could say I went for an early morning ride on his chaser, took a fall and was brought here?" she suggested.

"You are positive genius," he grinned at her.

"The only problem is my clothes," she said, remembering the smoke-stained state of her riding skirt and habit shirt.

"Lady Diana will loan you something—you're much of a size and she will not blab. Now all we have to do is rehearse my speech to Filmore—since you're not twenty-one yet, I shall have to ask his permission."

"Supposing he does not give it?" she said, the glow fading from her face.

"Then we shall elope to Gretna." He laughed and kissed her again. "Perhaps that is what we should do, anyway—then we would not have to wait the three weeks for the banns."

"Don't seem to have done much waiting as far as I can see," came an acerbic female voice as the door opened a fraction again.

"Is there no privacy in this house?" he growled and headed to the door. "What do you want, Grandmama?"

"Miss Hilton in the guest room, so we can put some gloss on whatever story you're planning to tell her guardian," Lady Stalbridge said from around the door, pushing a dressing-robe into his hands. "And don't try and tell me she is not in this house. I heard you come in last night."

Jonathan sighed and tossed the dressing-robe to Janey. "We'd better do as she says. I'll see you later, my love."

"Congratulations!" Lady Diana greeted Janey cheerfully as she came into the guest room, followed by her maid carrying an armful of gowns, a wolf-hound the approximate size and colour of a small donkey and the two puppies. "You don't mind dogs, do you?" she said airily as she sat down upon the end of the half-tester bed, and the wolfhound bitch immediately jumped up beside her.

"No," Janey said with a slight smile, turning from the window. "Not in the least."

"Didn't think you would." Lady Diana smiled back at her as her maid calmly began to lay out gowns over a *découpage* screen.

"Jono said you'd had a fall from a horse this morning and needed to borrow a gown?" There was a slight question in her brown eyes.

"Something like that," Janey replied, feeling herself blush.

Lady Diana laughed. "Well, I for one don't care what you're doing here so early in the morning. Perry tells me you're to marry Jono and that's the best news I have heard in months. I'm so glad Jono's going to marry you. I've been terrified for years that old Sutton would die and he'd marry Susanna. She was all wrong for him, you know."

"I am rather afraid that is what his family will say about me," Janey said with a sigh.

"They won't—at least, not once they've met you," Lady Diana said with what Janey was coming to realise was her usual bluntness. "And you've already got Lady Stalbridge's approval, which is half the battle."

"Have I?" Janey said, startled.

"Oh, yes. She's been going on at Jonathan since the ball about not marrying trade—knows him like the back of her hand, you see."

"You mean that telling him he must not do something almost guarantees that he will."

"Exactly!" Lady Diana laughed. "I didn't realise you knew him so well already."

"Two of a kind, I am afraid," Janey replied a little ruefully.

"That's what Derwent wrote to me in a letter just after he first met you," Lady Diana said. "He said Jonathan had just met the woman he ought to marry, but he was not sure he realised it yet. Remarkably perspicacious for Perry—he does have his moments, even if he does like to play the fool."

"Yes," Janey said as she sat down upon the other corner of the bed and remembered exactly how Lord Derwent had been made aware of their engagement. "And he is very kind."

"Yes." Lady Diana smiled fondly. "Now let's sort you out a gown for facing up to Mr Filmore—what's it to be? Penitent and demure or brazen it out?"

Janey thought for a moment. Then she laughed. "Brazen, definitely brazen. I am afraid Mr Filmore will never believe me as a penitent."

"Right! Teresa—give Miss Hilton the cherry wool to try on," Lady Diana ordered. "And then attend to her hair for her," she added as she got up. "I hope to see you later, Miss Hilton. Good luck."

Chapter Fourteen

"So what do you suggest I should have done, Piers? I took risk enough over the insurance upon those ricks for your sake!" Mr Filmore roared at his son later that day in the drawing-room of Pettridges Hall. "Refuse him permission! Have her committed when he has made it clear enough he would have the hounds of hell at my heels if I try anything of the kind! We are ruined, and it is your fault alone—if you had left the tables alone, we would not be in this pickle."

"Well, how was I to know he would want to marry her?" Piers said disgustedly, slumping into a chair. "We made it clear enough what she is! The granddaughter of one jumped-up millhand and daughter of another, who is accustomed to eating in kitchens! A girl dragged up in a boarding house!"

"Dear God! You are such a fool!" Annabel said, throwing down her sketch book. "She might have been that when she came here, but she acquired the manner of a lady better than you ever managed to appear a gentleman, though you were born to it! All you had to do was flatter her when she first came here—but no—you had to be your usual boorish self!''

"Don't damage your sketch book, dearest." Mrs Filmore sighed, as Annabel stamped her foot upon it. "You are so clever with your pen. That Leonardo you copied was hard to tell from the original."

"Oh, yes, she's quite the little forger, aren't you, sis?'' her brother hissed. "And it wouldn't have suited you if I married her, would it?''

"What do you mean, Piers?" Mrs Filmore said mildly, looking up from her netting again.

"Nothing," he said sullenly as his sister shot him a look.

"Shut up, Piers!" Annabel flared. "You may spend the rest of your life as a pauper if you wish, but I am not going to!''

"That is enough!" Mr Filmore roared. "If you cannot behave better, I suggest both of you go to your rooms and consider how you might ingratiate yourselves with Jane since, I assure you, her generosity will be our only hope of avoiding ruin.''

Outside, Janey hastily withdrew the hand she had just put upon the brass door handle and tiptoed back down the hall. So Jonathan's suspicions had been right. Mr Filmore had had designs upon her fortune, once she had made it clear there was no hope of her marrying Piers. She sighed. Three weeks of the Filmores' attempts to ingratiate themselves did not fill her with joy. But then she smiled—three weeks. In three weeks she would be Jonathan's wife and she could tell the Filmores to pack their bags and leave.

Lord Derwent had already intimated that he would

be more than interested in renting Pettridges House
after Janey moved to Southbrook, as Lady Diana
liked the look of the downs for exercising her horses.
Her smile widened. She was looking forward to having the Lady Diana as a neighbour.

And with Jonathan's plans for his silk mill, and the
improvements to both estates to be carried out, there
would be plenty of work for the men and more prosperity for the whole village. And he had promised her
he would help her build a proper school for the children. If it had not been for the riots, and John Avery's
unnecessary death, she would have been almost perfectly happy.

"Well, one good thing," Perry said late the following afternoon, as he and Jonathan strolled through the
overgrown gardens of Southbrook house, "if what
Miss Hilton overheard is right, and old Filmore
wanted to prove her insane, and Piers wanted to marry
her, neither of 'em can have wanted her dead."

"No," Jonathan said slowly, a frown furrowing his
brow. "But there is still something about this whole
business that makes me uneasy—something we have
all missed."

"Don't worry—you said yourself no one knows
who would gain by her death—so what reason would
anyone have to harm her now?"

"Yes, I suppose you are right—but I'd still like to
take a look at that Tower. But I don't like to bother
Avery—not until his brother is buried."

"A bad business, that—"

"Yes, and it could have been avoided but for that
hothead, Crowne." Jonathan sighed. "He still thinks

they have quelled the riots here with fear, whereas the only reason they have stopped is because every farmer in the district has made concessions. But even that's not enough. I'm beginning to think these Reform fellows are right. It is time for some changes in the way things are done. No one in England should starve—we're supposed to be the most advanced nation in the world, after all.''

Lord Derwent laughed.

''What are you laughing about?'' Jonathan said, frowning as he bent and picked up a stick for Tess, who was bouncing at his heels.

''You. You're starting to sound like Miss Hilton, Jono. You're definitely in love. Never thought I'd see it.''

''Nor did I.'' Jonathan grinned and threw the stick for Tess. ''And do you know, Perry, the odd thing is, I'm enjoying it.''

''Miss, there's another note come for you,'' Kate said with a grin three days later. ''He'll have written the county out of paper soon.''

Janey laughed and took the note, which was addressed in the strong, slanting hand that was becoming so very familiar to her.

She broke the seal, and scanned the brief message, her smile broadening.

I MUST see you alone. Come to the waterfall at noon. All my love, Jonathan.

She took paper, pens and ink from her writing-box and wrote a swift note in reply, to the effect that she wanted nothing more than to see him alone and that she would be at the waterfall at noon. For the last

three days, it had seemed everyone in the neighbourhood had wished to call with their congratulations,
including the Norrises and the Huttons, who had been
so effusive and different in their manner to her, and
so sycophantic to Jonathan that Janey had been hard
put not to laugh.

"I think I preferred them when they were fawning
over the Filmores," Jonathan had muttered darkly.
"At least then I wasn't expected to talk back to
them."

Still smiling, she handed her note to Kate and asked
her to get one of the stable lads to take it over to
Southbrook.

"What is it, Jono?" Lord Derwent asked as they
came in from the garden and Jonathan, having read
the note handed to him by Brown, went suddenly
ashen.

"I don't know," he said slowly. "There is note
here from Miss Hilton, saying she will meet me as
arranged at the waterfall."

"Well, that's nothing to be alarmed about, is it?"
Perry laughed.

"No, except that I did not arrange the meeting,"
Jonathan said grimly.

"Where are you going?" Perry said as Jonathan
took to his heels.

"The waterfall," Jonathan shouted back over his
shoulder. "There is something wrong, Perry, I know
there is."

A few minutes later, they were both running
through the gardens.

* * *

The sun was already high in the bright clear winter sky when Janey reached the top of the cliff and looked down at the pool below. She shivered in the chill air and realised with a slight sense of disappointment that Jonathan had not arrived yet.

She took a step forward and then turned, a smile on her lips as she heard a twig crack in the woods behind her. "Jonathan—"

The greeting died on her lips as she recognised the figure stepping out of the trees with some surprise. "Annabel? What brings you here?"

"You." Annabel gave her childish little giggle. "I am afraid I played a little trick upon you, Jane, I needed to get you alone. The note was from me."

"You..." Janey stared at her, unease making her scalp prickle. All her instincts were screaming danger—danger of the most basic kind. "But the note—the writing—"

"Was not at all difficult to copy." Annabel smiled and stepped closer to her.

Janey retreated a half-step and then froze as Annabel pulled a pistol from her black fur muff. She stared at it. It was one of her sleeve pistols, which in her haste to meet Jonathan she had forgotten to bring with her.

"You left them on your dressing-table, which was very helpful of you, Jane." Annabel smiled.

Janey ignored her, her attention now fastened upon the pearl ring Annabel wore upon her trigger finger.

She stared, seeing suddenly, as if in a picture, the woman bending to retrieve it after she had hurled it down at Edward's upturned face.

"It was you—it was you at the Tower." Recollection came with swift and total clarity. "You and Edward planned to kill me, didn't you?" she said, fighting against the panic she could feel growing inside her.

"So you have finally remembered. I was always afraid you might, though I would have denied everything, of course, and no one would have believed you anyway," Annabel said calmly. "You are right, of course. Edward and I had planned it all. We had met in Town, you see, but I could not possibly marry him when he had no money—"

"So you thought to get mine," Janey said flatly.

"Yes. I did not see why Piers or Papa should have it all simply to pay off Piers's stupid gambling debts. It is so boring to be poor, Jane. But, of course, as usual, you had to ruin things by going to the Tower on the wrong day. I was very angry—I was very fond of Edward at the time. Not that it matters now—with your money I shall be able to do far better for myself."

"You won't get my money, it goes to a trust."

"No—" Annabel shook her carroty head "—after your death, a previously unknown codicil to your grandfather's will shall accidentally be discovered— in which everything is left to me, his beloved goddaughter. His handwriting is no more difficult to forge than Mr Lindsay's, you see."

"I see." Janey swallowed, her gaze fixed upon the barrel of the pistol, which had not wavered for a moment. "But I am not dead, Annabel. And if you kill me, Jonathan will not rest until my murderer is found. He has suspicions enough of your father already."

"Oh, *I* am not going to kill you. You are going to

kill yourself by jumping from the cliff to drown in the pool—your coat is going to be found here upon the cliff top, neatly folded, and a note with it. A note in which you most touchingly make your farewells to this world and explain that you cannot abandon Mr Grey's memory by marrying another or be separated from him a moment longer.''

"Jonathan will never believe it," Janey said fiercely.

"Why not? It will be in your handwriting." Annabel smiled. "Take your coat off, Jane, I am getting cold standing here."

"And if I do not—"

"Then I shall shoot you in the head—and the note will do just as well, though I should prefer it if you would jump. There is always the risk with a gunshot wound that someone may argue it was not self-inflicted."

Janey undid the buttons of her coat as slowly as she dared. The one thing Annabel did not know was that she had replied to the forged note. Dear God, let her note have reached Jonathan, she prayed. If it had, then he might arrive here at any moment—

"Hurry up!" Annabel snapped, her face pale, but her grip upon the pistol still steady.

Janey shrugged off her coat and bent slowly to put it down. The ground was wet and muddy; there was not even a handful of dust and gravel to scoop up into Annabel's eyes. And the woods remained silent, empty. Jonathan might not even have received her note yet, she thought bleakly. If he had not been at home—

"Jump," Annabel said coldly, cocking the pistol.

Janey turned and looked down, her heart pounding as she stared into the foaming water. Annabel did not know she could swim. It could be done, she told herself. She had seen it done by a Cheyenne, leaping from a fall higher than this to escape his pursuers. And she and Daniel had leapt from rocks and trees to swim in pools and creeks when she was a child.

But then she had not been wearing a gown and petticoats—if she got caught in the roll of water at the base of the fall—stop it, she told herself as she began to shake. She had to stay calm. If she panicked, she would die. At least it was a chance—and a chance was better than a bullet in the head.

After one last glance at the woods, she took a breath, pinched her nose and made two rapid strides and leapt as far out as she could, praying she would at least miss the rocks at the base of the fall.

It was like hitting stone, icy stone that shattered and closed over her with a roar as the force of her fall sent her down, and down, her skirts billowing up over her head like the petals of a flower. Oh, God— they were wrapping about her face and arms, she could see nothing—and then the air in her skirts took her upwards again towards the light. She broke the surface, coughing, spluttering, and then was tumbled over and over by the roaring water.

It was useless, she thought, as her head broke the surface a second time and she gasped in a breath, she could not even try to swim because of her stupid, stupid skirts. And then the water swept her down again, down and down into the darkness. Into the mercifully calm darkness, where the current tugged her skirts away from her head and arms. She still could not use her legs properly—but at least she could move her arms.

Go deep, a trapper had told her once, that's the only way out of a roll. Her lungs bursting, she dragged herself downward and forward in agonising strokes, praying that she was going away from the fall. She couldn't do it, she thought, as a redness seemed to explode behind her eyes, and her lungs felt as if they would burst. She had to breathe—she had to—she kicked her constricted legs frantically, and reached up with her hands towards the distant light and roaring noise. She had to breathe.

The roar was deafening as her head broke the surface. She had gone the wrong way, she thought, despairing, as the air sliced into her burning lungs like acid. And she had no strength left to fight the churning water—but it wasn't churning—it was calm. She was behind the fall, between the curtain of water and the cliff. There was rock no more than a yard or two away. A yard or two that was like a mile as she fought against the downward pull of her skirts, and the numbing, seductive cold that made her want to shut her eyes and give up.

And then her fingertips found the rock, found a hold. She managed to pull herself halfway out of the water, but then could do no more. She was too cold, her skirts too heavy, the rock too slippery with weed. She could not get any further up the rock. She was so cold, so very, very cold. She lay shivering, her face pressed to the shiny black rock, praying that Annabel would not come down to make sure she had drowned.

* * *

"My God!" Lord Derwent said in horror, some fifteen minutes later, as he stared at Janey's coat and read the note Jonathan had pushed into his hand. "You don't think she has really taken her life?"

"No, I don't! Janey! Janey!"

It was Jonathan's scream of her name that brought Janey back from the brink of unconsciousness.

"Jonathan—" she breathed his name against the rock.

It was only as he called again and again that she realised he could not hear her or see her for the roaring, white sheet of water.

"I'm here," she tried to shout, to move, but her body would not work properly.

And then suddenly, something was nudging her, licking her face, snuffling at her.

"Tess—" She half-groaned, half-sobbed the spaniel's name. "Mark, Tess—mark, please—"

The spaniel started to bark, short, sharp shrill barks that reverberated against the cliff.

"Tess has found something—listen," Perry said, his face as white as Jonathan's as he scanned the dark waters of the pool. "Where the devil is the dog?"

"Behind the fall." Jonathan was already running, his booted feet slipping and sliding on the wet rocks.

"Janey—don't be dead, Janey." He groaned as he edged around the fall on a ledge of rock and saw her sprawled motionless upon the black rock, like a stranded mermaid, the hem of her gown still drifting on the cold dark water.

"I'm not—" she tried to say, tried to smile as he came into the range of her vision. But no sound came out of her blue lips, except the chatter of her teeth.

"It's all right, my love," he said as he pulled her

up into his arms and rocked her against the wonderful warmth of his chest. "It's all right, you are safe now."

She shut her eyes and let the darkness swallow her.

He was still there beside her, the following morning, or perhaps the morning after that; she was not sure what day it was when she opened her eyes again in the guest bedroom at Southbrook.

"Jonathan?" She tried to sit up and failed, finding herself as weak as a kitten.

"Just lie still and rest, my love." He stroked her cheek with his finger.

"Annabel, she—"

"I know. She's been arrested. She cannot hurt you," he said soothingly. "Piers told me everything in an attempt to save his own neck. He arrived at Southbrook just after we found you. He knew all about Annabel and Edward Grey's liaison and had always had suspicions about the accident in the Tower—and then last week he found one of Annabel's practice copies of the codicil and realised she might try and harm you again. But I already guessed it the moment I read your note. Somehow I knew it was her—" His voice dwindled to a growl for a moment. "And I knew, the moment I read it, what she had in mind—I have never run so fast in my life, Janey. And I was still too late. I thought I had lost you."

"It's all right." She reached up with her fingers to touch his face.

"Yes—" he caught her hand and held it to his lips "—everything is going to be all right now, I promise you."

*   *   *

And he had kept his promise, she thought with a smile, some months later, as she stood beside a rather sheepish-looking, flower-bedecked Brutus in the late evening sunshine beside the now well-tended lawns of Southbrook and watched the children of the village race about between the long trestle tables laden with food and bedecked with garlands of greenery and flowers. It had been a good idea of his to have a harvest supper for all the tenants and their labourers.

"Happy?" Jonathan said softly, coming up behind her and putting a hand about her waist, which was just starting to thicken.

"Yes." She smiled and leant her head against his shoulder. "We must do this every year."

"So long as I don't have to make speeches," he pretended to grumble. "I have to make enough of those in the House these days. I had no idea being a Reformer was going to be such hard work."

"You are not wishing you had not crossed the floor to the Whigs?" she asked.

"No, my dear dangerous radical." He smiled and kissed her. And then, sobering a little, he asked, "Did you see the paper this morning?"

"No."

"The ship the Filmores took for India after Annabel's trial—it was wrecked. There were no survivors."

"Oh—that's awful," Janey said and meant it. She had not liked the Filmores enough to feel grief, but she would not have wished such a fate upon anyone.

"Is it?" He looked at her quizzically.

She shrugged. "I have everything I want, I should not have begrudged them their lives."

"I do," he said with feeling. "In fact, I'd cheerfully have hung the lot of them——"

"No, you wouldn't," she said with total confidence. "You were as glad as I was that Annabel was judged insane and did not have to hang."

"No, I was not, I'm no——"

"Galahad." She smiled and sighed. "I know, you are a wicked cynic who cares for nothing but your own pleasure. Now off you go and make your speech."

"What speech?" he groaned.

"The one in reply to the children who are coming to thank you for your generosity with a special poem."

"Must I? I hate being thanked—and I am not very good with children."

"Then you had better start practising." The little push she gave him was augmented by a hefty nudge in the back from Brutus's large black head.

"*Et tu, Brute,*" he muttered darkly at the horse before starting to walk towards the group of children. Then he halted in mid-stride and swung round to look at her.

"Janey? Do you mean——?"

"Yes," she nodded, her heart soaring at the joy written on his face.

And then she was in his arms, being kissed so soundly that she entirely failed to notice Brutus had begun to chew contentedly upon the brim of her new wide-brimmed straw hat, and even when she did, she did not care. And neither did he.

*   *   *   *   *

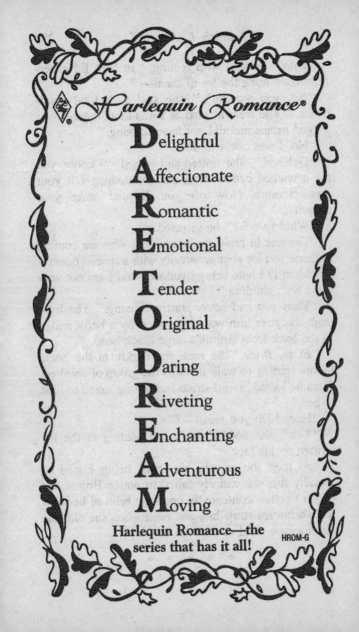

Harlequin Romance®

Delightful

Affectionate

Romantic

Emotional

Tender

Original

Daring

Riveting

Enchanting

Adventurous

Moving

Harlequin Romance—the
series that has it all!

HROM-G

HARLEQUIN PRESENTS®

**The world's bestselling romance series...
The series that brings you your favorite authors,
month after month:**

Helen Bianchin...Emma Darcy
Lynne Graham...Penny Jordan
Miranda Lee...Sandra Morton
Anne Mather...Carole Mortimer
Susan Napier...Michelle Reid

and many more uniquely talented authors!

Wealthy, powerful, gorgeous men...
Women who have feelings just like your own...
The stories you love, set in exotic, glamorous locations...

HARLEQUIN PRESENTS,
Seduction and passion guaranteed!

Visit us at www.eHarlequin.com

HPGEN00

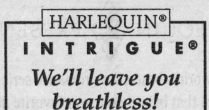

HARLEQUIN®

INTRIGUE®

We'll leave you breathless!

If you've been looking for thrilling tales of
contemporary passion and sensuous love stories
with taut, edge-of-the-seat suspense—
then you'll *love* **Harlequin Intrigue!**

Every month, you'll meet four new heroes
who are guaranteed to make your spine tingle
and your pulse pound. With them you'll enter
into the exciting world of Harlequin Intrigue—
where your life is on the line
and so is your heart!

THAT'S INTRIGUE—DYNAMIC ROMANCE AT ITS BEST!

 HARLEQUIN®

INTRIGUE®

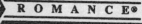